In the Secret Cabin Where Slaves Passed on to Freedom,

Becky found herself trapped.

"Now that I'm virtually your prisoner, I hope you're satisfied," she said scathingly.

Mike grinned. "Prisoner is a bit dramatic, don't you think? Why not think of yourself as my guest?" he said quietly.

"Fine," Becky snapped. "If I'm your guest, I'm free to leave."

For a large man, Mike moved with catlike swiftness to block her exit. "I wouldn't advise it," he warned. "I'll use force if necessary to keep you here."

"You wouldn't dare," she hissed.

"Wouldn't I?"

Emerald eyes clashed with sapphire ones. Then Mike's mouth crushed hers, demanding and receiving a response. Becky didn't want the kiss to end, as her mind flashed warnings her body ignored . . .

Dear Reader,

We, the editors of Tapestry Romances, are committed to bringing you two outstanding original romantic historical novels each and every month.

From Kentucky in the 1850s to the court of Louis XIII, from the deck of a pirate ship within sight of Gibraltar to a mining camp high in the Sierra Nevadas, our heroines experience life and love, romance and adventure.

Our aim is to give you the kind of historical romances that you want to read. We would enjoy hearing your thoughts about this book and all future Tapestry Romances. Please write to us at the address below.

The Editors
Tapestry Romances
POCKET BOOKS
1230 Avenue of the Americas
Box TAP
New York, N.Y. 10020

Sweet Possession

Elizabeth Turner

A TAPESTRY BOOK

PUBLISHED BY POCKET BOOKS NEW YORK

An *Original* publication of TAPESTRY BOOKS

A Tapestry Book published by
POCKET BOOKS, a division of Simon & Schuster, Inc.
1230 Avenue of the Americas, New York, N.Y. 10020

ISBN: 0-671-61447-9

First Tapestry Books printing June, 1986

10 9 8 7 6 5 4 3 2 1

POCKET and colophon are registered trademarks
of Simon & Schuster, Inc.

TAPESTRY is a registered trademark of Simon & Schuster, Inc.

Printed in the U.S.A.

To my parents,
Anna and William Bolleau,
who showed me love can last a lifetime

Sweet Possession

Chapter One

Indiana 1850

THE BETTER SHE KNEW HIM, THE LESS SHE LIKED HIM.
He was indifferent, insensitive, and callous.

Becky Foster's full mouth tightened. She sighed as
she slipped another bloom into a chipped enamel
pitcher. It had been her idea and at the time seemed
sheer inspiration. There was no one to blame but
herself.

Her father used to berate her for being a strong-
willed female. In retrospect, he had been a better
judge of her character than Becky cared to admit.
Dear wise Ben Sloane had cautioned her against her
plan; her brother, Adam, had been more blunt. He

1

had told her she was crazy. She had refused to listen and now it was too late. Marshal Frank Denby had taken the bait.

It seemed so simple. All she had to do was attract the marshal's attention and win his confidence. Convinced she shared his anti-abolition sentiments, he would confide any suspicions he might entertain of the underground railroad operating in the vicinity of Oak Ridge. Being forewarned would aid not only Ben and herself but others along the route as well. If only she didn't feel like such a hypocrite, pretending to care for a man she was growing to despise.

Becky shoved a daffodil into the crowded container with enough force to shear the leaves from the stalk. So far the plan was a dismal failure. The lawman was proving as closemouthed as any of the clams in Boston Harbour.

Maybe she shouldn't have come this afternoon. Maybe she should have waited for another day. Flowers were a flimsy excuse for a visit and she knew it. Still, she hadn't been bold enough to come both unexpected and emptyhanded. She had meant to bake Frank's favorite molasses cookies, but there just hadn't been time.

The outside door opening broke through her absorption. She squared her shoulders; it was too late now for second thoughts. She gave the colorful spring bouquet a final glance, and picking up the makeshift vase, moved toward the sound.

Her soft-soled slippers carried her noiselessly out of the back storage room, down a dim corridor, past two empty jail cells, to the doorway leading into the outer office. She paused on the threshold, her smile of greeting fading. She stared unabashedly at a man who seemed to fill every corner and crevice with his powerful presence.

Even viewed from the back, he was magnificent. Her brother Adam was tall, well over six feet, but this man was even taller. His hair, so thick and so black it gleamed, curled loosely above the collar of his shirt. The light blue fabric was stretched across the broadest shoulders she had ever seen. Their wide expanse tapered to a trim waist. Soft worn cotton pants molded firm buttocks and sheathed superbly muscled thighs. A tiny seed buried deep in the innermost part of her began to unfurl. To her amazement, Becky found herself interested in a man in a way she hadn't been in a long time—a very long time.

The stranger's attention was focused on a handbill tacked to the wall. It was no different from a dozen others that circulated with increasing regularity as southern slaveholders attempted to staunch the steady trickle of slaves fleeing to freedom. The man was studying it so intently, Becky wondered if he might be a slavecatcher in pursuit of a victim. Then her large green eyes lit with silent approval as she watched him rip the handbill off the wall and crumple it into a tight ball.

"The marshal won't like that."

At the soft taunt, the man whirled to face her. A livid scar cut a diagonal swath across one cheek, marring an otherwise handsome face. On closer inspection, one cheekbone seemed flatter than the other. Becky surmised it might have once been shattered by a cruel blow, perhaps the same one that left its indelible brand on his flesh. However, far from

3

repulsive, Becky found the man's face incredibly intriguing.

"Do you always sneak up on people?" Irritation roughened his voice.

"Occasionally." A small smile tugged at the corners of her mouth. "There are times I've found it most revealing." She walked over to the desk and set the bouquet next to a stack of neatly piled papers.

"I was told to wait here for the marshal. If it would make you more comfortable, I can leave and come back later."

Becky eyed the stranger curiously. "Why would I want you to leave?"

"Women often find my face offensive, especially pretty women like yourself. Like I said, I can come back later."

In spite of the bold words, she sensed a wealth of hurt and bitterness not far below the surface. "It's kind of you to flatter me." Spreading the full skirt of her lilac muslin gown in a graceful arc, Becky sat down on a roundbacked chair next to the desk. "Please, don't leave on my account. I've seen burn scars before and they don't bother me in the least."

Surprise flickered across the scarred countenance. Eyes, thickly lashed and as blue as sapphires, searched her upturned face. Becky returned the look unflinchingly. Why is it, she wondered, men are always the ones blessed with long eyelashes? After what seemed an eternity, the taut lines of his face relaxed and the defensive blaze burning in his eyes was extinguished.

A friendlier note seeped into her voice. "Are you just passing through Oak Ridge, or will you be staying awhile, Mister . . ."

"Ryan. Mike Ryan," he supplied. "That all depends on whether or not I find work, Miss . . ."

"Foster. Rebecca Foster," Becky mimicked. Her eyes sparkling with amusement, she extended her hand. "Shall we declare a truce, Mr. Ryan?"

Mike Ryan accepted her outstretched hand, his humor restored. "I think our first bout would have to be declared a draw," he said, grinning.

Becky found herself responding with unusual warmth, acutely aware of the sunburst of laughlines etched at the corners of his eyes and the flash of even white teeth. The man had a decidedly unsettling effect on her. A sixth sense warned she was treading dangerously close to quicksand and she'd better scurry to safer ground. She withdrew her hand and cleared her throat.

"You mentioned looking for work, Mr. Ryan. Exactly what do you hope to find here in Oak Ridge?"

"That's a good question," he admitted with a wry twist to his mouth. He settled his large frame against the edge of the desk, his arms casually folded across his chest. "I've had every kind of job you can imagine, plus a few you probably can't. Someone mentioned there were a few cattle ranches in these parts, and I thought maybe I could hire on."

"Here in Indiana, whether you raise livestock or crops, they're still called farms," she corrected absently.

The kernel of an idea was planted, but before it could take root, the door burst open and Frank Denby strode into his office. The marshal shot a cursory glance at Mike, a glance that managed to convey both annoyance and aversion, and then turned his attention on Becky.

"Becky! What a pleasant surprise!" he exclaimed, crossing the space that separated them. Capturing both her hands in his, he pulled her to her feet. Not usually demonstrative, Becky was unprepared for the hard swift kiss he pressed to her soft mouth. It was over in an instant. Out of the corner of her eye, she saw the darkened scowl on Mike Ryan's face and turned to catch the satisfied smirk on Frank Denby's.

"Springtime certainly agrees with you. You look pretty as a picture."

"Why, thank you." She smiled and inclined her head to acknowledge the compliment. "Frank, I don't believe you've met Mr. Ryan. He has something to discuss with you."

The marshal relinquished her hands reluctantly and stepped back to study the stranger. Becky looked from one to the other. How different the two were. Frank Denby's description of medium build, average height, brown hair, and brown eyes, could easily match those of six other men. Some women she knew considered him handsome, but his cleancut features left her unmoved. Mike Ryan, on the other hand, though physically flawed, embodied a compelling blend of strength and sensitivity.

The air between the two men seemed to crackle with animosity as they silently took each other's measure and found it lacking. Frank's eyes narrowed speculatively on Mike's scarred cheek. The corners of his mouth turned down in obvious distaste. Becky's anxious gaze shifted to Mike. His rugged face could have been carved in granite for all its hardness, his eyes held the warmth of twin glaciers. She fervently hoped never to see their coolness directed at her.

6

"Well, Ryan, what can I do for you?"

"I just arrived in town this afternoon, and I'm looking for work," Mike explained in a carefully bland voice. "I thought maybe you might have heard of someone looking for an extra hand."

"This is a marshal's office, not a club for down-on-their-luck cowhands."

"Frank!" Becky gasped, appalled by the lawman's rudeness.

"I don't recall anyone saying they need an extra hand," Frank began, making a grudging attempt to mollify her. "Maybe in the fall . . ."

"Thanks for your time," Mike replied stiffly. He made a movement toward the door before the lawman's voice stopped him.

"Where you from, Ryan?"

Mike favored the smaller man with a long hard stare. His answer was so long in coming the marshal shifted his weight uneasily. When Mike spoke, his voice betrayed no emotion.

"I was raised in Boston but I've been living in Texas the past ten years."

"A drifter!" Frank snorted. "I thought so." He perched on the edge of his desk, one leg casually dangling over the edge. Picking up a pencil, he toyed with it while he talked. "That's real interesting. With the North being anti-slavery and Texas siding with the South, what side of the fence does that find you on?"

"I didn't realize the time had come to choose sides."

"Well, it's high time you did," Denby retorted irritably. "Let's set one thing straight, Ryan. I don't know what your politics are, but I don't take kindly to abolitionists. They're troublemakers! They won't be happy 'til they see the whole country split in two. And for what?" He didn't wait for an answer. "To free a bunch of niggers who'll be helpless as a litter of newborn kittens.

"Abolitionists!" Frank spat the word. "Not only do those fools condone slaves running away, they help 'em do it. So help me, if I ever catch one I'll see 'em tarred, feathered, and run out of town on a rail."

The strained silence was broken by the sound of a pencil snapping in two.

"You still haven't answered the marshal's question, Mr. Ryan." The taunting ring was back in Becky's voice. "Which side do you favor?"

Mike regarded her, his expression unreadable. "Since you're both so curious, I'll set your minds at ease," he replied coolly. "I'm opposed to slavery. I believe it's wrong for one man to be able to own another. If that's what you consider an abolitionist, then that's what I am."

"I knew it. I just knew it!" Frank crowed. "Good thing you won't be staying around Oak Ridge very long. We'd be bound to tangle sooner or later and you'd come out the loser."

Mike Ryan's rigidly clenched jaw betrayed his struggle to control his anger. "I'd best be going," he said, his voice tight. "Good afternoon, marshal, Miss Foster." He gave a curt nod in Becky's direction. His hand was on the doorlatch when her voice stopped him.

"It's *Mrs.* Foster," she corrected softly. "I'm a widow. Good day, Mr. Ryan."

Their eyes met briefly and for a split second before

he disappeared into the street beyond she imagined she saw his stony gaze relent.

Becky left the office a short time later after promising Frank to attend the annual fair scheduled to be held in a fortnight with him. Her eyes scanned the street. It didn't take long to find what she was looking for. A large chestnut gelding was tied at the hitching post of the general store. Becky walked toward the store and prayed her guess was right and that the sleek animal belonged to Mike Ryan.

With this in mind, she pushed open the door. The clear tinkle of a bell announced her arrival to the two men standing at the far end of one of the counters. Becky strolled toward them, the full skirt of her dress swaying as she moved. Even as an adult, she felt the lure of the store. It was a veritable treasure trove. In addition to the laden countertops, the walls were lined from floor to ceiling with shelves and drawers containing every conceivable item a person needed to exist in rural Indiana. Anything one could not raise on their land, or barter for, could be found here. Bolts of calico and gingham, buttons and lace, vied for prominence amidst hammers and saws, hooks and nails. At the back of the store, an assortment of mismatched chairs surrounded a blackened potbellied stove. This was the forum where the men gathered to air their views and debate their differences.

As she drew near, the men ceased their conversation. The younger of the two, a clerk of eighteen with straw-colored hair, smoothed his white apron and hurried out from behind the counter to greet her. With a look bordering on adoration, his eyes swept over her trim figure before lingering on the exquisitely lovely face crowned with a cluster of amber curls.

"Gee, Mrs. Foster, you sure look pretty today," he gushed before a stricken look spread across his freckled face. "No offense, ma'am. I didn't mean that you don't always look pretty. I just meant, I mean . . ." he stammered in embarrassment.

"No offense taken, Jeff," Becky reassured him. "I understood what you meant. This is a new dress and I think it's sweet of you to notice."

The dull red flush in his cheeks deepened when he realized the exchange was being observed by an interested third party. He made an attempt to become more businesslike. "What can I do for you this afternoon, Mrs. Foster?"

"As long as I'm in town, I thought I would drop in to see if my order from Philadelphia has arrived yet. Could you please check for me?"

"Sure thing. Be happy to." His head bobbed with each word. "I wasn't here this morning, so I'll have to look in the back. It'll only take a minute." Eager to please, he darted off in the direction of a back storeroom.

"I'm in no hurry, Jeff," Becky called after him. "Take your time."

She found his youthful admiration flattering. A smile hovered on her lips as she turned to the store's other occupant. "Why, Mr. Ryan. Fancy running into you again. I thought by this time you'd be halfway to Indianapolis."

"Yes, this is quite a coincidence," Mike agreed dryly. He rested his palms on the counter and leaned his weight against it. "Tell me, Mrs. Foster," he said, crooking one dark brow, "do you weave some kind of magic spell? Is every man in town subject to your charm? If so, you must leave a trail of broken hearts wherever you go."

His sarcasm stung. With difficulty, she managed to keep her smile in place. "If I do possess such a charm, Mr. Ryan," she replied, "you must be immune to its power. I get the distinct impression you are not a man to give his affections freely."

"The lady is indeed wise, as well as beautiful." His cynical tone belittled the compliment.

Becky longed to rip the complacent look off the rugged face. An angry flash flared briefly in her emerald eyes before it was doused. "Let's put personal differences aside," she said crisply. Dropping her voice to a conspiratorial level, she edged closer. "Something you said in the marshal's office started me thinking. Are you still interested in finding work here in Oak Ridge?"

He nodded, a puzzled frown creasing his forehead.

Becky moistened her lips with the tip of her tongue in an unconsciously provocative gesture. "Perhaps I can be of some help."

"Go on," he encouraged. "I'm listening."

"You might find it worthwhile to check at the Sloane farm out on the river road. Ben Sloane has a rather large place and has been without a foreman for some time. There is one slight problem, however," she cautioned, a mischievous curve to her mouth.

"What sort of problem?" Mike asked warily.

"Ben doesn't know he needs a foreman, at least not yet."

"What kind of trick is this?" he demanded, his voice rising in irritation.

"Shh!" Becky held her finger to her lips and shot a

quick glance toward the storeroom. "It's no trick, I assure you. It's entirely up to you to persuade Ben you're the very person he's been looking for without his even realizing it. Anyone bearing a name as Irish as Michael Ryan should by right have inherited the gift of gab. Consider this a true test of your heritage."

She moved away from him and was idly examining a spool of lace when an apologetic clerk returned emptyhanded. "I searched high and low, but I can't find your order anywhere. Mr. Curtis might know about it. He's at the barber shop. I'd be happy to run over and ask him," he volunteered helpfully.

"Don't bother, Jeff. I'll be in town again on Friday." Giving her youthful admirer a smile that made him lightheaded, Becky left the store without a backward glance. In so doing, she failed to see she had in fact successfully erased the complacent look from Mike Ryan's face.

Chapter Two

HER PERCH ON THE BUGGY SEAT PROVIDED AN EXCELLENT view. Becky's eyes swept over the throng milling about the sun-dappled grove. She tried to convince herself she wasn't seeking anyone in particular. Nevertheless, she felt an undeniable stab of disappointment at not finding a certain tall rugged stranger.

"You haven't heard a single word I've said." Frank Denby's plaintive voice brought her back to the present.

"I'm sorry," Becky apologized. "I was just thinking that everyone in the county must be here today." Everyone but one, she added silently.

13

"You'd think folks would have better things to do than waste time on such foolishness," Frank grumbled as he placed his hands at her waist and swung her to the ground.

"Leo Briggs and his family have been coming to Oak Ridge for as long as most people can remember," she pointed out.

Leo Briggs was part peddler, part gypsy. Each spring the appearance of his gaily painted wagons was as predictable as the jack-in-the-pulpit. Along with trinkets and potions, he brought eagerly awaited news from other parts of the country.

While Frank got the picnic hamper and quilt from the buggy, Becky adjusted the wide emerald-green sash that circled her slender waist and smoothed the wrinkles from her gown of white lawn sprigged with tiny flowers.

"Let's stake us out a spot," Frank said, grasping her elbow and steering her toward a stand of birch trees. Becky waited as he spread the quilt beneath the leafy boughs and settled the basket in one corner.

"Shall we socialize?" Becky asked.

"Sure thing. Always like to remind folks I'm around." He tucked her hand in the crook of his arm. "Makes 'em think twice before startin' trouble."

Becky stifled a groan. The man's over-inflated self-importance was beginning to nettle her already, and the day had only begun. She pasted a bright smile on her face, determined to keep it there. She would not allow his sour outlook to curdle the day's pleasure.

It did seem as though the entire population of Oak Ridge and the surrounding countryside had turned out for the event. After weeks of working sunrise to sunset tilling fields and planting crops, people welcomed the brief respite. Children scampered about noisily while the grownups gathered in small groups to share ideas and exchange gossip. To anyone watching, it was evident that Becky was enjoying herself. Just as obvious was the fact that her companion wasn't. More than once her smile and tact soothed injured pride and diverted angry outbursts.

At the edge of the grove, they saw Hannah Sloane. She was kneeling on a faded patchwork quilt, diligently unloading the contents of a wicker basket. Her plain but kindly face lit with pleasure when she looked up and saw Becky. "Lord, child, don't you look a sight. You're even prettier than your ma was."

"Thank you, Hannah." Becky's voice grew husky at the mention of her mother.

"Would you believe we just got here?" Hannah went on. "One of the mares decided to foal just before we set out."

Becky nodded in sympathy. As a fellow farmer, she was acquainted with its myriad problems. Actually, the farm wasn't hers, but Adam's. Father's will had seen to that. Nor could it ever belong to her. This knowledge never failed to bring a bitter taste to her mouth. Even in death, Matthew Brantford couldn't resist the final opportunity to remind his children they had been a disappointment. Though Becky dearly loved her home with its rolling acres, she had fled to live with a cousin in Boston the day of her mother's funeral. Adam, on the other hand, wasn't happy raising livestock, preferring the faster pace of city life instead. After Becky had returned to Oak Ridge and as soon as he was able, Adam had left the management of the ranch in her capable hands and moved to New Orleans. This arrangement suited both of them.

"Where's Ben?" Frank asked.

Hannah turned her attention back to her task, her dislike of the lawman apparent to Becky. "He stopped to talk to a friend. He ought to be along in a minute or two."

"It looks as though you brought enough food to feed an army," Becky said, attempting to fill the uncomfortable breach with small talk.

"Don't know about that, but no one's goin' home hungry on my account. Don't you go forgettin' we have an extra mouth to feed nowadays."

Becky happened to glance beyond Hannah's shoulder and saw two men approach. Her eyes slid from Ben Sloane's stocky frame to the powerful one of the man next to him. Mike. Her heart raced at the sight of him.

Frank saw them too. "Well, Sloane, I hear you've gone and hired yourself a foreman," he said as soon as they were within earshot. "Hope you did some checking up on him first. A man can't be too careful."

"I appreciate your concern, marshal," Ben replied easily. "Don't worry. I think I'm a pretty fair judge of character."

"Suit yourself," came the brusque return.

The lawman's attitude rubbed Hannah the wrong way. Bristling, she rushed to Mike's defense. "Ben and I are lucky to have Mike working for us. We've never said anything to her, but we're grateful Becky sent him out our way."

Instantly Becky became the target of four pair of eyes. A dull red flush crept upward from beneath

Frank's shirt collar until it suffused his face with angry color.

"Is that true, Rebecca?" he demanded.

"Yes, it's true," she returned his look calmly.

His eyes narrowed with suspicion. "Why didn't you tell me this sooner?"

Impatience tinged her voice. "Because I was afraid all too much importance would be placed on a perfectly innocent remark."

"What are you talking about? What remark?"

"After I left your office, I chanced to meet Mr. Ryan at the general store. I casually mentioned Ben might be able to use some help. I can hardly be responsible, can I, for what happened afterward?"

"No, I suppose not," Frank admitted grudgingly, unable to find a flaw in her logic though still irritated with the results. "A woman, especially one living alone, has to be careful. You don't want to encourage the wrong sort of people."

"You're right, Frank." Becky nearly choked on the docile reply. "I'll be more careful."

Ben cleared his throat. "Becky's always been a mite," he paused and flashed her a grin, ". . . impulsive."

"Ain't that the truth," Hannah chuckled. "As a young 'un she was always getting herself into more scrapes than Adam and two of his friends put together."

Becky laughed. It was true. As a young girl she had been a hopeless tomboy, much to her mother's despair. She caught Mike watching her, a peculiar expression on his face. Her mouth still curved in amusement, she raised a delicately shaped brow and asked, "Is something the matter, Mr. Ryan? Or are

17

you just having a difficult time picturing me with pigtails and scraped knees?"

Before Mike could answer her, Frank's hand bit into her waist. "Becky's a grown woman now," he snapped. "It's high time she learn to think things through before jumping in head first." With a curt nod, he pulled her along with him.

Becky resented his highhanded treatment. It made her feel as if she were a recalcitrant child in need of a firm hand. However, short of creating a scene, there was little she could do but go meekly.

"Come back later, honey," Hannah called after her. "I'll save a piece of fudge cake for you."

Becky shot Hannah a grateful smile. Of the three people watching, only Ben guessed the anger and frustration that writhed beneath her smooth surface.

At an unspoken signal, families began to regroup. Women put aside their purchases to set out their culinary masterpieces, each determined to outdo her neighbor. The aroma of hickory-smoked ham and fried chicken caused stomachs to rumble in appreciation. Jars of pickles and preserves were set out along with an impressive array of pies and cakes. At last quiet blanketed the grove, smothering further conversation until appetites were appeased.

Afterward both children and adults succumbed to the peculiar form of lethargy that comes to those who have consumed a large quantity of food in a relatively short span of time. Leo Briggs's wiry figure moved among the groups, stopping frequently to relay messages from kinfolk who had since moved away from Oak Ridge.

As so often happened, talk invariably turned to

politics. What began as a desultory debate heated to near crescendo proportions.

"Mr. Briggs!" a woman's voice called out imperiously. "Come here, please. I would like to have a word with you."

Heads swiveled toward the sound. A woman of indeterminate age was seated on a cane-backed chair at the base of a large oak tree, the skirt of her lavender taffeta gown spread decorously. A coronet of braids crowned her head, their wintry gray the same shade as her eyes. From her manner, Margaret Nelson could have been a grand duchess conducting court.

"Ah, Mrs. Nelson," Leo Briggs greeted her, his expansive smile a blinding slash of white in his swarthy face. He favored her with a gallant bow. "It's a pleasure to see you again. Might I add, you look younger with every passing year."

"Save your flattery for the young or the foolish," she said, dismissing the compliment with a regal flick of the wrist. "I am well aware your travels take you all over the country. In your opinion, Mr. Briggs, do you feel the majority of the population are willing to accept the compromise measures Senator Clay has proposed to the Senate?"

Earlier in the year, Senator Henry Clay, a Whig from Kentucky, had presented a series of measures before Congress. These were designed to pacify both North and South by concessions to each side. While the extension of slavery was the chief issue, another was the passage of a more rigid fugitive slave law. At the mention of this controversial topic, people ceased their private conversations to form a loose semicircle around the two.

Of their own volition, Becky's feet pushed to the front of the group to better hear his reply. Frank stuck to her side like a burr, but for once she scarcely noticed.

Leo Briggs smoothed his bushy mustache with a forefinger. "Understand now, this is just my opinion," he ventured. "I think the plan is doomed. Clay's supporters are like rats leaving a sinking ship. Unless something drastic happens, and happens soon, it doesn't stand a snowball's chance in hell—if you'll pardon the expression," he added quickly.

"You seem quite confident, Mr. Briggs. However," Margaret Nelson sighed, "I'm afraid that's the way I see the situation too. With both North and South so determined to have everything their way and neither willing to bend, well, quite frankly, it frightens me to think where all this will lead."

"I don't see what all the fuss is about!" Frank was unable to remain quiet. "For the life of me, I don't see what's so terrible about allowing slavery in the new territories. What's more, I don't see what's so wrong about slaveowners wanting tougher laws to deal with runaways. Folks have a right to protect their property."

Margaret Nelson's beringed fingers tapped the handle of her fringed parasol. She directed a frosty look at the lawman until he began to shift his weight from one foot to the other. "Your attitude doesn't surprise me, marshal. I've heard it often enough before," she replied in a bored tone before her chilled gaze shifted to Becky. "And your sentiments, my dear, I assume are in total accord with the marshal's?"

"Naturally," Becky returned, silently marveling at how easily the lie sprung to her lips.

"Hmph!" The older woman snorted. "Birds of a feather flock together, my mother used to say." The dowager's gaze left Becky and drifted to the scarred stranger who stood somewhat apart from the others. Her powers of observation had not diminished with the years. She had noticed the way his eyes strayed to the pair, and it had aroused her curiosity.

"You there," she addressed him. "You must be Michael Ryan, Ben Sloane's new man."

"That's right, ma'am." Mike drew himself up to his full height and met her look.

By the time her inspection was over, Margaret Nelson's silver eyes gleamed with anticipation. "Over the years, we've become well acquainted with each other's viewpoints, particularly in regard to the slavery dispute. Where do you stand, Mr. Ryan? Are you anti-slavery, or do you agree with the marshal and Mrs. Foster?"

Mike flicked a contemptuous glance over the pair in question. "No," he replied without hesitation. "My sympathies lie in the opposite direction. I strongly believe slavery is morally wrong, and I feel the time has come for the government to recognize it for the evil it is."

"Well said, Mr. Ryan," Margaret Nelson applauded. "I admire a person who isn't afraid to speak out for his beliefs, and," she cast a disparaging look at Frank and Becky, "one who has the sense to know right from wrong."

Becky returned the dowager's cool stare with one of her own. But it was difficult to stand meekly by and allow herself to be the target of the woman's barbed remarks, remarks that found a way to slip through her armor of pretended indifference and wound. She wished she could take this woman into her confidence. Intuition told her Margaret Nelson could be trusted, but her promise to Adam stood in the way. No one but Ben must know of her involvement with the underground railroad. No one. Adam had insisted. It was far too dangerous. The more people involved, he had said, the greater the chance of discovery.

Becky felt someone watching and, turning her head, discovered it was Ben. He had an uncanny knack of being able to read her thoughts. His lined face and solemn dark eyes conveyed both sympathy and understanding. Becky managed a wobbly smile of gratitude in return.

Next to her Frank shifted restlessly. "That old biddy," he grumbled. "You'd think she was queen of England from the way she carries on. If it wasn't for all her money, folks wouldn't give her the time of day. Look," he said, "could you excuse me for awhile? I want to find my deputy and see what he's been up to. Can you amuse yourself 'til I get back?"

"Don't worry," Becky said quickly. "I'm going to find Hannah and collect that piece of cake she promised to save me."

Even in a crowd, Pete Mitchell's flaming red hair and burly figure were hard to miss. Frank soon caught sight of his deputy standing at the edge of the grove where the wagons and buggies were tied. As he drew closer, he noticed Pete wasn't alone. His bright head was bent to catch the words of a dark-haired companion. Frank recognized her as the wife of a merchant from a neighboring village. The woman was the first to observe his approach and a guilty look crossed her face before she mumbled an excuse and hurried off.

It took only minutes for Frank and his deputy to attend to their business matters. Frank was about to return to the gathering when Pete's comment stopped him.

"By the way," there was a smirk in the deputy's voice, "I just heard a juicy piece of gossip I thought you might be interested in."

"Yeah, what's that?"

"I recalled you sayin' how you didn't trust the new man Sloane hired. Well," he shoved his hands into his pockets and rocked back on his heels, "I heard it was none other than Becky Foster who sent him out their way." He waited for the explosion he was sure would follow.

"What of it?" Frank growled irritably.

"Nothing, Frank," Pete denied hastily. "I was just wondering what to make of it. That's all."

"There's nothing to make of it. Becky told me she felt sorry for Ryan, that it can't be easy for anyone with a face like his to find work. She only did it out of pity."

"Sounds like a woman," Pete admitted and then gave Frank a playful nudge of his elbow. "If you don't mind my sayin' so, Becky Foster's one hell of a woman."

"Just don't go forgettin' whose woman she is," Frank warned. "I know your reputation with the ladies, Mitchell. If you know what's good for you, keep away from Becky Foster. She's private stock!"

The threat hung in the air even after the men had left.

Mike Ryan rose slowly from his crouched position, unmistakable fury stamped on his face. He had gone to water the horses and had stooped to examine the axle of a wagon when he had overheard the lawmen talking. Ben Sloane's name caught his attention, but Becky's held it. He had followed the rest of the conversation with interest. It had been an enlightenment.

Pity! The one thing he hated most. So that was what lay behind Rebecca Foster's well-meant suggestion. Pity! In her eyes, he must be some kind of freak, an oddity who belonged in a circus sideshow. Anger boiled within him until it became a frothing rage, ready to scald anything or anyone in its path.

What a fool she was, Becky chided herself as she strolled the perimeter of the wooded grove. She moved slowly, needing time to sort her jumbled thoughts. She had dawdled as long as possible with Hannah, all the while hoping Mike would return. And what would she have said if he had, she wondered. If she closed her eyes she could recall the cold contempt on his face when he looked at her. His unspoken criticism cut like a whip. His opinion shouldn't matter, her brain asserted. But it did, came her heart's rebuttal.

Head bent, preoccupied, her mind failed to register the handsomely tooled boots blocking her path in time to avoid a collision.

"Well, well," the boots' owner drawled, while a large pair of hands steadied her shoulders.

Becky's eyes flew up to meet narrowed sapphire slits that held a dangerous glitter.

"Fancy running into you," he continued mockingly, still not releasing her. "Or should I say fancy you running into me."

She cringed inwardly at the expression on his face. She kept silent, waiting for him to speak.

Mike shook his head in disbelief. "How can you just stand there so innocent and so damn beautiful?" The end of the sentence trailed away. His hand left her shoulder to grasp her arm. "I've got a few questions to ask, and I expect some honest answers." With this, he propelled her toward a footpath that veered into the woods away from the festivities.

"What on earth do you think you're doing?" she demanded, trying to jerk free from his grip.

"Let's say we're adjourning to my office where we can have our conversation free of interruptions."

Becky cast a glance over her shoulder, but no one seemed aware of her dilemma and came to her rescue.

Her action didn't go unnoticed. "What's the matter, Mrs. Foster?" he jeered. "Afraid what people might think?"

Anger must be contagious, she thought, because his ill humor was having an unwanted effect on her own disposition. "This is a small town, Mr. Ryan," she retorted. "People love nothing better than gossip."

"Far be it from me to compromise the lady's precious reputation," he mocked. "If that happens, I'll do the gentlemanly thing and offer matrimony." He gave a harsh discordant laugh that ricocheted off the trunks of the trees.

Sounds from the grove dulled and faded before he released his hold on her arm. Mechanically Becky rubbed the place his hand had been. "What do you have to talk about that requires my undivided attention?" she asked with a slight lift of an eyebrow.

He scowled down at her from his impressive height.

"Did you, or did you not," he interrogated in a clipped precise tone, "deliberately follow me into the general store that first afternoon in town?"

"This is why you brought me out here?" Her eyes widened in incredulity. "All you had to do was ask in a civilized manner, and I would have been happy to give you your answer. But no, you couldn't do that. You had to literally drag me off into the woods like a . . . a . . . barbarian."

His jaw clenched tightly, making the scar on his cheek even more livid than usual. "Did you, or didn't you?"

Becky's chin raised a notch. "I did."

Her prompt admission caught him off guard. He had been prepared for a lengthy inquisition and, if that failed, more drastic measures falling just short of strangulation. Mike crossed his arms over his wide chest and glared down at her. "Why?"

"Because Ben needed someone to help him even though he's too stubborn to admit it," she answered simply.

"And that's the only reason?"

"That's the only reason."

"Liar!"

Becky recoiled from the epithet. Color slowly ebbed from her face. "How dare you," she gasped. Her hands curled into tight balls, the nails biting into the flesh of her palms. Drawing a ragged breath, she spoke in a voice that shook with emotion. "If you think I'm going to stand here and listen to your insults or let you browbeat me, you're in for a big disappointment." She whirled on her heel only to find herself roughly hauled against a chest of granite.

"What about pity?"

She blinked. "Pity?"

"Yes, pity," he grated.

"That's absurd!" In spite of the tension, the notion struck Becky as so ludicrous she felt the wild urge to laugh. "Pray tell, why would I pity a hulk like you?"

Attuned to every nuance of her expression, Mike had seen amusement dance in the emerald eyes though he could find no humor in the situation. His grip on her slender shoulders tightened. He wanted to shake her until her teeth rattled, until she finally admitted the truth and pleaded for mercy. He wanted her to know he wouldn't tolerate being an object of pity—or amusement.

"If memory serves me," he ground out, "Denby said you felt sorry for me. That it can't be easy for someone with a face like mine to find work and that's the reason you sent me to see your friend."

Becky's head snapped up at the mention of Denby's name. Things began to make sense. "You're hurting me," she said with quiet dignity and, although Mike didn't release her, his hold loosened. Her next words were chosen with care. "Pity never entered into it. It's quite obvious either the marshal is lying or I am. The choice is yours, Mr. Ryan. Who will you believe? Frank Denby or me?"

Confusion and frustration played across his features like sunlight and shadow filtering through the spread boughs. "Convince me it isn't pity you feel when you look at me," he challenged softly.

"How?" It came out a whisper.

Mike cupped her face in his hands. Their eyes locked, the gauntlet thrown, the challenge accepted. Ever so slowly his head lowered to hers, as though still giving her time to reconsider and retreat from his advance. His mouth hovered mere inches from hers, so near she felt his warm breath caress her cheek. Her lips parted, not ready yet eager to meet the assault. A lambent flame in the dark blue depths of his eyes grew hotter and brighter. Tentative at first, his mouth touched hers, unable to comprehend her easy capitulation without a struggle. The kiss deepened, triggering an explosion that rocked the very ground they stood on. His mouth moved over hers, demanding and receiving total surrender. Both were breathless when they finally broke apart, neither feeling victorious, neither unscathed.

Becky dropped her eyes. "I'll be missed," she murmured. Gathering her full skirts in both hands, she turned and fled, for once eager to return to Frank Denby and away from the havoc this man could wreak upon her emotions.

Chapter Three

HER JOB WAS FINISHED; BEN WOULD DO THE REST.

Becky nervously fingered the whistle deep in the pocket of her jacket. The slender wood cylinder felt satiny smooth and oddly reassuring. When it was time she would take it out and gently blow into it three times. The plaintive call of a whippoorwill would sing on the night breeze, alerting Ben his journey could begin.

Yet she hesitated. There was safety here, hiding behind the cabin setting in the midst of a clearing waist-high in weeds. The screech of an owl pierced the stillness, startling her. One hand flew to her breast where she could feel her heart flutter like a trapped bird's.

"Ninny," she scolded herself. "What's wrong with you tonight? Stop being so jittery."

Everything was going according to plan, Becky reminded herself. A short time ago she had met the runaway, or passenger as he was sometimes called, at Willow Creek and guided him through the woods to a prearranged spot. Ben waited inside the cabin. At her signal, he would take their passenger to the next station concealed beneath the floor of an innocuous-appearing wagon that had been craftily designed for this particular purpose.

Becky glanced skyward and wished once more the night was dark and cloudy. Instead the moon hung like a giant silver medallion suspended in midnight blue velvet. As she watched, a wispy cloud trailed across the shiny surface like a diaphanous veil pulled across the heavens by an invisible hand. She waited until the moon's light was partially obscured and then began to skirt the cabin. Halfway around the clearing, a brisk breeze sent the cloud skittering off, leaving the night swathed in moonlight, and Becky clearly visible.

"Stop!" The command rang out.

Becky froze, momentarily paralyzed. Her head swiveled toward the sound and her eyes picked out the dark shape of a man silhouetted against the cabin. He took a step toward her, releasing her from her immobility. The woods offered sanctuary; she darted for cover.

"Stop, or I'll shoot!"

Panic gripped her, but her feet seemed encased in

lead. The faster she tried to flee, the slower her feet responded. Heavy footsteps crashed behind her, quickly closing the gap between them. Just a bit further and she would be safe. Becky was as familiar with the woods as she was with the shelves of her own pantry. The hollowed trunk of a maple would provide the perfect hiding place until her pursuer tired of his search.

She would have made it too, she told herself later, if her foot hadn't caught in a gnarled root and sent her sprawling. A heavy body fell on top of her, pushing her into the musty leaf-strewn ground. Frantically Becky squirmed to free herself. Desperation lent her strength, but she was no match for her opponent. Their bodies locked in silent combat, rolling over and over until they were stopped by the broad base of a tree. Her wrists were secured in an iron grip and pinned against the ground on either side of her head. Mike Ryan sat on top of her, his weight effectively subduing further struggle.

The floppy-brimmed hat shielding her identity was lost in the scuffle. A torrent of amber curls spilled free, framing her lovely face, her eyes wide with fear. They stared at one another in mute recognition.

"What the hell are you doing here?" Mike rasped finally.

Becky's mind was blank. What excuse could she possibly find to explain her way out of this . . . this mess? What was Mike doing here anyway, she wondered. Where was Ben?

"Well . . ." he prompted impatiently.

"Get off," she managed to gasp.

Mike took his time getting off of her, at least that's

the way it seemed to Becky. Reaching down he caught hold of her arm and pulled her to her feet. She breathed in great draughts of air and tried to collect her scrambled wits.

"Are you all right?" he demanded gruffly.

"No thanks to you," she retorted, venting her frustration on the hapless bits of twig and leaf that clung to her clothing.

Mike folded his arms across his massive chest in an already familiar gesture and raised a dark brow. "Is this the latest in women's fashions?" He circled her slowly, noting her attire.

Becky endured his inspection in silence, conscious of the way his eyes traveled the length of her, taking in the dark high-necked sweater visible above the collar of a jacket many sizes too large, to the oft-mended pants that once belonged to Adam.

"If I had known it was only you masquerading as a boy, I would have used more restraint," he said, plucking a dried leaf from her hair.

Becky glared at him. "If you've had your evening's entertainment, I'll be on my way. Wish I could say it's been a pleasure." She turned to leave, not really believing she'd get away so easily, but hoping just the same.

"Not so fast," his voice lashed out, stopping her before she could put one foot in front of the other. "For the last time, what are you doing out here?"

With a toss of her head, Becky flung the tangled mane of hair over her shoulder and decided to brazen it out. "I was out for a walk."

His harsh humorless laugh grated on her nerves. "Surely you can do better than that."

"I hardly think I owe you an explanation, Mr. Ryan," she said stiffly.

"I'm not letting you out of my sight until I know what you've been up to. You're coming with me."

"I am not!" Becky dug in her heels, a determined jut to her jaw.

Without another word, Mike picked her up and tossed her over his shoulder, as effortlessly as if she were a sack of flour.

"Put me down!"

Mike ignored her demand and walked purposefully in the direction of the cabin.

Infuriated, her fists pummeled his back. "I said put me down, you . . . !" She let loose a string of expletives learned long ago from Adam.

A firm swat across the buttocks silenced her tirade and brought the sting of tears to her eyes.

With his foot, Mike kicked open the door of the cabin and dumped her unceremoniously under the open-mouthed stare of Ben Sloane.

"Becky!"

Becky stared back, anger making her eyes shine with emerald brilliance. She was angry at Mike for his crude treatment of her, angry at herself for being caught in this ridiculous situation. She even felt an unreasonable anger at Ben for being witness to her humiliation.

"I found her snooping around outside," Mike said without preamble.

Ben cleared his throat. "Well, Rebecca, what have you to say for yourself?"

"I was out for a walk," she muttered sullenly.

"She was spying on us. My guess is that she'll head

straight for Denby and tell him what she found out. It won't take him long to figure out what we're up to."

"Is that right, Becky?" Ben questioned.

Becky released a pent-up sigh of relief. Mike's suspicions provided the excuse she needed. All she had to do was pretend he was right and play along with the notion. "What an imagination you have, Mr. Ryan," Becky drawled, warming up to her role. "I hate to disappoint you, but I have no idea what you and Ben are up to. I've never been good at riddles," she smiled sweetly into Mike's scowling face, "but Frank is. He's quite clever." She watched with satisfaction as the two men exchanged worried glances. "What are you going to do about it?"

Mike's fierce expression told her exactly what he'd like to do given the chance. Becky fought an instinctive urge to back away.

"You certainly have a knack for complicating things, Becky," Ben sighed.

"*I* do!" She rounded on him indignantly only to be silenced by the warning in his dark eyes. If anyone had a talent for complicating affairs, she wanted to scream, it was Mike Ryan, not her. Why had Ben brought him along anyway? The two of them had always managed just fine on their own.

"Well, there's only one thing to do." Ben ran his fingers through his snowy hair. "Since I know the route, I'll deliver the package. Mike, you'll have to stay with our guest until I get back."

Mike frowned, obviously unhappy with the situation. "You're the boss," he acquiesced with reluctance.

Ben looked from one to the other and slowly shook

his head. Judging from the anger on one face and the rebellion on the other, he would place his money that it would be far more exciting here than on the lonely journey to Potterville.

"See you both later," he said and then was gone.

A heavy pall fell over the cabin. Becky sighed. Nothing was going right. The last place on earth she wanted to be was in the cabin, cooped up for hours with a man who quite clearly despised her, yet a man whose kiss she couldn't forget.

"Now that I'm virtually your prisoner, I hope you're satisfied," she said scathingly.

"Prisoner is a bit dramatic, don't you think? Why not do as Ben said and think of yourself as my guest."

"Fine," Becky snapped. "If I'm your guest, I'm free to leave."

For a large man, Mike moved with catlike swiftness to block her exit. "I wouldn't advise it," he warned. "I'll use force if necessary to keep you here."

"You wouldn't dare," she hissed.

"Wouldn't I?"

Emerald eyes clashed with sapphire and were the first to look away. Becky knew with absolute certainty his was no idle threat. Turning away, she stalked to the far end of the cabin. Convinced he had made his point, Mike pulled out a chair and sat down at the rough-hewn table.

When Becky glanced over her shoulder, she found him shuffling a worn deck of cards. She pivoted and approached the table slowly. Dropping down in the chair opposite him, she propped her chin in her hands and waited for him to look up. He ignored her. Not a flicker of an eyelash betrayed he was aware of her presence. All his attention was concentrated on a game of solitaire. Becky's eyes narrowed thoughtfully. More drastic measures were called for. Before she could weigh the consequences, she reached out and mussed the neat columns of cards until they were scattered in hopeless disarray. Mike's head jerked up.

"Now that I have your attention," she said in dulcet tones, "I have a question for you."

"Lady, you sure know how to court danger. Without Ben here to protect you, you're walking a fine edge."

"You don't scare me," she said with bravado.

"Then that's your mistake," he growled. "What's your question?"

Becky leaned forward slightly. "How are you going to stop me from telling Frank everything that's happened tonight, particularly about me being kept here against my will?"

"No problem, provided Ben backs me up." Mike scooped up the cards and began reshuffling them.

Becky fumed at being summarily dismissed. She rose so abruptly her chair teetered precariously. "Your plan better be good!"

"It is." Mike placed the queen of hearts on a black king. "I doubt, however, you'll find it to your liking."

Frustration spawned a restless energy. Becky paced the cramped confines, observing her surroundings with disinterest. Constructed from logs, the cabin was one large room separated into sleeping quarters by a dingy scrap of burlap suspended by a piece of twine. Besides the table and two chairs, a bed with a sagging cornhusk mattress was the only other piece of furniture. A fireplace, its stones blackened with use, occupied an adjacent wall. The cabin's sole window was covered with heavy oiled paper to prevent light from escaping. This had been the first home of her parents, Matthew and Amanda Brantford.

A covert glance told her Mike was still engrossed with his game and oblivious to her presence. The air inside the cabin grew warm and stifling. Becky tugged the buttons of her jacket free of their openings and shrugged it off, tossing the garment carelessly across the foot of the bed. She closed her eyes and arched her back to relieve the knot of tension between her shoulder blades. Her waist-length hair felt hot against her neck. Raising her arms, she lifted the heavy mass and emitted a soft sigh as the air touched her neck.

The muffled sound drew Mike's attention. He watched, his actions arrested, as she lowered her arms sending the dark gold tresses rippling down her back like spilled honey. God! She was a beauty, he thought. In the lamplight, her profile was delicate and pure, each feature finely carved by a consummate artisan. Her skin had the translucence of ivory touched lightly at the cheekbones with coral. The sweetness of her lips still lingered in his memory. Even dressed as a boy, she was lovelier than one woman had the right to be. Sweater and pants clung to all the appropriate places, molding the ripe fullness of her breasts and hugging the gentle curve of waist and hip. Mike found himself wondering what it would be like to lose himself in her sweet essence.

"Damn, stupid fool!" Mike cursed under his breath and forced his concentration back to the game at hand.

Becky sent him a questioning glance. She couldn't

possibly have heard correctly. Gnawing her lower lip, she debated whether to ask him to repeat what he had said. But judging from the vehement manner he was slapping the cards down, she prudently remained silent. Her pacing resumed.

Her thoughts were unruly, always returning to dwell on Mike Ryan. He was a difficult man to ignore. No, not difficult, Becky amended, impossible. Her eyes traversed the broad expanse of his shoulders and then wandered over the ebony strands curling loosely over the edge of his collar. Her imagination fondled the stray locks, finding them like thick coils of silk beneath her exploring fingertips.

God! What was wrong with her, she wondered in exasperation. She hadn't been the same since she first set eyes on him. What set Mike Ryan apart? His physical strength? Becky gave her head a negative shake. Though Pete Mitchell lacked Mike's commanding height, he was his equal in brawn. His appearance? Becky again shook her head. In all fairness, she had to admit Frank Denby's clean even countenance held a certain appeal, at least to a number of women in Oak Ridge. His moral convictions? She stifled a giggle. Surely no one could match Reverend Tucker's fervent sense of right and wrong, good and evil. What was it about Mike that could cause her stomach to flutter as though she had just stepped off a tightrope into thin air? The answer eluded her.

"Your pacing is wearing on my nerves," Mike said, breaking through her reverie. "I don't suppose you play poker?"

Becky stopped to stare at him in amazement. Then, before he had time to reconsider, she pulled out a chair and sat down. "Five card stud or draw?"

It was his turn to be surprised. "Ladies' choice." He shrugged, recovering his composure.

An hour later Mike threw down yet another losing hand in disgust. "I didn't think ladies were given poker lessons."

A smile of pure glee curved her mouth. "If you have any complaints, you'll have to take them up with my brother, Adam. He taught me everything I know about the game."

"I might just do that," Mike agreed amiably, lounging back in his chair. "From what I've heard, your brother doesn't spend much time around here."

"We keep in touch." Becky rose to her brother's defense. "Adam knows I'm perfectly capable of managing the farm in his absence. He trusts my judgment completely."

Mike rocked the chair back on its legs and eyed her lazily. "When I met you in the marshal's office I never would have guessed in a million years you'd turn out to be a farmer."

"Just what did you think?" Curiosity prompted her to ask.

Mike shrugged, a rueful smile played across his mouth. "You looked more the type to live in a big house in the center of town and spend your days organizing church socials."

"In other words," Becky laughed in delight, "you thought I knew more about sipping tea than shipping cattle."

Her accurate assessment brought forth an engaging grin, one Becky returned with equal warmth. Her smile gradually faded, and she became serious. "First impressions are often deceiving, Mr. Ryan. Situations and people are not always as they appear on the surface."

Becky regretted the words the instant they were spoken. Before Mike could probe beneath her cryptic remark, she hurriedly changed the subject.

"It's getting late. How much longer will Ben be?"

Mike's expression hardened. "What's the rush? Is your lover waiting?"

His assumption slapped her. Stunned by the unjust attack, Becky could only stare at him, her eyes turbulent pools of hurt and anger. Suddenly the thought of remaining in the restrictive confines of the cabin another moment was intolerable. Jumping to her feet, she overturned the chair in her haste, and ran across the room. The latch balked under her trembling fingers, but at last gave way and the door swung open. The weathered planks were wrenched from her grasp and slammed shut. An involuntary gasp escaped as she felt a sharp stab of pain in the palm of her hand. Looking down, Becky saw a long splinter of wood protruding from the soft flesh.

Mike's glance followed hers. Seeing the cause of her distress, his anger abated somewhat. "Give me your hand," he ordered.

Reluctantly Becky extended her hand, palm up. Mike reached deep into the pocket of his pants and withdrew a penknife. She watched as he opened a blade and flinched at the touch of its cold steel against her warm skin.

"Hold still!" Mike instructed in a tone that brooked no disobedience.

It was over in an instant. The offending splinter was removed in a deft motion that caused a prickling of tears behind her eyelids. A ruby red bead of blood marked the site. Mike blotted the drop with a hand-kerchief and then inspected her palm to make certain no tiny fragment remained to fester later.

Becky's eyes, brilliant with unshed tears, met his. "Thank you," she said in a choked whisper.

Ever so slowly, Mike raised her hand. Becky was torn between the urge to snatch it free and the desire to let it rest in his forever. His eyes held her captive. She watched spellbound as his irises darkened to the color of the midnight sky.

"You're a witch," he murmured. "A sweet wicked witch."

Mike turned her hand and pressed a tender kiss to the sensitive spot at the base of her thumb. Though his kiss was gentle, Becky felt as though a bolt of lightning had struck her. She drew in a shuddering breath. Her body swayed toward him. The contact was electrifying. He wrapped his arms around her, holding her tightly.

His mouth crushed hers, demanding and receiving a response. Her lips parted eagerly. With deliberate thoroughness his tongue explored the hollows of her mouth. A low moan escaped when his lips left hers.

Becky didn't want the kiss to end. She was greedy for more, so much more the need was terrifying in its intensity. All the passion, all the desire lying dormant since David's death surged to break free.

Mike's fingers twined through the strands of dark gold silk. "Witch," he breathed. "Work your magic, weave your spell. Love me."

It was beyond Becky's power to deny his plea. His words broke through her carefully constructed barri-er, sweeping inhibitions and logic away in a swirling current. All she wanted at that moment was to be a woman again, complete and whole, purged of the lonely void that had been her companion for the last three years. Her passion-filled eyes gave Mike the answer he craved. Picking her up in his arms, he carried her to the bed where he reverently placed her on the sagging mattress.

This is insanity! Her mind flashed the warning her body ignored. That was her last coherent thought before his mouth lowered to once again claim hers. He kissed her eyelids, the corners of her mouth, the sensitive skin just below her earlobe.

"Michael," she sighed.

Mike framed her face with his hands. "I want you as I've never wanted a woman," came the ragged admission. "I want no barriers between us." His hands left her face and Becky felt their calloused strength against her ribcage as he removed first her sweater and then her camisole.

"Perfect," he breathed. The rest of her clothes quickly followed.

He stood tall and powerful, looking down at her, memorizing every graceful curve and line. His look bordered on adoration. It was a look reserved for a rare work of art, a masterpiece.

Never taking his eyes from her, Mike removed his clothing. Now it was Becky's turn to worship. He could have been the model used for a superbly sculpted statue, with his magnificently proportioned body of muscle and sinew.

Becky held her arms out and he came to her, the mattress yielding beneath his weight. Their lips met. Slowly, caught up in the urgency of his kiss, she became aware of his hands cupping the swell of her breasts. His mouth left hers to nibble a path down her neck to the soft mound of one breast where it stopped to tease and tantalize the rosy peak.

Pleasure burst within her. Weaving her fingers through his thick glossy curls, she held him to her breast as her body began to move to an ageless rhythm. No words were necessary as together they celebrated the ancient ritual.

"Michael." Her whisper filled with joy and wonder floated on the stillness as they lay spent in each other's embrace.

Reality crept back slowly, bringing reason with it.

Becky stirred in the cradle of Mike's arms. Guilt and shame that had been mysteriously absent earlier rose up to engulf her. Good Lord! What have I done, she asked herself. Whatever possessed me to behave no better than an animal in heat? Becky had always taken quiet pride in the knowledge that during her marriage, she and David shared a loving and mutually satisfying relationship. But love played no part in what had just transpired. This had been a coupling, a frantic urgent release of long-denied emotions. I'm no better than Loretta Porter and her whores at the Satin Slipper, she admonished in disgust.

Pulling free from his arms, Becky scrambled off the bed and grabbed her clothes. Keeping her back turned, she dressed quickly, grateful Mike couldn't see how her fingers fumbled with the simple fastenings. She heard him swing his legs to the floor and reach for his clothing.

The silence was painful. What did one say after a quick tumble in the hay? She swallowed, but it felt as though a hard lump was lodged in her throat. What must Mike think of her? A tramp? A woman of easy virtue? His low opinion could only match her own. Should she try to explain it was the first time she'd been with a man since her husband had died? Could that be the reason for her abandoned response?

"Mike . . ." she began hesitantly.

He cut her off. "If you expect me to be a gentleman and say I'm sorry, forget it!"

Becky studied her hands, a curtain of hair falling about her shoulders to hide her face. "If anyone is to blame, it was me," she said softly.

"How noble!" he scoffed. "We're both adults, Mrs. Foster. What happened between us wasn't rape, or even seduction. You wanted me, and I wanted you. It was that basic."

"Whatever the reason, it mustn't happen again."

"Your wish is my command." Each word was laced with sarcasm. He strode to the table, sat down, and picked up the deck of cards, the episode dismissed. Instead of relief, his casual disregard of the incident made her feel worse.

"Please understand," she tried once more. "I'm not like that. I don't know what came over me."

"Then let me enlighten you," he snarled. "This isn't the first time I've made love to a woman only to have her regret it later. You have a reputation to protect here in Oak Ridge. It wouldn't do for people to know you've taken a scarfaced lover. Besides," his eyes pierced her like shards of blue ice, "Frank Denby wouldn't want any more to do with you."

It was useless to protest. He had a point, Becky conceded in defeat. Let Mike think what he wanted.

One word to Frank about a dalliance of any sort and their relationship would be severed. She had worked too hard to sacrifice it all.

With a harsh discordant laugh, Mike returned to his cards. Becky resumed her pacing. Neither spoke another word until the door swung open and a weary but triumphant Ben Sloane appeared.

"How did things go?" Mike asked, getting to his feet.

"Like clockwork," Ben answered. "Did you two manage to get better acquainted while I was gone?"

Becky nearly choked at his choice of words. Feeling a blush flood her cheeks, she turned her back and busily arranged the cards on the table into a neat pile.

"Mrs. Foster was curious how we were going to stop her from going to the marshal and telling him we detained her against her will."

Ben shot a troubled look in her direction. "Surely we can take her word that she won't mention it."

"Don't count on it," Mike argued.

Becky flung her tousled hair over her shoulder and turned to confront the two men. "Mr. Ryan has a plan all worked out," she said coldly. "Why don't you ask him what it is? He refuses to tell me, but maybe he'll tell you."

Ben shoved his hat back from his forehead with a weary gesture. "Let's hear it, Mike."

Mike glanced at Becky's mutinous expression before answering. "From what I've gathered, the marshal regards the lady as his private property. He wouldn't like knowing there was a trespasser."

"What are you getting at?" Becky demanded, her voice rising.

Mike's gaze raked over her, beginning with her disheveled amber curls and traveling down her trim shapely figure. Becky's hands clenched into tight fists at her sides as she forced herself to endure his insolent perusal.

"If you tell Denby what happened tonight," Mike said, "I'll tell him my version."

"Which is?" she asked through gritted teeth.

"I'll tell him you asked me out to your place on some false pretext and then invited me to spend the night. When I told you I wasn't interested, you flew into a rage and threatened to get even. Ben, I'll need you to supply my alibi. You'll have to tell Denby we were together, that we spent the night in the bunk-house playing cards."

"You can't! You'll ruin everything," Becky cried in protest. She turned to her old friend for support. "Ben, are you just going to stand there and let him blackmail me?"

"Honey," Ben shook his head, "I don't like this any more than you do, but what else can I do?"

Becky glared from one to the other. "Ohh!" She gave in to the childish urge to stamp her foot.

"The decision's yours," Mike told her, unmoved by her antics. "What's it going to be?"

Becky drew in a deep breath and summoned a creditable air of arrogance. "You leave me little choice but to go along with your outrageous threat. Now am I free to leave?"

Ben massaged the bridge of his nose between thumb and forefinger. For the first time since his return, Becky noted the tired slump of his shoulders. "The woods are no place to be roaming about at this hour." Each word was dragged out with effort. "I'll sleep better knowing you got home safely. I'll take you there."

Becky nodded, eager to agree with anything that would bring this night to an end. She had brushed past Mike on her way to the door before his voice stopped her.

"Go home and get some rest, Ben. You look all done in." Mike's voice carried authority. "I'll see Mrs. Foster home."

"If you don't mind, honey," Ben gave Becky an apologetic smile, "I think I'll take Mike up on his offer. I finally have to admit I'm not as young as I used to be."

Becky managed to return a feeble smile and bit back her objections. "Well," she rounded on Mike, "what are we waiting for?"

She grabbed her jacket and stalked out of the cabin, leaving the men to follow. Once outdoors, she sucked in a lungful of cool night air. After the stuffiness of the cabin, it was a blessed relief. A horse whinnied impatiently, and she saw that two horses were saddled and waiting. Ben mounted one while Mike got on the other and extended his hand to her. Becky hesitated, loath to have even this casual contact.

"What are you waiting for?" he mocked. "I thought you were in a hurry." The moonlight lent his scarred face a sardonic cast as he stared down at her. "Of course," he said, shrugging, "if you want Ben, as exhausted as he is, to insist on seeing you home. . . ."

Becky accepted Mike's hand and swung up behind him in the saddle. "You don't have to look so damn smug," she hissed under her breath.

"Tch, tch," Mike clucked his tongue reprovingly. "I didn't think ladies knew how to swear."

"I never claimed to be a lady," Becky flared.

Mike chuckled softly and nudged his horse to follow Ben's down the narrow overgrown track that led to the main road. Once there, they parted company, Ben going in one direction, Mike and Becky in the other.

The steady clip-clop of horse's hooves had a soothing effect on Becky's jangled nerves. Her earlier turmoil dissolved into a strange tranquillity. It was a beautiful night. High above, the moon reigned in pale splendor while a host of stars shimmered in abeyance. Isolated farmhouses stood mute sentinels to their slow trek homeward. How easy it would be to imagine she and Mike were the only two people in the universe. Becky's arms grew heavy with the desire to steal tighter around his waist. She wanted to mold her body to his and rub her cheek against the coarse fabric of his shirt.

Enough! she admonished, realizing the treacherous bend of her thoughts. She sat up straighter in the saddle and interjected a peevish note in her voice. "Can't we go any faster?"

"Not unless you want to wake everyone from a sound sleep to wonder who's fool enough to be galloping by at this ungodly hour."

Becky could not think of a suitable rejoinder, and they lapsed back into silence.

Mike circled the house reining to a halt near the

steps of the back porch. Becky caught his hand and swung to the ground. Mike gazed down at her, his expression unreadable.

"You may or may not be a lady, Rebecca Foster," he released her hand at last, "but you sure are one hell of a woman." He gave what resembled a jaunty salute, and nudging the gelding into a canter, disappeared from sight.

Chapter Four

REVEREND THADDEUS TUCKER MOPPED THE PERSPIRA-
tion from his brow with a snowy linen handkerchief.
Then, nonplussed by either the heat or his congregation's inattention, he forged ahead with an earnest if
uninspired sermon.

Becky was one of the few present who appeared
impervious to the sweltering July heat that had
plagued southern Indiana for over a week. She managed to look crisp and fresh in a gown of delicate
white India muslin, its wide skirt trimmed with three
deep flounces which like the bodice were embroidered

with dainty pink rosettes. A straw chip bonnet was perched at a saucy angle on top of her amber curls.

Unfortunately Becky wasn't as immune to the temperature as she appeared. She shifted her weight subtly and noted the starch in her crinoline was beginning to wilt. Drat! If she were truly a witch as Mike Ryan so snidely implied, she would place a curse on the person who decreed it fashionable that ladies wear layer after layer of stiff petticoats. Giving her ivory-handled fan a lethargic wave, she scanned the assembled worshippers.

By chance her gaze rested on a couple and their small son seated to her right several pews ahead, Tom and Sally Weston. Tom would always occupy a special place in her affections. Surely, Becky reflected, every woman remembers the first man who kissed her. Before her mother's illness had claimed all her time and energy, she and Tom had been childhood sweethearts. If she hadn't fled to Boston and met David Foster how different her life might be. The tow-haired boy of three resting against Tom's shoulder might easily have been her son.

Once again she made an effort to concentrate on Reverend Tucker's text, and once again failed. This time her attention was diverted by the flight of a blue-tailed fly. She watched while it looped lazy circles and then came to rest on the collar of Ben Sloane's jacket. Poor Ben! He was having a horrible time staying awake. His head nodded and bobbed like a sunflower in a breeze. Finally he gave up the valiant attempt and his head slumped forward to rest chin on chest. She frowned. Was that a snore? It had to be. Next to him, Hannah's eyes rolled heavenward, whether in supplication or contrition Becky could only guess, and then with unerring accuracy Hannah jabbed her elbow into Ben's ribcage. Ben woke with a start to give his wife a reproachful if somewhat bewildered look. Moments later he was dozing again.

Mike Ryan observed the episode with an indulgent smile. Turning his head slightly, he noticed Becky also watched Ben with fond amusement. Try as he might, Mike hadn't been able to forget the night at Willow Creek. He couldn't forget the spill of honey gold hair around bare shoulders. He couldn't forget the satiny texture of her skin. But most of all, he couldn't forget she had been kindling in his arms, igniting instantly to burn with brilliance all too quickly extinguished.

It would never happen again. Becky had made that clear. Nor was he surprised. Countless times, he caught himself wondering if things might have been different without the damning scar that crossed one cheek. But he knew the answer. His mouth compressed into a bitter line. Hadn't Claire, his own fiancée, been unable to hide her shock and revulsion once the bandages had been removed? It was a look he had seen many times since. Why should Becky Foster be any different?

A murmur started at the back of the church, growing louder as it rippled forward. A slightly-built man with sparse brown hair and a receding hairline purposefully made his way up the side aisle brandishing an official-looking sheet of yellow paper. Reverend Tucker, astounded by the interruption, halted his sermon in midsentence. Jed Rawlins handed over the telegram with a flourish. Upon reading the missive, Reverend Tucker took out his handkerchief and blotted beads of perspiration that dotted his upper lip. He cleared his throat and read the message a second time.

Jolted from their lethargy, the congregation fairly buzzed with whispered speculation. An expectant hush fell as the minister held up his hands and signaled for silence.

"My dear friends," he intoned solemnly. "I have just received word that President Zachary Taylor is gravely ill. Our prayers are asked for his recovery. Let us bow our heads for a moment of silent prayer that the Almighty in his infinite wisdom and mercy will look down in favor upon his faithful servant."

All heads bowed obediently. Becky offered up a hasty prayer while her mind raced. Newspapers, of course, had reported President Taylor's leaving the Independence Day festivities in Washington after complaining he was ill. Until now, however, no one had any idea of the seriousness of his condition. Should anything happen to Taylor, Vice-President Millard Fillmore would serve the nearly three years that remained of Taylor's term. Heaven knew, Zachary Taylor left much to be desired in a president, but there was no doubt the man violently opposed the Compromise Measures. With Taylor in office there was no chance of their passage, but with Fillmore the situation could literally change overnight.

Reverend Tucker prudently abandoned his sermon and brought the service to its conclusion. People spilled down the church steps to gather in clusters on the lawn. Becky was one of the last to leave the church. She stood on the top step and scanned the groups until she spotted Ben. Then she lifted her skirts and quickly descended the stairs.

"That poor man." Hannah clucked her tongue in sympathy. "I had no idea he was so sick."

"It's most unfortunate," Margaret Nelson agreed. "Jed," she directed her question at the telegrapher, "did the telegram mention what was wrong with President Taylor?"

"Cholera."

"Cholera, my foot!" a man snorted in disbelief. "The old fool most likely ate too much at that fancy Independence Day shindig and came down with a case of indigestion."

"Will!" the man's wife admonished. "What a thing to say."

"It's true, Emma," Will Connally returned. "Taylor may have made his mark as general, but he doesn't know a darn sight more about being president than I do. Sixteen months in office and what has he done? Nothing!"

Impatient with the aimless drift of the conversation, Becky raised her voice and addressed her old friend. "Ben, if Zachary Taylor should die and Fillmore become president, what do you think will happen to the Compromise Measures?"

Ben's dark brows knit thoughtfully. "I don't read tea leaves, honey," he cautioned, "but my guess would be that Fillmore won't waste a minute getting those bills approved."

"What makes you so sure, Ben?" Tom Weston spoke up.

"Way I see it, Tom, Fillmore is in a rather shaky position. No one outside New York State even heard of the man until the Whigs picked him to be Taylor's running mate in '48. Now Fillmore finds himself in the middle of a situation where on one hand the South threatens secession, and on the other the North promises to preserve the Union at all costs. A compromise is the only way out."

A flurry of discussion greeted Ben's statement. Becky edged away, needing time to sort out her conflicting feelings. Talk of a civil war was being heard with frightening regularity, so perhaps a compromise was the best solution. However, it would have a direct bearing on her since an essential element was a more stringent Fugitive Slave Law. Although this would prove unpopular in the North, southern slaveholders would rejoice. Under the revised law, it would be the responsibility of the federal government and not the individual state to assist in the return of runaway slaves. Knowing Frank Denby, he would track down any rumors of the underground railroad with a fanatic's zeal. Her friendship with him would be invaluable. Though she might loathe his pompous ways, Becky resolved to give Frank no cause to suspect her growing dislike.

"Politics bore you?" Mike's voice sliced into her thoughts. He stood somewhat apart. The sun glinted on his glossy blue-black hair, bringing to mind the sheen of a raven's wing. In tan well-fitting breeches, white linen shirt, and navy broadcloth jacket he looked exceedingly attractive.

"Not at all!" Becky retorted, waving her fan with sudden vigor to cool the warm surge in her cheeks. "Actually I find politics fascinating."

"So fascinating you walked away?"

"What about you?" she countered. "I don't see you in the midst of all the talk. Bored?"

He ignored the jibe and stared off with a faraway look that caused her to wonder if he had forgotten her presence.

"Maybe I view this morning's news differently than most folks," he said at last.

"In what way?"

"I fought beside Taylor at the Battle of Buena Vista. If he dies the country will lose one of its greatest generals."

"You were at Buena Vista?"

Mike nodded, already regretting his admission. He didn't like to think about that time.

"I remember reading about it. If memory serves me, Santa Anna's men outnumbered Taylor's forces four to one."

"I was too busy at the time to count."

"Nevertheless, it was a stunning victory. It made Zachary Taylor a national hero."

"Sorry to interrupt. Did you forget our plans for this afternoon, Rebecca?" Frank Denby's tone was full of censure.

Becky summoned a smile. "How could I forget our picnic when I've looked forward to it all week?" She tucked her hand in the crook of his arm and drew him away. "Wait until you see . . ." Her voice trailed off as they strolled out of earshot.

Mike scowled. What a conniving little bitch! She had tricked him into thinking she was interested in him. Maybe she was, at least until another man came along. Damn her pretty little hide! The way she made up to Denby, you'd think her life depended on it. How long would it take before she told him about the night at Willow Creek?

"They make a rather handsome pair, don't they?"

Mike turned to find Margaret Nelson at his side. The dowager watched his reaction with avid curiosity.

"I suppose." He shrugged.

"I can't offer you a cozy picnic on a riverbank, Mr. Ryan, but it would please me greatly if you would be my guest for dinner this afternoon."

"Why?"

"Because, my suspicious friend, you interest me," she answered smiling. "Now will you humor an old lady and be her dinner guest? And please, call me Maggie."

Mike chuckled. "I never could refuse an attractive woman."

"Blarney!" she retorted with a dry laugh.

Two days later, Becky stood on the back porch and waited for the dust to settle after Jed Rawlin's hasty departure. Normally Jed would have lingered. Not even a gaggle of women at a quilting bee loved gossip more than the spindly myopic telegraph operator. This time, however, his visit had been brief. Thrusting the cable at her, he tossed down a glass of cold water before riding off to spread the news that Zachary Taylor was dead. Tomorrow, Millard Fillmore would be sworn in as thirteenth president of the United States.

Becky reached into her skirt pocket and withdrew the envelope, then ripped it open. As she had guessed, it was from Adam. The message was brief.

EXPECT TWO PACKAGES. STOP.
ARRIVING TUESDAY. STOP.
SHIPPING NORMAL ROUTE. STOP.

ADAM

57

Tuesday! That's today! Her brain worked feverishly. This was Adam's way of informing her he would be sending two runaway slaves northward to be met at Willow Creek and transported to the next station. To avert suspicion, two packages bearing the name of an exclusive New Orleans shop would be sent to Becky in care of the general store.

Ben would have to be told. Becky refolded the telegram and placed it back in its torn envelope. Taking only time to grab a wide-brimmed straw hat from a hook inside the kitchen door, she headed toward the stable.

The sun scorched through the thin cotton of her blouse and perspiration trickled between her breasts as Becky rode across the fields separating her property from the Sloanes'. Queen Anne's lace, buttercups, and yarrow nodded drowsily in the summer heat. A haze of dust kicked up by the mare's heels marked her progress. At last the roof of the Sloane ranch appeared below the crest of a hill. Now if her ruse worked she would find a chance to talk to Ben without being overheard.

Her light rap on the screened door was answered almost immediately.

"Becky!" Ben's face creased in genuine pleasure. "What brings you out on such a hot afternoon? Don't you know you could get sunstroke?"

"Stop acting like a mother hen," Becky laughed. She stepped into the kitchen and looked around, fully expecting to see Hannah. "I thought I'd write to Adam when I remembered there was a journal article you wanted to send him."

Ben grinned. "Let me get you a glass of lemonade. Then you can tell me the real reason for your visit."

58

"I never could keep any secrets from you, Ben Sloane." Becky gave the man who was more father than friend an affectionate hug. "Where is Hannah, by the way?"

"She went into town to help plan the next church social."

Becky swept off her hat and brushed aside the damp tendrils of hair that had escaped from the long single plait falling across one shoulder. "I'm glad to see you had the good sense to stay out of the heat."

"Now listen to who's talking," Ben teased as he poured lemonade into tall glasses. Handing one to her, he ushered her into the room he jokingly referred to as the library. "I was trying to get caught up on my bookkeeping." He gestured to the untidy mound of ledgers and papers that littered the rolltop desk.

Becky sighed as she sank into a worn but comfortable leather chair. "Just let me sit here for a minute and enjoy this. After the ride over, I'm absolutely parched."

Ben lounged back in the remaining chair and reached for his pipe. The fruity aroma of tobacco pleasantly filled the air. With the window shades drawn to keep out the sun's searing rays, the room was a comfortable oasis. For a time, Becky and Ben were content to sip their drinks in companionable silence.

Considerably refreshed, Becky leaned forward and spoke in a low voice. "I just received a message from Adam."

Ben nodded, calmly puffing on his pipe, and waited for her to continue.

59

"He said to expect two packages." Becky paused. "Tonight."

"Tonight?" He frowned. "It isn't like Adam to give such short notice."

"The same thought ran through my mind," Becky admitted. "I imagine in the confusion of President Taylor's illness, the message was delayed."

Possibly, Ben thought to himself. Still, Adam was a planner, it wasn't like him to let things go until the last minute.

"Adam's telegram wasn't the only reason for Jed's visit," Becky went on.

"President Taylor?"

Becky nodded. "He died this morning. Millard Fillmore will be sworn into office tomorrow."

"If the Compromise Measures pass, and I believe they will, we're going to have to be mighty careful." Ben's deep voice sounded troubled. "No one, absolutely no one, other than myself and Adam must know you're involved with the movement."

"What about . . ."

"Not even Mike." He puffed on his pipe and blew out a cloud of smoke. "I know you're wondering why I included him last time. Truth is, I just can't keep up with things as well as I'd like. Thought I might need his help from time to time. The spirit's willing, but the body isn't what it used to be."

Becky's eyes misted. "You'll never grow old, Ben."

"Everyone grows old, honey," he said, giving her a fond smile. "I'd bet my last cent that Mike Ryan can be trusted, but I gave Adam my word. I've never seen him so fired up about anything like he was about keeping your part in this a secret."

Becky played with the end of her thick braid. Did

Ben realize how hard it was butting heads with Mike each time they met?

"Look," Ben said, trying to cheer her up, "Adam will be home in a few months. Let him meet Mike for himself and we'll take it from there."

Becky sighed. "All right," she agreed reluctantly.

"Good!" Ben relaxed back in his chair and pointed the stem of his pipe at her. "Now I don't want any arguments when I tell you I'm going to take care of tonight's delivery myself."

Objections bubbled to the surface but before they could burst forth there was a knock on the door.

"Let me see who it is." Ben rose to his feet. "Remember, you're only here to borrow that journal."

Becky tucked her legs underneath her and waited. The muted sound of male voices filtered into the study, and presently she heard footsteps approach. Thinking they belonged to Ben, Becky was surprised to find Mike's large frame instead.

She drank in the sight of him. An unruly tangle of curls fell boyishly across his forehead. His shirt was unbuttoned nearly to the waist and revealed a mat of dark hair covering a hard muscled torso. Skin deeply bronzed by the sun made the sapphire hue of his eyes a startling contrast. He exuded a virility that made her pulse erratically skip a beat.

A slight movement from her drew his attention. "Ben didn't say he had a visitor."

"I hardly think Ben regards me as company."

"No, I suppose not," Mike agreed, his mouth twisting in a parody of a smile. "You seem to have bewitched him as well."

Circling the rim of her glass with an index finger,

Becky matched his unblinking stare. "Is something wrong, Mr. Ryan?" she challenged.

"Wrong?" he echoed. "What could be wrong when I'm in the presence of a beautiful woman? Once again you surprise me. I didn't think it proper for a *lady* to allow the sun to tint her skin the color of wild honey or streak her hair the shade of ripe wheat. If I seem confused, it's because I can't decide whether you look more a golden gypsy or a tawny kitten."

It would have been easy to respond to the husky seductive timbre of his voice if it hadn't been for the cool mockery in his eyes. "You have the rare talent for turning a compliment into an insult."

"You're a smart woman. Perhaps too smart for your own good."

"Stop talking in riddles. What are you trying to say?"

"I got an uneasy feeling watching you and the marshal on Sunday. It started me thinking about something you said once about first impressions being deceiving. I may have sorely underestimated you."

"In what way?"

"You're far too intelligent not to have figured out what was really going on the night I caught you snooping outside the cabin. Let me remind you, it would be foolish to mention any conclusions to your boyfriend."

"I'm not an idiot! Only an imbecile would tell Frank what you and Ben are up to. Your blackmail threat was a stroke of genius. You are to be congratulated."

"As long as we understand each other there shouldn't be any problems."

The tide of Becky's temper rose. She set her

lemonade down with a thud that sent the liquid sloshing against the sides of the glass. "You chose the perfect weapon," she said, springing from the chair in a swift feline movement. "Frank is extremely jealous. Your accusations would plant a doubt in his mind that all the denials in the world couldn't erase. It would be my word against yours and Ben's. While Frank would never believe you, he'd never doubt Ben. It wasn't easy winning Frank's trust. I will *not* allow you to spoil things for me."

"Far be it from me to stand in the way of true love."

His mockery fanned her anger. With a toss of her head, Becky sent the long braid whipping over her shoulder. "If I were you," her tone was clipped, "I'd be very careful not to make any mistakes. Nothing would give Frank greater pleasure than to lock you behind bars."

"What about you, Becky? Would you like that too?"

"You stubborn pigheaded Irishman!" she flared. "All I'm trying to do is give you fair warning that Frank Denby would like nothing better than to see your hide nailed to the barn door."

"Why the warning?"

"Because," she advanced toward him, arms folded across her chest, oblivious of the way her blouse gaped in front. "Because," she repeated, "I want the satisfaction of saying I told you so when Denby throws away the key."

Mike's gaze dropped from her flushed face to the deep cleft between her breasts. Before she could guess his intent, he reached out and brought her braid back over her shoulder. Ever so slowly his fingers slid down the thick silky rope until they rested along the velvety swell of her breast. Her skin burned beneath his touch, a sensation both exciting and distressing. She watched his gaze shift and travel to the throbbing pulse at the base of her throat. Her breathing became shallow. When his eyes raised to her mouth and lingered there, her lips parted, ready to receive the sweet pressure of his.

Footsteps clattered on the stairs; the mood was shattered. Mike dropped the golden plait as though it singed his fingers. Feeling flustered, Becky half-turned and toyed with an ornately carved pipe rack on the desk.

"I found it!" Ben announced, waving a dog-eared journal. "I asked Hannah to put this where it wouldn't get lost, then I couldn't remember what she did with it." His triumphant grin faded as he glanced from one to the other. The tension in the small room was palpable. Ben shook his head in disgust. The two couldn't be left alone five minutes without arguing.

"I'm glad you found it." The words came out in jerks. "Adam will appreciate it." She took the magazine from Ben. "Don't bother, I can see myself out."

It took all her willpower to walk when she wanted to run. Every fiber, every cell, screamed with the need to put distance between herself and Mike Ryan. As soon as the house was out of sight, she kicked the mare's flanks. Distance. She needed distance.

No sooner had the door shut behind her when Ben rounded on Mike. "What happened?"

"Nothing."

"Don't give me that!" Ben spoke sharper than Mike had ever heard him. "Becky was upset. What did you say to her?"

Mike shrugged. "I reminded her it wouldn't be a

good idea to run to Denby with any ideas she might have about us being involved in the underground railroad."

"Why the blazes did you do that?" Ben slammed his fist on the desk.

"Come off it, Ben." Mike's temper began to heat. "Becky wasn't on a snipe hunt the night I caught her nosing around. She was on to something and was checking it out. Everyone in town knows she and Denby are pro-slavery. There's talk she has him on the brink of proposing. She must be chafing at the bit to tell him everything she knows."

The color drained from Ben's face, leaving it pale and drawn. Wearily he sank into a chair. "What did Becky have to say?"

"She didn't need a reminder she was being blackmailed." Mike tugged his hand through disheveled curls. "I know you're fond of her, Ben, but you have to stop thinking of her as a child. She's a grown woman. Think how much trouble she could cause."

"All right. You made your point." Ben absently rubbed his chest with the heel of his hand.

How strange, Mike thought, that even such a sensible man could be influenced by a beautiful woman.

Chapter Five

THE SOLITARY WAGON CRAWLED ALONG THE DARK, rut-filled road. Mike had come one, maybe two miles, and already it seemed like twenty. The night was dark as pitch, and the air felt thick and heavy. Beneath the thick scar on his face, his cheekbone throbbed. A sure sign of rain.

He swore softly as the wagon bounded in and out of a deep groove and thought of the human cargo hidden beneath the wagon's false bottom. Tonight's journey would not be easy one. At least the shorter of the two runaways had a generous supply of body fat to cushion the worst of the jolts. Mike gave a low

66

chuckle, remembering the unlikely pair, one tall and rangy, the other as round as he was high. Then Ben's face intruded into his thoughts and the humor faded. It hadn't been easy for Ben either. He was a proud man. It was hard to admit he didn't feel up to making tonight's trip and ask Mike's help. Ben blamed it on the heat. Still Mike worried about him and knew Hannah did too.

Just then the wagon hit a particularly deep rut. At the same time, a high-pitched wail pierced the stillness. Hair-raising, Mike's superstitious Irish grandmother would have called it. Mike brought the skittish team to a halt and jumped down from the seat. Flinging aside the sacks of feed, he opened the trap door. Two pair of eyes stared back at him.

"What's wrong?" Mike demanded.

"Baby's comin'."

Mike's startled gaze swung to the other figure. Good Lord! Was it possible? Could the rotund shape he assumed to be male really be a woman about to give birth? The fugitive, in answer to his unspoken question, clutched her abdomen with both hands and moaned.

Now what, Mike asked himself, absently rubbing his scarred cheek. There was a storm brewing and it would not hold off much longer. Already the wind was starting to pick up.

"We're turning around," he said.

"We cain't turn aroun'. We come too far." The taller one pushed himself into a sitting position. "I done promised Celia our chile be no slave of Virgil Madden."

"Be sensible. We have nearly twenty miles over roads like this. Then you'll have to hide out for two days in the root cellar of a deserted farmhouse before someone takes you to the next station. Is that what you want for Celia? Besides, once this storm breaks, it won't be a fit night for man or beast."

"We cain't turn aroun'." The man shook his head stubbornly.

"There's a cabin not far from where I first met you. You'll be safe there."

"Please, Isaac." The woman's voice was barely audible. "Listen to the man."

Isaac nodded with obvious reluctance. Without a word, he lay down and put his arm around her.

Mike lowered the trap door in place. He wasted no time in turning the team around and heading back the way they had come. By the time they reached the cabin, the wind was whipping the branches into a frenzy. He helped the man Isaac out of the cramped space and then went ahead to open the door of the cabin. Isaac followed carrying the woman. Mike groped along a shelf just inside the door for matches and lit the lantern, then pointed to the bed. No sooner did the woman's body touch the thin mattress when it was convulsed in another spasm of pain. The man stroked her forehead and waited for the pain to pass.

"Ole Hattie tol' us the chile weren't due for another month and we couldn't wait."

"Don't worry. Everything will be all right. I'll think of something."

But what, Mike wondered, raking his hand through his hair. He felt helpless. He didn't know the first thing about women having babies. Celia needed a doctor. Perhaps Doc Nolan would come. Or would he? Mike wasn't sure. The man seemed awfully timid and cautious. He might be unwilling to make an exception and bend the law. It would be a damn shame if Isaac and Celia had come all this way only to be sent back to the hated Virgil Madden.

Long strides carried Mike back and forth across the cabin. What would Ben do in a situation like this? He tried to put himself in the other's shoes. If not a doctor, what about a midwife? Midwife! The word brought his pacing to an abrupt halt. Mike remembered a nearly forgotten conversation with Ben. Ben had boasted Becky Foster was the best midwife this side of the Mississippi. Mike had scoffed at the notion, but Ben had defended his claim. Clara Horton, Ben said, swears if it weren't for Becky she would have died last winter while birthing her youngest. Forget that idea. Mike resumed his pacing. Becky would never come, especially if he were the one to ask. Behind him, the woman tried without success to stifle another cry. In that instant Mike made his decision. Becky would help. He wouldn't give her a choice.

Heavy brocade panels hung limply on either side of the open window. Not even the slightest breeze stirred the stagnant air. Leaning forward, her palms resting on the sill, Becky stared into the night. She might as well try looking through a bottle of ink. By now Ben was on his way to the next station. She tried to reassure herself there was no need to worry. Thus far all had gone smoothly. She had met the two runaways by the creek and guided them through the woods to wait in the shed near the cabin. Ben would do the rest. This was the same plan they had used many times before, yet a nagging uneasiness persisted.

With a sigh, she turned from the window. She

crossed the room and lay down on the large brass bed where she tossed and turned trying to find a comfortable position. Her nightgown felt like it was made of flannel instead of sheer batiste. She was considering how deliciously wicked it would feel to take it off and sleep nude when the first whisper of cool air caressed her body. With yet another sigh, this one of pleasure, she closed her eyes and willed her body to relax. Soon she fell into a fitful slumber.

Becky woke with a start, her heart racing. She wasn't sure what had wakened her, or how long she had slept. The drapes billowed freely into the room, and she climbed out of bed and walked over to the window. Then it came to her. It was a loud crash that forced her fully awake. But what had caused it? Surely the wind must have knocked something over or slammed a loose shutter against the house. Whatever it was, Becky knew she couldn't go back to sleep until she had investigated.

She cautiously stepped into the hallway and her toes encountered something cool and gritty. A flash of lightning momentarily illuminated the darkened house with an eerie pale glow. Becky looked down and found soil and bits of foliage spilled across the hallway floor. A brass planter lay on its side nearby. Becky's heart pounded. No breeze could have knocked the planter from the small table at the top of the stairs. Fear caused the skin at the nape of her neck to tingle and sent tiny tendrils skittering down her spine. In that split second, Becky knew she was not alone.

Before she could react, a large hand snaked out from behind and clamped over her mouth. Her assail-

ant's other arm encircled her like a steel band mercilessly pinning her arms against her sides. Becky was
drawn back against the rock-hard strength of her
captor. Her feet virtually left the floor as she felt
herself propelled backward into the room. Panic and
desperation drove her to twist and squirm in an
attempt to break free.

Becky kicked out with her bare feet and her effort
won a grunt of pain from her captor, but not her
freedom. Still she resisted. She kicked again, this time
her feet caught and tangled in the folds of her
nightgown. She was flung face down across the bed.
She drew in a deep gulp of air to scream and was
horrified to have a gag wedged between her jaws and
tied securely in place. The heavy weight of a man's
body pressed her into the feather mattress, making
escape or even struggle impossible. Becky felt her
arms pulled behind her back and her wrists tied. Next
her ankles were bound together rendering her totally
helpless. The crushing weight lifted and she was rolled
onto her back.

Chest heaving, eyes wide pools of fright, she recognized her tormentor. Mike! Why would he do this?
Was he mad? Did he really mean to harm her? All
these questions chased through her mind.

She was afraid of him. Mike could see it in her eyes,
and he had half expected it. What he hadn't expected
was the gut-wrenching pain that her lack of faith
brought forth.

"I'm not going to hurt you." His voice was rough
with emotion.

He drew back and his gaze chanced to fall on her
rounded breasts that nearly spilled out of the bodice.

71

Her nipples were barely confined and the gossamer fabric did little to conceal their impudent contour. With fingers that were suddenly clumsy, he jerked the satin straps of her gown back into place.

"Where are your clothes?" he asked.

At her uncomprehending look, he repeated more sharply, "Your clothes? Unless you want to go out dressed in your nightgown."

Becky turned her head to the right and nodded toward a rosewood armoire in one corner. Mike left to return a moment later with a dress slung over one shoulder and holding a pair of slippers. Without further ado, he picked Becky up, put her over the other shoulder, and bounded down the stairs. Outside a strong gust of wind whipped her hair about her face, obscuring her vision. Becky had the sensation of being lowered into a pit. Shaking tousled strands from her eyes, she looked up in time to see a jagged streak of lightning split the ebony sky. In that strange half-light, Mike's scarred face took on a menacing look. He had begun to lower the trap door before it finally occurred to her fear-clouded mind what he was doing.

"Please," she whimpered, her voice muffled by the gag. "Please, don't."

The latch clicked shut.

The wagon began moving, slowly at first, then rapidly picking up speed. For Becky, every bump in the road was torture. Her body was jostled unmercifully, leaving her bruised and battered. The coarse burlap beneath her offered another brand of torment. It chafed her skin until it was raw and tender. The odor of jute, dust, and the sweat of countless former occupants filled her nostrils.

Added to this was the growing horror of being enclosed in a small dark space. Becky felt as though she were inside a coffin, its lid closed. It was getting harder and harder to breathe. Blood roared in her ears. Hysteria beat at the edges of her consciousness. She prayed for the journey to end. She was too preoccupied fighting off demons to notice the wagon had stopped until the trap door was opened and light poured into her prison.

Eyes enormous, their pupils dilated, stared up at Mike from a chalk-white face. Recognizing Becky's terror and knowing he had been the cause, Mike came close to hating himself at that moment. He bent to lift her out, then deposited her on the wagon's edge. With deft movements, he untied the gag and sliced through the cords binding her wrists and ankles. Not stopping to question his actions, only responding to an overwhelming need to comfort, he gathered her in his arms.

"There, there," he murmured against her hair. "It's all right." He repeated the words over and over until her tremors ceased. He continued to hold her until a final shudder rippled through her slender frame and she pushed away.

Calmer now, Becky glanced at her surroundings for the first time. She saw the cabin and knew where they were, though the reason for being there was still unclear.

"Why did you bring me here?" she asked, her voice shaky.

"I need your help. I heard you were good at birthing babies. Is that true?"

"I've delivered some."

Mike studied the tips of his boots, then swung his gaze back to hers. "There's a woman inside the cabin who's about to have a baby."

Becky gasped. "You don't mean one of the fugitives was a pregnant woman?"

"The baby wasn't due for another month or so. All the bouncing over rough roads must have brought on her labor."

"We're wasting time. Give me my clothes."

Mike shoved the dress and shoes into her hands.

"Turn around," she ordered. She slipped the pale blue gingham over her nightgown and hurriedly fastened the buttons. "I don't suppose it ever occurred to you to simply knock on my door and ask for help. No," she continued, recalling her fright, "something that simple and decent isn't your style, is it, Mr. Ryan? You prefer more drastic measures such as kidnapping or blackmail. Tell me, what would you have done if I had refused to lift a finger to help?"

"Guess I never thought about it," he admitted. "I was counting on once you got here you wouldn't turn your back on us."

Becky found a length of grosgrain ribbon in her pocket and used it to tie her hair at the nape of her neck. "Let's go," she said, stepping into her shoes.

Mike picked up the lantern in one arm while the other circled her waist. Heavy drops of rain pelted them as, with heads bent against the wind, they made their way across the narrow tract separating shed from cabin.

Upon entering the cabin, Becky took in the situation in a glance. The man, tall and ramrod straight, had assumed an almost military stance at the bedside.

He stared back at her with a certain mixture of fear and wariness in his dark eyes. The woman lay quietly, waiting and watchful.

Becky approached him and extended her hand. "I'm Becky Foster."

He looked hard at the proffered hand before slowly reaching out and accepting the gesture of friendship. "They calls me Isaac. This here is Celia. We jumped the broom."

Becky smiled at the euphemism the slaves used for marriage, pleased he had accepted her. Instinct told her the woman would do likewise.

"Hello, Celia." Becky turned her full attention on the woman. Rather a girl soon to become a woman, she noted. The girl wasn't much more than sixteen. Wiry dark hair was pulled back from a pretty round face with lively black eyes and a full sensuous mouth.

"I's sorry to be such bother."

"Nonsense. How are you feeling?"

"A mite better, ma'am. The pains don't hurt none like before in the wagon."

"What can I do?" Mike offered.

"Why don't you and Isaac take a look around and see what you can find in the way of supplies? Perhaps someone thought to stash a basket of food in the wagon. When you're done with that, we'll need a fire started and water brought in."

While the two men did as she asked, Becky set about making her patient more comfortable. She stripped off the layers of clothing, folded some, and used it as a pillow. Celia was caught up in another spasm.

Becky rested her hand on the distended abdomen

and felt the womb contract and relax. "Don't be afraid, Celia. Everything is going to be just fine. Trust me."

Her words of encouragement were met with a tremulous smile.

The door crashed open. Isaac and Mike returned dripping wet, but pleased. Isaac's arms were full of firewood, gray and dry with age, while Mike carried a wicker hamper and a serviceable though threadbare blanket.

In no time at all, a kettle of water simmered lazily over a crackling fire. The rich aroma of coffee pervaded the air. Becky sniffed it appreciatively, grateful for Ben's addiction.

After giving a huge yawn, Celia dozed off. The others sat about the rough-hewn table to enjoy the repast.

"When did you eat last, Isaac?" Becky said, watching him spear another slice of ham.

"We had berries this mornin'." He broke off a hunk of bread.

Outside the storm unleashed its fury. Thunder boomed like cannon fire. Rain and wind lashed the weathered planks. But inside, the cabin was a cozy haven. The three seated at the table presented an unlikely trio, but all felt the unique camaraderie that stormy summer night. Encouraged by Mike's interest, Isaac told of a lifetime spent in bondage and the struggle to escape. Becky's eyes were moist when his narrative ended.

An agonized groan from Celia broke the spell. Becky went to her side and felt the familiar tightening of a swollen womb.

"It's going to be awhile yet. I know it isn't easy, but

try to relax. Do you want a boy or a girl?" Becky asked, hoping to distract her.

"A boy," said Celia.

"A girl," Isaac contradicted.

Celia and Isaac exchanged a smile that said this was a longstanding bone of contention.

Celia grimaced, her hands plucking at the mattress. "I's sorry for bein' such a fraidy cat, Miz Becky."

"You have nothing to be sorry for, Celia. Every woman who ever lived is frightened when her time comes. Mark my words, the first time you hold that new life in your arms you'd gladly go through this all over again."

"You sound though you knows all 'bout it."

"Experience is the best teacher, Celia."

"How many little ones you got?"

Mike froze in the act of shuffling his ever-present deck of cards. He eavesdropped unabashedly.

"I had a baby girl." Becky's voice was so low he had to strain to hear it. "She died."

Stunned, Mike slowly let out his breath.

Distress was evident on Celia's expressive features. "Me and my big mouth. Isaac always sayin' I ast too many questions."

"What happened is in the past," Becky said briskly. "Instead concentrate on the future. Think of happy things. Think of your child growing up free."

The hours passed. Celia's labor progressed at a slow unpredictable pace. Isaac hovered at her side, offering words of encouragement and praise. With the pains spaced at lengthy intervals, Becky decided to give the couple a few moments privacy.

"Seeing Celia's in such capable hands, Isaac, I'm going to step out for some fresh air."

With nary a glance in Mike's direction, Becky slipped out the door. Except for the desultory rumble of thunder, the storm's fury was spent. A cool rain fell softly. Becky stood under the narrow overhang, her back pressed against the rough planks. Absently she watched rivulets of rain stream off the roof to be soaked up by thirsty soil.

"I thought you could use this." Mike was at her side, holding a steaming tin cup of coffee.

Becky accepted it with a grateful smile and took a sip. They stood side by side, close but not touching. Becky tried to pretend indifference, but failed miserably. She was keenly aware of his clean masculine scent, the heat radiating from his skin. Instead of intimidating, she found his size bespoke of strength and his presence was comforting.

"About the girl," Mike cleared his throat. "Is everything all right?"

"As far as I can tell, things seem normal. Of course," she kept her tone casual, "coming a month early, the baby is likely to be small. We can only hope that won't present problems."

"Becky?" Mike said with unaccustomed hesitancy.

Becky turned her face up to his and waited for him to continue.

"You would have come tonight even if I hadn't forced you?" It was part question, part statement.

"Yes, Michael," she said with exaggerated patience. "I would have come even if you hadn't trussed me up like a Christmas goose." A tantalizing smile curved her lips.

Mike dug his hands into his pockets and gave her a sheepish grin. "I guess an apology is in order."

Becky shook her head. "There's no need to apologize. You only did what you felt was necessary."

An anguished cry came from inside. Wordlessly Becky handed her unfinished coffee to Mike and rushed to the bed. Celia claimed all her attention thereafter, her labor escalating at a rapid pace.

Feeling powerless to help his wife, Isaac wore a path in the floorboards. Mike mechanically shuffled and reshuffled the deck of cards, too distracted to distinguish a club from a heart. Becky alone remained calm and matter-of-fact. She confiscated Mike's knife and placed it in the kettle of boiling water along with her hair ribbon to use later.

Celia's pretty face contorted in a mask of agony. Beside herself with pain, she writhed and thrashed about. She was no longer capable of holding back the screams when the paroxysms ripped through her.

Of one accord both men got up and left.

"I can see the baby's head, Celia. Just hold on a couple more minutes."

One contraction barely loosened its hold when another began.

"Push!" Becky instructed. "Harder, Celia, harder!"

The girl squeezed her eyes shut, grabbed the edges of the mattress with both hands, and bore down.

The crown appeared first, then the head.

Becky smothered a gasp of dismay. A length of shiny rose-colored membrane was twisted around the baby's neck. The umbilical cord!

"Again, Celia. Push!"

Her strident command communicated its urgency to the men outside.

The shoulders of the infant were expelled next, quickly followed by the rest of the body.

No cry signaled a new life.

Driven by desperation, Becky swabbed the child's mouth with her fingers, freeing it of excess mucous. When this had no noticeable effect on the still form, she bent and covered its nose and mouth with her lips and breathed into the dusky body.

Please, God. Let this baby live, she prayed silently.

Seconds seemed an eternity. The tiny chest shuddered and the quivery cry of a newborn filled the cabin. Becky cradled the squalling infant in her arms before placing it next to its mother. Tears coursed unheeded down her cheeks.

She half-turned to include the men who had watched the drama from just inside the doorway. "It's a boy," she announced, her face radiant. "A beautiful healthy boy."

Chapter Six

DROPLETS OF RAIN CLUNG PRECARIOUSLY TO BROAD leaves only to lose their tenuous hold and slide to the ground. Their muffled drip and the steady turning of wagon wheels were the only sounds to mar the pre-dawn stillness. Becky sat next to Mike, his jacket around her shoulders warding off the early morning chill. She inhaled the clean freshly laundered air. The world seemed a wonderful place. She should be exhausted but she had never felt more wide awake, more exhilarated. She wondered what Mike was feeling. Did he share her good mood?

Mike chuckled softly. He sensed rather than saw

Becky glance at him curiously. "I thought Ben had taken leave of his senses when he bragged about you being a midwife. Looks like I was the crazy one." He grew serious. "You were incredible tonight. A doctor couldn't have done better."

"I bet a doctor wouldn't have been as scared."

"If you were scared, it didn't show."

"My husband was a doctor." The admission popped out. "I used to go with him sometimes when he made housecalls. Once, during a delivery, the cord was wrapped around the baby's neck. I only did tonight what David did then."

"You must have loved him very much."

"I did." Becky swallowed hard before continuing, "David was a very special person, an idealist. I never met anyone so dedicated. Even though he came from a wealthy family, money wasn't important to him. He studied medicine in spite of his family's objections. They threatened to disown him when he started a practice in South Boston instead of Beacon Hill."

Mike's silence lent her encouragement to go on. It felt good to be able to talk about the past. She had kept too many things bottled up for too long. It was time to let go.

"There was a typhoid outbreak two years ago. David could never say no to anyone who asked his help. He was out all hours of the day and night. It was no wonder, really, that he caught the fever too. David never even knew the baby was sick. They died only hours apart." Her voice broke.

For the second time that day, Mike wanted to take her in his arms and comfort her, but held back. What did one say at a time like this? What words would erase the pain?

"I don't know what got into me," Becky said with a self-deprecating laugh. "I'm not in the habit of boring people with my life's story."

"If I lived to be a hundred," Mike smiled, "I doubt if I'd find you boring."

His words warmed her. "You're easy to talk to."

"Anytime."

Her earlier elation returned. "Do you know what?" she rushed on. "I'm starving. Is it possible, Mr. Ryan, that I could persuade you to join me for breakfast? Unless, of course, at your ripe old age," she said, a teasing sparkle dancing in her eyes, "you feel the need for rest more than the need for sustenance?"

"Ah, Mrs. Foster," he answered in a thick Irish brogue. "Tis a hard decision ye face me with. A good meal, or a soft bed?" he pondered aloud as he drew the wagon to a halt at the steps of the back porch of her home. He climbed from the seat, reached up, and swung Becky down to stand in front of him. He made no attempt to remove his hands from the narrow span of her waist. Her hands tarried on his broad shoulders, savoring the play of muscle beneath the thin layer of cotton.

"Which will it be, Mr. Ryan? Bed or breakfast?"

The instant the words were said, Becky could have died of embarrassment. Instead of light and bantering, her invitation seemed bold and brazen. She didn't mean it the way it sounded. Or did she, an inner voice questioned.

"A difficult choice, Mrs. Foster," Mike answered, laughter lacing his lilting baritone. "But if choose I must, then I choose a good meal in your company, rather than time on a solitary bed. Why stand here talking when we could enjoy a feast?"

Becky took his large work-calloused hand and led him toward the darkened house.

Crimson fingers of dawn were creeping across a dun-colored sky when Mike sipped the last of his coffee. His eyes roamed leisurely around the cheery kitchen. Sunny yellow walls and milk-white woodwork formed the backdrop for a profusion of greenery. Plants were everywhere, some hung from the ceiling in front of the window, others stood in large pots along the floor. A few lined the windowsill and exuded the pungent smell of herbs.

"I feel like I'm in a garden," Mike said. "I like it."

"Thank you." Becky smiled at the compliment. "It's a hobby of mine. Would you like more coffee?"

Mike shook his head, but a smile softened his refusal. "You're a woman of many talents, Mrs. Foster, and cooking numbers among them. In case you failed to notice, my appetite was more hearty than polite." He gallantly referred to the platter of buttermilk pancakes and sausage links he had devoured.

"Ah, Michael," Becky said, laughing as she tried to imitate his brogue, "I see ye have indeed inherited the Irish gift of gab along with a touch of blarney as well."

His laughter joined hers. It felt good to be with her, to share something as simple as a meal, or a memory. Never once did Becky make him feel less a man because of his ugly scar. And that felt best of all. It would be easy to let down his defenses with this woman and . . . the laughter faded. Careful, Ryan, he cautioned himself. You're going too fast. You're going to get hurt. But it was impossible to be careful when a woman with the face of an angel and the most beautiful green eyes this side of heaven was smiling at him.

"If I don't get back soon, Ben will worry." Mike rose to his feet.

Becky pulled a lacy knit shawl from a peg near the door and threw it over her shoulders, then followed him out onto the porch. She drew in her breath at the spectacle that greeted her. The sun was the artist, the sky its palette. The heavens were awash in vivid hues of fuchsia, scarlet, and magenta dappled with indigo. What a glorious sight! Mike stood by quietly. He too was affected by the magnificent display.

A gentle breeze swirled a long honey-brown curl teasingly across her cheek. Before she could brush it aside, Mike caught the silken strand. Becky turned toward him; her lips parted but no sound escaped. Around and around his finger, Mike carefully wound the curl, each twist bringing her inexorably closer. Their bodies touched. His mouth hovered over hers. Becky's hands were poised against his chest, waiting.

Drawn like a moth to a flame, Mike reached out to cup her face. He gazed searchingly into her eyes. There was doubt and fear there, the same doubt and fear that shadowed his own. He lowered his head and breached the chasm. His mouth moved over hers, teasing, cajoling, coaxing. Though she didn't pull away, neither did she respond. Disappointment pierced him. It wasn't enough. He wanted all of her, the unconditional surrender of body, mind, and soul. Just when he would have released her, he sensed a change. A tiny spark ignited and burst into an all-consuming blaze. Reservations melted in the torch of passion, leaving her soft and malleable. Her arms crept upward and twined around his neck. Her fingers wove into the thick ebony locks. She was his.

They clung together long after the kiss ended. When they finally drew apart, they stared deeply into each other's eyes, trying to gauge the other's innermost secrets. Becky ventured a tremulous smile. The happiness shining there was more eloquent than words. Mike's smile mirrored hers. As delicate as a butterfly's touch, Mike placed a farewell kiss on her rosy lips.

"Sweet dreams, love," he whispered.

Dreams. Sweet dreams.

Becky was floating, drifting aimlessly through uncharted depths. Images drifted past, vague images with no recognizable shape or form. The images solidified into textures. Rough rocky crags gave way to smooth tan beaches. Just beyond, a sapphire sea shimmered with crystal brilliance. Textures merged and formed a face. A face where scarred uneven flesh blended with smooth. A face where vibrant blue eyes sparkled with laughter. Mike's face. Becky woke with a smile.

For the remainder of the day, Becky went about humming snatches of tunes and was uncharacteristically absentminded. Even Brewster, her foreman and longtime fixture at the Brantford place, noticed her distraction. He dropped by and found her in the midst of baking an enormous batch of cookies.

"I was wonderin' about fall roundup," he said, twirling the brim of his hat. "About how many hands are you plannin' to hire on this year?"

"Oh, five or six dozen ought to do it."

Brewster scratched his bald head. "Beggin' your pardon, Mis' Becky, but ain't that a mite too many?" At her blank look, he added, "Since your pa died, we never needed more than five or six men."

"How silly of me, Brewster." Becky laughed at her mistake. "Just do whatever you think best."

"Yes, ma'am," the bandy-legged man agreed. Must be the vapors affecting her mind, he decided with a shake of his grizzled head.

After nightfall, Becky paid a visit to Isaac and Celia, bringing with her a basket of food and baby things. The bloom was back in Celia's face, foretelling a quick recovery. The infant, Celia reported proudly, was content to eat and sleep. Isaac kept to the background, quiet and withdrawn.

"Folks back home sure be surprised to hear this chile's already borned," Celia giggled.

"Why is that, Celia?" Becky asked, watching the baby stretch its tiny arms.

"Ole Hattie sweared my baby won't come for 'nother whole month. Ole Hattie knows all 'bout these things, and she never wrong. No sirree!"

The infant awakened and made his demands known. As Celia put the child to her breast, Becky said her farewells and promised to return the next day. Isaac offered to walk her to the edge of the clearing.

"Is anything wrong, Isaac? You haven't said more than two words."

"Nothin's gone like we plan it. I's beginnin' to wonder if Canada is only a place in a fairy story. Maybe in the end, I have even less than I start with."

Becky's heart went out to him. His fears were well

founded. Should Isaac and Celia be caught, a permanent separation would be the least of the punishments meted out by an irate master.

"My friend, Ben Sloane, will be coming to see you soon. Together we'll find a way to help you north. You've come too far. You musn't give up hope."

Isaac's doubts faltered under the force of her conviction. She reminded him of a Quaker widow they had met along the way. Soft on the outside, steel on the inside.

"I jus' got to feelin' sorry for myself."

"Goodnight, Isaac. Don't worry so. Things will work out, I just know they will." Becky watched him return to the cabin and disappear inside. Satisfied it gave no clue to the activity within, Becky made her way back home.

Restless, Becky wandered from room to room. Maybe she had been wrong to give Isaac a false sense of security. Helping Isaac and Celia to the next station was risky, but it could be done. The baby, though, presented an added complication. Of course, Ben could drug the infant with laudanum, but that would be dangerous for the still fragile life. Even with friends lending help along the way, the journey was a grueling one. Much of it was on foot which meant sleeping in the open and hiding in fields more often than not. Becky didn't think that Celia and her premature baby would survive such a trip.

There had to be another way. Becky began to fluff pillows and rearrange bric-a-brac, hardly aware of what she was doing. She formed and discarded a half dozen plans. A clue hovered in the back of her mind, but continued to elude her like the answer to a riddle. She frowned and threw herself down on the sofa.

There had to be a way, there just had to be. She hugged an embroidered pillow to her stomach and smoothed it absently. The action reminded her of Celia the night before. Celia. It was something the girl had said. Becky's brow furrowed in concentration. Finally, it came to her. Celia had said no one expected the baby for at least another month. Ole Hattie's predictions, the girl had chortled, were never wrong. Becky jumped up and flung the cushion aside. That was it! The missing piece of the puzzle suddenly fell into place. It had been there the whole time. Searchers would be scouring the countryside, tracking down a man and an obviously pregnant woman. They would not be overly suspicious of a man, woman, and a baby. At least not yet, not if they acted quickly. Was it possible to slip the three past the authorities and speed them on their way?

"Yes," she answered out loud.

Hurrying to the desk, Becky pulled out pencil, paper, and train schedules. Hours passed before she had all the details of her plan worked out. She would still have to sell the idea to Ben and overcome his objections. It was a bold, daring scheme with much depending on her acting ability, but it would work. Becky was certain.

It seemed as though she had scarcely closed her eyes when she was awakened by an insistent knocking. Groggy, she pulled on her robe and groped her way downstairs toward the sound. Becky pushed aside the muslin curtain and peered through the glass panes of the back door. Recognizing the familiar figure, she threw back the bolt to admit Ben Sloane.

"Can I bum a cup of coffee, lady?" his deep voice rumbled.

"Ben." She shook her disheveled curls in exasperation. "Do you have any idea of the time?"

"I know it's early, honey, but early or late is the only time for visiting our guests. Wouldn't want to be seen coming or going from that direction and make people curious. I was going to go last night," he explained, doffing his hat, "but I fell sound asleep."

"Let me put the coffee on." Becky yawned. "Are you hungry? Can I fix you some breakfast?"

"Coffee's fine, honey. Hannah will think I'm sick if I don't do justice to her bacon and eggs."

"So, you've been to see Isaac and Celia?" Becky glanced up from measuring coffee into an enamel pot.

"They're the reason I'm here." Ben sat down at the large oak table. "The cabin is safe enough for right now, but we have to make arrangements to ship them north as soon as possible. I hate like the devil to drug a brand-new baby, and such a little one at that, but what else can I do? If it starts crying, it would give them away."

"The baby won't be a problem," Becky announced smugly, getting out cups and saucers. "I have a plan all worked out."

Ben raised a dark shaggy brow. "Out with it."

Becky outlined her plan over coffee and biscuits. The amazement on Ben's lined face gave way to admiration. "It's risky. It's crazy. But it ought to work. If anyone can carry it off, honey, you can."

Pleased with his reaction, Becky relaxed back in her chair and refilled her coffee cup. When she looked up, she caught Ben eyeing her anxiously. "All right, Ben," she sighed. "What else is bothering you?"

"You and Mike," he said bluntly.

Becky took a swallow of the hot coffee and scalded her tongue. "What about us?"

"Ever since the other night, Mike has been singing your praises. He can't seem to say enough good things about you and keeps pumping me for more. One doesn't have to be a genius to figure out Mike's falling for you. And falling hard."

Becky shifted uncomfortably and didn't meet his look. "So?"

"So, it's dangerous!" Ben's cup clattered against the saucer. "Can't you see the chance you're taking? For the past year, you've done everything imaginable to worm your way into Denby's confidence. Do you want to spoil it all now? Just when it could pay off big!"

"No, of course not, Ben, but . . ."

"But nothing! Becky, you should know better than anybody how jealous Denby is when another man so much as looks at you. It's not exactly a secret Denby hated Mike the minute he set eyes on him. All Denby needs is to see one calf-eyed look between the two of you, and it's all over! He'll want nothing more to do with you, and he'll hound Mike's trail until he finds trouble. Is that what you really want, honey?" He covered her hand with his.

"Oh, Ben, you know it isn't," she said miserably.

"All I'm asking is that you don't do anything rash that might jeopardize your friendship with the marshal. Use that friendship. Make it work in our favor. It's not only our safety I'm thinking of, Becky. Think of Isaac, Celia, the baby, and all the others who will come after them. Lives could depend on your relationship with Denby. Everyone can see you've got him wrapped around your little finger. He's sure to tell you if he hears a rumor of the underground railroad being in Oak Ridge. When he does, we'll lay low for awhile. Adam can send passengers by another route, maybe one further east 'til things cool off."

Ben's reasoning made sense. "What is it you want me to do?" Becky already knew the answer.

"Make a clean break with Mike. Tell him in no uncertain terms you want nothing more to do with him."

Becky pulled her hand out from beneath his and walked to the window. Outside dawn heralded a new day, but Becky was blind to its beauty.

"I'll do whatever you think best." Her voice was flat and lifeless.

"Glad that's settled." Ben heaved a sigh of relief as he got to his feet. "You always were a sensible one, honey. I knew you wouldn't let us down."

For the first time, it occurred to Ben the attraction might not be entirely one-sided. While he didn't cotton to them arguing all the time, he hadn't been prepared for the opposite either.

He walked over and stood beside her. "I know it must be lonely for you since you lost David. Mike's as fine as they come. Under normal circumstances, I'd do everything I could to encourage a match between the two of you. But you know as well as I do, these aren't normal times. Personal feelings have to be put aside."

"I know, Ben. I'm not blaming you for any of this."

Ben put his arm around her shoulders. "Think of this as only temporary, honey," he said, trying to soften the blow. "All in good time, Mike will learn the truth, and he'll not only understand, but respect your decision."

"I hope so, Ben," Becky breathed fervently. "I really hope so."

Late afternoon sunlight filtered through the overhanging branches to form a mosaic pattern on the dusty road. It was near dinner hour and Main Street wore a somnolent look. Only the general store remained open in the hope of attracting some last-minute trade. Ben had agreed Becky's meeting with Mike should take place on neutral ground, a place where others could intercede if things got out of hand. Ben had promised to send Mike into town on an urgent, yet nearly forgotten errand. The fact that Mike's gelding was tied to the hitching post in front of the store attested to his plan's success.

Becky had dressed for the confrontation with care. A perverse desire to make this occasion as unforgettable as it was unforgivable goaded her on. After much debate, she had chosen a gown of pale green watered silk that deepened the color of her eyes and heightened the creaminess of her skin. A mere wisp of a bonnet crowned the mass of tawny curls. Her look of cool elegance was deceiving. Inside she was a bundle of nerves. Her stomach knotted with tension; her gloved hands were clammy with perspiration. Becky pulled the buggy to a stop in front of the store and climbed down. Drawing a deep breath, she squared her shoulders and entered the building.

The tinkle of the bell above the door announced her arrival. Mike's head swiveled at the sound. Seeing Becky, he drew himself to his full six feet three inches.

She approached slowly, her full skirts swaying with each step. Golden rays of sunlight sifted through the screened door, bathing her in their glow, lending her an ethereal beauty that was breathtaking. She looked too lovely to be real. Her graceful slenderness brought to mind a Dresden figurine he once admired in a shop window. Both shared the same fragility, but there the likeness ended. Becky wouldn't shatter into a million shards of glass if caught by a sudden draft. She possessed an inner strength and resilience that would bend but not break. She paused in front of him.

"Are you real? Or are you just a vision conjured up to torment me?" he asked huskily, his strong sun-browned fingers reaching up to gently stroke her cheek.

A lump rose in her throat and threatened to choke her. Her carefully rehearsed speech was forgotten.

Mike's handsome mouth curved into a smile. "I think you're a green-eyed witch who has cast a spell over me. I can't seem to get you out of my thoughts. You even haunt my dreams."

Her resolve began to crumble and she fought the urge to throw herself into his arms. Dear God, why does this have to be so difficult? She forced herself to remember Ben's warning. Lives could depend on it. It took all her determination to step away from his touch.

"Where's Jeff?" Becky glanced around the deserted store.

Her cold demeanor chilled the warmth in his eyes. "He ought to be back in a minute. He's checking on a shipping schedule at the railroad depot."

"Good. I'm glad we have an opportunity to talk privately."

"What is it you want to talk about?" he asked, his tone guarded. She might have faltered like an actress missing her cue if Mike hadn't prompted, "Well, what is it?"

Nervously, Becky ran the tip of her tongue over suddenly dry lips. Then raising her chin at a haughty angle, she threw herself into the role she had reluctantly agreed to play. "This entire business with the underground railroad has been a terrible mistake. I must have been insane not to tell Frank everything I knew from the very beginning."

"I was always surprised you didn't." Mike watched her through narrowed eyes. "What stopped you?"

Becky gave a delicate shrug. "Ben and I are dear friends. I would not want to be responsible for getting him in trouble. Besides," she added, "you're forgetting your blackmail threat. I value my relationship with Frank too much to see it destroyed by lies."

"So what are you trying to say?" Only the icy glitter in his eyes betrayed his mounting anger. "Are you going to Denby with everything you know? Are you going to watch Isaac dragged back to Louisiana in chains? Are you going to stand by while Celia and the baby are auctioned to the highest bidder?"

"I'm not the monster you seem to think," Becky defended. "I give you my word. I'll keep Isaac and Celia's whereabouts a secret. All things considered, I feel a certain responsibility for their welfare."

"How noble!"

"One more thing, Mr. Ryan, and hear me well. Never, but never, involve me in one of your schemes again. If the thought so much as crosses your mind, I'll report you to the authorities. Do I make myself clear?"

"Perfectly."

Becky seemed about to leave when another thought occurred to her. "I hope you aren't under the mistaken notion there could ever be anything between us," she said with false sweetness. "That would be quite impossible. I'm not proud of the fact that I gave in to my base instincts. Call it impulse if you will. Or curiosity. Whatever the name, it's over and done with. Good afternoon, Mr. Ryan."

A final glance at his face told her that her words had struck their target with devastating accuracy. Her composure stretched to the breaking point, she whirled to flee.

"Not so fast!" Mike caught her arm and jerked her against his hard length.

Becky could feel the heat of his anger burn through the thin silk of her dress. She looked up fearfully. His expression was formidable; it could have been carved out of stone. Only his eyes were alive, shining with the brilliance of twin sapphires.

"Take your hands off me." Her voice shook. "You're wrinkling my gown."

He released her so abruptly she fell backward against the counter. "Rest easy. I wouldn't dream of forcing unwanted attention on you. You played me for a fool, lady, but never again," he vowed.

"At least we understand one another."

Becky was almost out of the door when he called out. "Stick with Denby. He's more your type."

The door slammed behind her. Oblivious to the direction she was heading, Becky's feet propelled her down the boardwalk that ran the length of town. Intent on blinking back the film of tears, she narrowly missed colliding with Margaret Nelson.

"My dear, do be more careful," the widow chided.

"Mrs. Nelson," Becky gulped. "Are you all right? I'm so sorry, it was all my fault. I wasn't paying attention to where I was going."

"No damage done, Rebecca." Wintry gray eyes studied her distraught face. "Are you sure that you are all right? You look upset."

The woman sounded genuinely concerned. Becky felt a hysterical giggle well up at the absurd idea. The woman despised her. "I'm just fine, thank you." Becky managed a strained smile and hurried down the walk.

Margaret Nelson frowned as Becky walked away. Something had ruffled the feathers of the self-possessed beauty, intuition told her. She wondered what it could have been. Minutes later she opened the door of the general store and found Mike. Her greeting died on her lips when she saw the ominous set to his face. He was furious. It was not a force to be trifled with.

"I . . . ah . . . needed some embroidery floss."

Mike gave no indication he heard her. He slammed his clenched fist into his open palm, the sound as sharp as the retort from a rifle.

"Damn little bitch!" he swore under his breath.

"I presume you mean Rebecca," Maggie said dryly.

Mike's vision cleared and he noticed Maggie for the first time. "Yes," he bit out, "Rebecca."

"We literally ran into each other just a moment ago," she remarked. "Judging from the way you both look, I'd wager it was quite a battle."

"If it's possible, I'm even angrier with myself than I am with her."

"I'm afraid I don't understand."

"Like a fool, I believed Becky Foster was more than a spoiled selfish little brat. I was wrong."

"There now, it can't be all that bad. After all, you're not the first man taken in by a pretty face. It's the wise man, though," she counseled, "who not only learns from his mistakes, but profits by them. Don't waste your time on Rebecca, Mike. She's not worth it."

Chapter Seven

"FRANK, WE'VE BEEN OVER THIS A DOZEN TIMES."

"I still don't see why you have to go rushing off to Chicago."

"I explained that before and I'll only be gone two weeks, three at the most. I'll be home in plenty of time for the Connolly wedding."

"Can't your cousin get along without you?"

"Not very well since I'm to be the baby's godmother at the christening. Cousin Rose would never forgive me if I let her down."

Becky mentally crossed her fingers at the lie. Cousin Rose was seventy if she was a day. In truth, there really was a Cousin Rose in Chicago who would dearly love a visit from Becky. However, it was Detroit, not Chicago, that was Becky's ultimate destination. The falsehood merely provided a convenient excuse to travel north.

"Three weeks seems like a long time just to get a baby baptized."

"It's not often I have a chance to visit Chicago. I hear it's growing even faster than Indianapolis. Cousin Rose wrote to say she plans to take me to an opera and promised to take me shopping at one of the large drygoods emporiums that recently opened."

"Well, I guess nothing I say is going to change your mind," Frank conceded grumpily. "I better make sure all your luggage gets aboard."

Frank strode away leaving Becky standing on the platform of the railroad depot amidst a handful of passengers and a larger group of idle bystanders. Becky felt a hand at her elbow and turned to find Ben beside her.

"Ben! I didn't expect you to see me off."

"I was going to come into town anyway," he muttered. He held a small parcel wrapped in brown paper and tied with string and thrust it at her. "Here. Hannah baked these for you."

"Please tell her I said thank you," Becky said, touched but not surprised by the thoughtful gesture so typical of Hannah Sloane.

Out of the corner of her eye, Becky noticed Mike. He stood away from them, an unfriendly glitter in his eyes, a grim set to his mouth. Becky tried to ignore him, but there was an ache around her heart that refused to be banished.

"I hate like the devil to see you take this long trip." Ben's voice drew her attention. "Promise you'll be careful."

"I'll be careful, if you promise not to worry so. I'm a big girl now. I can take care of myself." Becky raised on tiptoe and brushed a fond kiss across his leathery cheek.

The hoarse blast of the train whistle and Frank Denby's approach ended further conversation.

"Better get on board or the train will leave without you," Frank said as he took her arm and steered her toward the passenger car, giving Becky time only to flash Ben a quick smile.

Before she could step on board, Frank pulled her to him. His mouth ground against hers in a hard, possessive kiss. His lips were hot and dry. Instead of being kissed, Becky felt as though she were being branded. The act was a show of ownership, rather than tenderness. She forced herself to endure it, telling herself she didn't feel anything, but she did. Revulsion. No one watching the display, however, guessed that when the kiss ended, the pink that stained her cheeks came from anger, not pleasure.

"I wanted to give you something to remember me by," Frank said, releasing her.

"You're not a man easily forgotten."

Frank preened, not realizing her words were not flattery but innuendo.

Then there was no time left. Becky barely had a chance to settle into the narrow leather seat before the train began pulling away. She peered out the window and waved. Both Ben and Frank waved back. Mike was already stalking off in the opposite direction. With a pang of regret, she watched as his broad shoulders disappeared into the crowd.

It was dusk when Becky disembarked at the Indianapolis depot. She quickly made arrangements with a red-jacketed porter to store most of her baggage. Taking the remaining valise, she climbed into one of the carriages for hire. She gave the driver the address of a boarding house that catered to overnight guests, and sat back to view the many changes the city had undergone since her last visit. Indianapolis had multiplied eight times over since the days she had seen it through the eyes of a small child wedged between her parents. The advent of the railroad three years ago had given the growth spurt new impetus. Newspapers were beginning to nickname Indianapolis the *Crossroads of America.*

A short distance beyond the capitol, the driver turned onto a side street and stopped in front of a prim two-story clapboard building. A lacy curtain fluttered at a downstairs window and dropped back in place. Becky paid the driver and, picking up her valise, marched up the brick walk. The knocker scarcely struck the brass plate when the door swung open.

"Can I help you?" a rawboned woman asked, wiping her hands on a checkered apron.

"I'd like to rent a room."

The woman cocked her head to one side, making the knot of salt-and-pepper hair skewered atop her head tilt precariously. "For how long?"

"Only for three days. I'm waiting for my cousin to join me, and then we'll travel east together."

The woman studied her critically before standing back and allowing Becky entrance to the foyer. "All my boarders pay in advance. I don't hold with smoking, drinking, or men visitors."

"Agreed." Becky nodded. "If it isn't too great an inconvenience, I would like to take my meals in my room."

"I ain't no lady's maid. My guests take their meals in the dining room."

Becky loosened the drawstring of her purse and took out a bill of sizable denomination. Fanning herself with the currency, she asked sweetly, "Are you sure you couldn't make an exception just this once?"

The bill was snatched from her fingers in a twinkling and tucked into the bodice of the landlady's dress.

"Food's plain, but edible. Rest of my guests have already had their suppers, but I'll send my girl up with a tray. I'll show you to your room." She turned and trudged up a steep flight of stairs, leaving Becky to follow with her bag.

"By the way," the woman said over her shoulder, "name's Bertha Simpson. What's yours?"

Becky nearly tripped on a stair. "I'm Mrs. Ryan," she lied, saying the first name that came to mind. "Rebecca Ryan," she repeated, liking the sound of it.

Bertha Simpson led Becky down a corridor and unlocked a room at the end of the hall.

"This here's all I got left. There's a lotta fancier places, but you won't find none cleaner." The landlady departed with a jingle of keys.

Becky leaned against the closed door and glanced over her surroundings. Like the woman said, it was nothing fancy, but it would serve the purpose. All she had to do now was wait. Wait for Mike traveling at night by wagon to bring Isaac, Celia, and the baby to

Indianapolis. Then on the morning of the third day, Becky would slip away from the boarding house long before dawn. Her disguise in place, she would meet the trio at the railroad station where the final segment of their journey would begin.

"Where we goin', Mister Mike?" Celia asked.

Mike smiled at the woman in the gaily sprigged dress of yellow muslin. She bore scant resemblance to the frightened bedraggled girl of little more than a week ago. Isaac, too, looked much different in his new finery.

"We're headed for Indianapolis. Ben's instructions were to take and leave you at the railroad station."

"You means you goin' to up and leave us? Jus' like that?" Celia's dark eyes clouded with worry.

"Ben said you were to find an out-of-the-way spot at the depot and to just sit and wait. Ben's friend will meet you and take you the rest of the way north."

The three were silent as they entered the city limits. Celia cradled the baby while both men stared straight ahead. Mike was thankful the baby had posed no problems during the three days of travel and hiding. He would have hated to administer the drops from the brown stoppered bottle Ben had insisted he take along as a precaution.

"This here is the purtiest dress I ever owned." Celia sounded subdued as she fingered the folds of muslin almost reverently. "I ain't never had nothin' so purty. It looks like sumpin' Mis' Becky'd wear."

Celia failed to see Mike's face harden. "Mis' Becky sure one fine lady. She come see us ever' single day. Never come emptyhanded neither, no sirree. She always be bringin' us sumpin'."

"Woman!" Isaac glowered at her. "Cain't you ever keeps a secret?"

Celia clapped her hand over her mouth. "Now I done it! Me and my big mouth! Here I promises Mis' Becky not to tells no ones 'bout her visits and I go an' blabbers first chance I gets."

"Don't fret." Isaac regretted being sharp with her. "I sure Mis' Becky don't minds Mister Mike knowin'."

Mike's face remained impassive. If Celia's slip of the tongue surprised him, he gave no indication. He had been under the impression Becky wanted no more to do with the fugitives. Obviously he was mistaken. Maybe she pitied them, just as she once pitied him. Pity moved that woman to great lengths, Mike reflected bitterly. So Celia thought Becky a fine lady, did she? Well he had too, once upon a time. Now all he had to do was to get her out of his system. He would—or die trying.

Mike brought the team to a halt in front of the bustling depot. He waited while Isaac and Celia, clutching the infant, clamored down from the wagon. "Remember, do exactly as Ben said. Find an out-of-the-way spot and wait. No matter what happens, stay calm and say as little as possible." Mike repeated Ben's orders a final time.

The two men shook hands, and Celia managed a watery smile. "Good luck," Mike said gruffly and watched as they were swallowed by the crowd.

Up until this point, Mike had followed Ben's directions to the letter. Ben had been explicit. Leave Isaac and Celia at the station, he had said, and return at once to Oak Ridge. But how could he? Then he would never know what happened to them. What if Ben's friend never came? No, Mike decided, he couldn't leave until he was certain they were safely on their way.

Leaving the wagon where it was, Mike threaded his way through the mass of people. Most of the activity centered on the platform that ran the length of the station. Almost at once, Mike spotted the pair of runaways. Celia, hugging the babe to her breast, sat on a crate amidst a pile of mail sacks and baggage. Isaac stood next to her looking fiercely protective. Mike tossed a coin at a boy hawking newspapers. Tugging his hat low over his eyes, he hid behind the opened pages.

At first, Mike paid no attention to the small woman in widow's weeds who stood with her back toward him. She was deep in conversation with a man wearing the dark blue uniform and gold braid of a railroad official. It wasn't until the widow gestured toward Isaac and Celia that Mike's attention was captured. To better hear their conversation, Mike sidled closer and leaned against a post.

"Madam, you don't realize what you're asking. This is highly irregular," the conductor protested.

"Surely, sir, there must be something a man of your authority can do?" the woman asked in a soft musical southern drawl.

"Try to understand my position if you will," the official argued. "What would the rest of my passengers think if I allowed your slaves . . . er . . . servants to ride aboard my train?"

"I can't believe people would be so heartless, not even Yankees." The widow wrung her hands. "Whatever am I to do? Here I traveled all the way from Montgomery with dear friends that left just this mornin'. They continued their journey in one direction while I continue mine in another. My friends never would have gone off if they thought for one minute there would be a problem. They knew my servants would see to my comfort. Shortly I'll be needin' my girl's services. I can't leave them behind. Surely, sir, you can appreciate my position," she said, placing a hand over her rounded stomach.

"It is you, madam, who does not appreciate mine. Permitting niggers to ride on my train has never been allowed—and never will be." He would have left had it not been for the gentle pressure of her hand on his arm.

"You must be wondering what causes me to partake in a journey at this particular time."

The official shifted uncomfortably. "Really, madam! It's none of my business."

"You may rest assured, sir, only the direst of circumstances would force me to leave my home." The woman's voice wobbled. "Not long ago, I lost my beloved husband in a terrible, terrible accident. My darlin' Beauregard was riding in a hunt when his horse stepped into a gopher hole and threw him. Beauregard broke his neck. He died instantly." Her voice cracked and her slender shoulders shook with sobs.

The commotion drew a group of curious spectators. A ripple of sympathy was directed toward the grieving widow, heavy with child, while angry glances were darted at the official.

"There, there," the official soothed. He dug into his uniform pocket and produced a white linen square which he handed to the sobbing woman. "My deepest sympathy, madam. I had no idea, no idea. Please," he implored, unhappy at being the object of so many hostile glares. "Please try to console yourself. It isn't good to get this upset."

The widow accepted the handkerchief and sniffed her tears to silence. "You simply can't imagine how difficult a time this has been." Her voice quavered with a heart-wrenching conviction. "No matter where I went, no matter what I did, I was plagued with memories of my dear departed husband. I feared I was losing my mind. That's when the doctor ordered a change of scenery. This brings me to why I'm here on the way to Michigan to visit my mother's only living relative."

The widow beseeched the crowd of people who were avidly watching the enfolding drama. "Whatever shall I do?" She spread her hands in a helpless gesture. "All this traveling is so very tiring. There is no way I can tolerate the rest of the journey except by train. Why, I wouldn't know how to manage without my servants. They will be great comfort in a land of strangers. Having them with me is almost like taking part of my beloved Summerset along."

The official removed his cap and scratched his head. "I hate to add to your trouble, but . . ."

"Trouble!" The widow wailed pitifully. "I've had nothing but trouble since my poor Beauregard's untimely demise. We were so happy, and now he's gone forever." She broke into a fresh bout of weeping.

A fashionably dressed gentleman elbowed his way through the crowd. "Excuse me for intruding, madam, but I couldn't help overhearing your dilemma. Perhaps I can be of some assistance." He extended his hand to the widow. "I am Congressman Butler."

The official's gulp of dismay carried to all those within earshot.

The congressman turned his wrath on the hapless conductor. "I cannot in good conscience stand by and watch you harass this poor woman. An attitude such as yours should be reported to your superiors. Where is your sensitivity, man? Your compassion?"

The conductor's face turned beet red. He did not relish being cast the villain in this little melodrama. He cleared his throat and stammered, "I . . . ah . . . I'm only . . ."

The congressman dismissed the bureaucrat's attempt to explain with an expansive wave of his arm. "Certainly there must be some nook or cranny on your precious bit of machinery where this little lady's servants can ride in comfort without compromising your other passengers?"

"Well, hearing you put it that way gave me an idea." The conductor snapped his fingers and a young worker in railroad attire rushed up to him. "I want you to personally escort this lady's servants to the mailcar and see to it they are made comfortable."

"Yes, sir." The youth bobbed his head and scurried off to do as he was bid.

Before following the boy, Isaac and Celia took a long hard look at their benefactor. Celia's eyes rounded and she seemed about to speak when a gentle nudge from Isaac reminded her to hold her tongue. Wordlessly, they followed the youth.

Checking the time on his large gold watch, the official mumbled his apologies and hurried off, relieved to have the situation resolved.

The bereaved widow quickly recovered her compo-

sure. "I'm deeply grateful for your timely interces-
sion, Congressman," she said in a dulcet drawl. "You
are indeed a gentleman in the true sense of the word."

"My pleasure, madam, I assure you." He gave a
courtly bow. "My only regret is that we are traveling
in opposite directions. However, I would deem it an
honor if you would permit me to escort you safely on
board."

"Why, sir, I'd be delighted," came the sweet reply.
The widow half-turned to accept the congressman's
arm.

Mike let the newspaper drop. More than anything,
he wanted to see the face of the woman responsible
for spiriting Isaac and Celia under the very noses of
the authorities. He was disappointed to find her
features hidden behind a heavy satin-edged mourning
veil. His gaze fell from her face to the dainty gloved
hand that rested maternally on a burgeoning stomach.
The woman was pregnant! he realized. Small wonder
the congressman and the crowd were sympathetic to
her tragic tale. Mike wondered how much of it was
actually true. Even he had not been unaffected by her
performance. Indeed, he had been about to intervene
when the congressman had stepped forward in her
behalf.

As Mike slowly made his way back toward the
wagon, he shook his head. Isaac, Celia, and their
baby would ride to freedom in comfort and safety all
because of the courage of one small but determined
woman. The clever simplicity of the plan caused him
to smile. What could be more natural than for a
well-bred southern lady to travel with her servants?
And if that lady were in a family way, it was only
logical she bring a wet nurse for her expected child.

Mike's one regret was not seeing who she was. Her slight valiant figure dwelled in his thoughts the entire way back to Oak Ridge. The memory of her voice lingered like a haunting melody. Her drawl had been as soft as magnolias, as sweet as honeysuckle. He would never forget that voice. He'd know it anywhere.

Hard cup at saucer-prong up an ran the
from falls they the latter in a turned. Goose
hot ring to feet III as. They remote and or and
dear in the pockets welling. The have so her
it may her breath the all when it. Superior. Of
resolution Riggle but kills when eyes John it and
rest it.

Chapter Eight

IF SHE NEVER STEPPED FOOT ON A TRAIN AGAIN, IT WOULD
be too soon. A black cloud of smoke from the coal
furnace swirled past the window. Becky wrinkled her
nose at its acrid smell and wondered if its grime would
be embedded in her pores. She closed her eyes and
leaned her head against the seat, tired but triumphant. Except for the episode in Indianapolis, the
journey had been without incident. There was a lump
in her throat each time she remembered the poignant
farewell on the bank of the Detroit River. Then
suddenly there had been time only for a kiss for the
baby, a hug for Celia, and a handshake for Isaac

112

before the three were ferried across the river into Canada. They were gone from her life forever. Now she longed for home.

It was midafternoon when the train chugged into Oak Ridge. Becky leaned forward to peer out of the window, expecting to see Ben's familiar figure. There was no sign of him. Instead she spotted Frank.

No sooner had she alighted when he rushed up to give her one of the swift bruising kisses she had come to detest. "You know I should be angry with you," he said, releasing her and picking up her valise.

"How could I make you angry from two hundred miles away?"

"You didn't write once the whole time you were gone. People kept asking if I had heard from you, and what could I say? It made me look like a fool."

"Cousin Rose kept me so busy, I scarcely had time to sleep." Becky tried to salve his wounded pride. "Next time I'm away, I promise to do better."

"Next time!" he exclaimed in horror. "Don't tell me you're planning another trip?"

Becky laughed, genuinely amused at the notion. "Frank, it feels so wonderful to be home. I don't even want to think of leaving for a long, long time."

"Good!" Frank beamed his approval. "I took the liberty of hiring a buggy from the livery stable so I could take you home." He held out his arm and they made their way to the front of the station where the buggy waited.

Becky stood patiently while Frank and Jed loaded the trunks she had reclaimed at the Indianapolis depot into the back of the conveyance. Her gaze swept both sides of the tree-lined street still expecting to see Ben appear at any moment. She had been so certain he would be here to meet her. Knowing him as well as she did, she knew he would be eager to learn the details of her trip.

"You're wasting your time if you're looking for Ben." Frank's voice intruded. "Aren't you wondering how I found out when you were coming home?"

Becky tilted her head and studied the lawman's smug face. "You must be a mindreader. That's exactly what I was wondering."

"Truth of the matter is, I ran into Ben a few days ago. It took some fast talk on my part, but I finally convinced him to tell me when you were coming home." Frank helped Becky into the buggy before going around to the other side and climbing in. "Ben planned to meet the train himself, but I told him I'd save him the trouble. Besides," he smirked, "I thought you would like my way better."

"You're beginning to know me all too well."

"I'd like to get to know you even better," he said in an undertone. Uncomfortable with the intimate bend of the conversation, Becky tried to steer it along less personal lines. "Don't keep me in suspense any longer. I want you to tell me everything that's happened in Oak Ridge since I've been away. Don't leave out a single detail."

No further encouragement was necessary. Frank launched into a lengthy account of every event that occurred not only in Oak Ridge but the entire county as well. He was still talking when the buggy rounded a curve in the road and the graceful lines of her two-storied house came into view. Undiluted joy surged through her at the sight. She was home.

"You're not listening," Frank complained.

"Sorry." A guilty look crossed her face. "You caught me wool gathering. What was it you were saying?"

"I was reminding you that Mary Connolly is getting married Saturday. I'll be by at six to get you."

The Connolly wedding. She had forgotten all about it. She would have enjoyed it, without Frank as her escort. However, the thought of an entire evening in his company caused her spirits to sag.

Frank brought the buggy to a standstill in front of the house. After helping Becky down, he wrestled with the chore of unloading her trunks and hauling them inside and up the stairs to her room. Becky was waiting for him in the front hallway when he finished.

"Frank, I can't tell you how much your meeting me at the station has meant. I know how valuable your time is and I hate to be such a bother. That's why I asked Ben, not you, to meet my train. I won't keep you another minute. You must be anxious to get back to town."

"Pete can handle things once in awhile. I don't have to rush back."

Becky ignored his hopeful tone. "It's been a long trip and I'm exhausted," she explained with an apologetic smile.

"Yeah, sure. I understand." The scowl on his face said differently.

"I knew you would." Becky gave his hand a quick squeeze while opening the front door.

"You just be sure to get plenty of beauty rest. I want everyone to see me with the prettiest woman in the county come Saturday night."

Becky watched him leave with an enormous sense

of relief. Alone at last, she roamed from room to room, reacquainting herself with every piece of furniture, every piece of bric-a-brac. She made a mental note to thank Ben. He must have had Clara Horton send one of her girls out to dust and air out the place. Slowly she wandered upstairs and repeated the ritual. Her bedroom was the last stop on her inspection tour. The rosewood furniture gleamed beneath a fresh polish of lemon and beeswax. Muted shades of rose, moss green, and cream were repeated throughout the room in counterpane, draperies, and carpet. A giddy sense of well-being washed over her. She felt like a young girl again. Hugging her arms, she twirled about the room before collapsing on the bed. For the first time in weeks, she felt relaxed.

Turning her head slightly, her eyes rested on the mound of luggage waiting to be unpacked. Becky wrinkled her nose at the prospect. It could keep until tomorrow. A hot bath and a visit with Ben held more appeal.

The bath washed away much of her weariness along with the grime of travel. Dressed in a pearl gray riding skirt and rose-colored silk shirt, Becky snatched a lump of sugar on her way out the door. Her mare, Lady, whinnied loudly at the sight of her mistress. Soon horse and rider were flying down country lanes and across open fields in a wild burst of exhilaration. At last their pace slackened. As they topped the rise of a hill, Becky noticed that dark clouds were rapidly blotting out the blue of the sky. She wasn't about to let a summer shower interfere with her plans. She nudged the mare down the slope toward the Sloanes' farm.

Hannah saw Becky's approach from the kitchen

window and came out on the back porch to greet her. "Land, child! You're a sight for sore eyes."

"Thank you, Hannah," Becky said, smiling down at her. "You can't believe how wonderful it feels to be home again. Guess I must be more country girl than city girl."

"Ben felt bad about not meeting the train this afternoon. He was planning to until he let the marshal talk him out of it. Ben didn't think he'd be seeing you 'til tomorrow. Thought you'd be needing to rest up after your long train ride."

"I decided to play hooky when I looked at the unpacking I had to do. Besides, Lady and I both needed some exercise."

Hannah tucked a stray wisp of hair into her bun. "Don't know what's gotten into Ben since you left. He's done more fretting than a mother hen."

"Where is Ben, by the way?"

"He mentioned something about checking one of the steers. Why don't you look for him out in the barn?" Hannah suggested helpfully. "I'm fixing chicken and dumplings. No argument now, you're staying for supper."

Becky laughed. "Next to fudge cake, chicken and dumplings are my favorite food. Let me find Ben and we'll be back before you get it on the table."

"You've got plenty of time." Hannah cast a worried look at the darkening sky. "We're due for some rain. The leaves have been turning their backsides to the wind for the past hour. Take care you don't get caught in a downpour."

Becky shook her head. "You sound just like Ben. I won't melt."

As she rode toward the barn, fat drops of rain

started to fall, leaving dark splotches on her silk blouse. She was grateful the barn was only minutes from the house. Coaxing the mare through the opened door, she swung down from the horse's back. It took awhile for her eyes to adjust to the gloomy interior. Deep in the shadows a horse whinnied. The unexpected sound caused Lady to shy with fright. Becky stroked the velvety muzzle and murmured soothingly to the frightened mare. Leaving Lady munching hay in an empty stall, she hesitantly walked further into the dark cavernous building.

"Ben?" she called out. "Ben, are you in here?"

A large figure detached itself from the shadows of the furthermost stall. Becky's heart sank. It wasn't Ben she found, but Mike.

He stood impassive, silent, feet planted apart, arms folded across his chest. His stance seemed menacing, even hostile, daring her to come closer. Only pride kept Becky from fleeing. Stubbornly she raised her chin and squared her shoulders.

She approached him in slow measured steps. "Hannah said I might find Ben in the barn."

"He's not here."

"Oh." The response was woefully inadequate. Becky glanced backward over her shoulder. A steady gray curtain of rain was framed by the opened doorway, effectively cutting off any chance of a dignified retreat. Trapped. She felt trapped.

Mike's gaze followed hers, and he sensed her uneasiness. "What's the matter, Mrs. Foster? Afraid to be alone with me?"

"What an absurd idea," she scoffed. "Why should I be?"

His massive shoulders rose and fell in a shrug.

"Maybe it's my face. It wouldn't be the first time it has scared small children and squeamish women."

Becky's fear evaporated. "And that's what you think I am, a squeamish woman?" she asked, lifting a delicate brow.

"Could be." Mike shrugged again.

"Do you know what I think, Michael Ryan?" Becky stepped forward and gently traced the diagonal scar with a fingertip. "I think your scar bothers you far more than it bothers me."

Mike's fingers closed around her wrist and jerked her hand away. She felt the fury vibrating within him. His grip was a hairsbreadth away from being painful. With only the slightest pressure, he could snap the delicate bones caught in his hold. Becky had awakened a sleeping tiger, yet she refused to back down. She returned his angry stare without batting an eyelash.

"Whatever happened to your face scarred more than just your flesh, didn't it, Michael?" she challenged softly. "It scarred your soul as well."

He flung her arm down, his breathing heavy and labored. Not meeting her eyes, he walked to the opened door and stared broodingly at the driving rain. Becky's words had struck a raw nerve. It had been years since the so-called accident. Mike should be able to exercise more control than to lash out like a wounded beast. He remembered the fragile wrist and was horrified at his near violent reaction.

Becky came to stand beside him. Neither said a word.

The rain subsided as abruptly as it had begun. Becky didn't linger. She mounted Lady and fled to the relative sanctuary of the farmhouse.

Hannah's cozy kitchen was a welcome refuge. Becky's half-formed plan to cancel her supper invitation vanished the moment she spotted Ben at the round oak table. His tan weathered face broke into a wide grin the minute he saw her. He sprang from his chair to enfold her in an embrace, one Becky returned with enthusiasm.

"Let me take a good look at you, honey," he said, holding her at arm's length and eyeing her critically. "You look as though you lost weight. Even your face looks thinner."

"And you look as though you have a few more gray hairs from worrying too much."

Once more Ben gathered her for a gruff bear hug. "I can't tell you how good it is to have you home all safe and sound."

"For heaven's sake, Ben!" Hannah looked up from the stove and shook her head in exasperation. "The child only went to Chicago for a christening."

"Ben has old-fashioned ideas about women traveling alone," Becky said, smiling.

Hannah returned to stirring the contents of an iron kettle. "I told you I had a surprise for you, Ben. Becky dropped by just before it started raining. I'm afraid I sent her out on a wild goose chase."

"How's that?"

"I told her she'd probably find you out in the barn."

"But she found me instead." Mike completed the sentence, stepping into the kitchen. "Hope I'm not interrupting anything."

"You should know better by now," Hannah wagged her head. "Why, you're part of the family now." Mike took the platter of dumplings from her and placed it on the table. Hannah acknowledged his help with a smile. "Becky's joining us for supper," she explained.

For the first time, Becky noticed the table was set for four. She silently cursed her stupidity. She should have known Mike took his meals with Ben and Hannah. It was too late to back out. Not only would she offend the Sloanes, but Mike would think her a coward. With a sigh of resignation, Becky started to pull out a chair at the place Hannah indicated.

"Allow me." Mike held out the chair and waited for her to be seated. "Fate seems determined to throw us together," he said softly, for her ears alone.

"How unfortunate for both of us," Becky murmured in reply.

"Supper's ready," Hannah called out. She set an earthenware bowl filled with chicken and vegetables swimming in creamy gravy in the center of the table.

When all were seated, Ben bowed his head. The others did likewise while he said a simple grace. After the prayer, Ben passed the platter of dumplings. "Go ahead," he urged Becky. "Take two—they're small. You could stand to put on a few pounds. You're getting skinny."

Becky looked at the huge fluffy mounds and then back to Ben. "Hannah is going to put salt in your sugar bowl if you insult her cooking like that."

"You tell him, Becky," Hannah chuckled. "I don't take kindly to any complaints in my kitchen."

No sooner had Becky passed the platter to her left, when Ben handed her the ladle and held out the bowl of chicken. "Come on, Becky. Take a big helping. The biggest insult you can give Hannah is not to do justice to her meals."

"Ben's right about that, child," Hannah concurred. "Eat up."

Becky felt in the middle of a conspiracy to add inches to her waistline. A glance across the table at Mike's stony countenance did little to stimulate her faltering appetite.

"Tell us about your trip," Hannah said.

Becky gave a small shrug. "I don't want to bore you with all the details."

"Nonsense! We want to hear all about it. Don't we, Mike?" Hannah turned to him for support.

"By all means. Did you enjoy Chicago, Mrs. Foster?" he asked with exaggerated politeness.

Becky speared a chunk of chicken with uncalled-for zeal. "As a matter of fact, I did, Mr. Ryan. Chicago is an exciting city. Have you ever been there?" She popped the morsel into her mouth, pleased at having neatly turned the subject back to him. Actually, she had never been closer than a hundred miles.

"I've been there once or twice. Chicago impressed me as a big brawling town, not one I would think was to your liking. I would have guessed you would prefer a city more cosmopolitan, more refined."

"That just goes to show you how very little you know about me," she returned coolly.

"How was your Aunt Rose and the baby, Becky?"

"Fine."

"Funny," Hannah mused, "I always pictured your aunt as someone much too old to be having babies."

Becky's swallow of milk went down the wrong way. Ben patted her back and waited for her coughing to subside before answering. "I think Becky's aunt was more than a little surprised, too, to find herself a mother this late in life."

"Did you find time for the theater, Mrs. Foster? Or was it the opera?" Mike resumed his interrogation.

Becky dabbed at her watery eyes with a napkin. "Both."

"What about the shops? Were they up to your expectations?" The icy glitter in his eyes was chilling.

Becky nibbled a piece of carrot and fixed him with a cool stare. "The shops were more than adequate," she said at last. "I fail to see how the stores in Chicago could possibly be of interest to you."

"Stores are a reflection of the times." He leaned back slightly in his chair. "A person can learn a great deal from observing not only the newest trends in merchandise, but people's attitudes as well."

"Ain't that the truth," Hannah agreed. "Though I have to admit I never thought of it quite that way before."

"Take our general store for instance," Mike expounded. "It's a great place for observing how attitudes can change almost overnight." Although he addressed Hannah, Becky knew each word was directed at her.

Hannah nodded. "I know what you mean. Especially these days with folks talking about such things as secession, slavery, and abolition. Folks amaze me how they can change their minds from one day to the next."

"They amaze me too, Hannah," Mike said quietly.

Becky dropped her eyes and toyed with her food. The wistful note in Mike's voice cut her to the quick. He wasn't the only one who hurt thinking about the disastrous scene in the general store. When would the pain cease, she wondered.

Noisily, Ben cleared his throat and began talking

123

about Will Connolly's elaborate plans for his daughter's upcoming wedding. Hannah was full of questions and proved a good audience. Neither of the hosts remarked that their guests were unusually quiet for the remainder of the meal.

When the last crumbs of peach cobbler had disappeared, Hannah pushed back her chair and began to stack the dirty dishes. Becky was quick to help.

"You just join the menfolk while I do up the dishes," Hannah ordered. "You must be all tuckered out after your long train ride."

"Absolutely not!" Becky protested. "Where do you keep an extra apron?"

She wrapped a voluminous apron around her slender waist and rolled up her sleeves. As the men got up and left the kitchen, she felt Mike's brooding gaze sweep over her a final time.

The murmur of male voices and the fruity aroma of Ben's pipe tobacco drifted in through the screen door. Hannah and Becky were an efficient pair and soon put the last of the dishes in the cupboard. There was no excuse to avoid joining the men any longer. Becky was unable to cope with another verbal sparring match with Mike, so immediately made her excuses to leave.

"Hannah, thank you for the delicious dinner, but I really must be getting home."

"Not already." Hannah sounded disappointed. "Can't you stay and visit a bit longer? Mike will see you home if you're worried about staying until after dark."

"No, no, it's not that," Becky said hurriedly. "It's been a long day and I'm afraid it's starting to catch up to me."

"You're not getting away that easily, young lady," Ben objected. "I'm going to be the one to escort you home. On the way, you can finish telling me all about Chicago."

Ben could be so transparent at times it made her smile. "All right, Ben, since you insist."

"I insist." Ben's dark eyes twinkled with good humor. "Wait here until I saddle my horse. I'll be right back."

Hannah tried without success to carry on a conversation. All three were relieved when Ben reappeared.

"Good night, Hannah." Becky gave the older woman a kiss on the cheek. "Good night," she mumbled in Mike's direction and left.

Hannah and Mike watched them ride off in silence.

"I suppose it's time I left, too," Mike said, but made no move to leave.

"There's more coffee in the pot. Stay and have another cup with me."

"Sounds like a good idea." Mike didn't relish the thought of being alone with the memory of a green-eyed witch to plague him.

Hannah went inside and returned with two mugs. She handed one to Mike and sat down on a wooden rocker that was a permanent fixture on her back porch. Mike leaned a hip against the railing and let a long leg dangle back and forth.

Hannah heaved a sigh. "Don't know what's come over me. I just don't feel like being alone just yet."

There was a bleak look on Hannah's worn features that Mike found disturbing. "You look as if something is bothering you. If you care to talk about it, I've been told I'm a good listener."

"It's Becky," Hannah confessed, her brow furrowed. "Tonight she was the Becky I used to know, other times she's a stranger."

"In what way?" Mike was interested in spite of himself.

"When Becky was growing up, she was almost a daughter to me. You couldn't find a nicer girl. Then her ma took sick and Becky grew up almost overnight. She stopped going to dances. Even stopped seeing that nice Tom Weston. I never heard her complain once. About the time her ma died, Becky and her pa had a falling out. She left for Boston the same day her ma was buried. Becky's not the same person Ben and I saw off that day."

"People change, Hannah. After all, a lot happened to her while she was gone."

"Ben told you about her husband and baby dying?"

"No." Mike took a sip of coffee and stared past the dirt drive. "Becky mentioned it once." He could recall every small detail of that early morning ride. The way Becky's voice caught when she spoke of her child, her smile as radiant as the dawn, how she melted in his arms. A mistake, Becky had called it later. A bittersweet mistake he paid for dearly.

"Scares me to death to hear rumors about her marrying Denby. I just can't abide that man! In the old days, Becky wouldn't have given that pompous fool the time of day. I can scarcely believe my own ears when I hear her agreeing with all his crazy notions. I just don't know what's gotten into that girl."

"Both you and Ben still think of her as the little girl who used to come for milk and cookies." Mike's disapproval was evident in his voice.

Hannah gave him a sheepish smile. "Maybe you're right. Sorry if I talked your ear off."

"Anytime." Mike returned the smile.

"I don't dare say anything to Ben for fear he'll bite my head off. He's mighty prickly when anyone finds fault with Becky."

"Don't I know," Mike said with a humorless laugh. "I learned that the hard way."

"Maybe I'm jealous of Becky. I know how close she and Ben are, and I get to feeling left out sometimes. Nowadays when she comes visiting, it's Ben she wants to see, not me. Like the two of them share some kind of secret, and I'm only in the way."

"You're making a mountain out of a molehill. Becky probably wants Ben's advice on problems she's having at the farm."

"No, I don't think so. Becky's got a good head for business. She does just fine without Ben, or anyone else, telling her what to do. I know her foreman, Brewster, well enough to know he'd never take orders from anyone he didn't respect. Truth is, Becky does a better job farming than Adam did. Nothing against Adam, but he just wasn't cut out for country life. Becky, on the other hand, thrives on it."

"That's odd. With all her ladylike airs, I would have thought her better suited to a big house, servants, fancy clothes, and a constant round of parties to keep her entertained."

"Not Becky. She's a real homebody. Hadn't been for that fight with her pa, she'd probably have settled down with Tom and had half a dozen young'uns by now."

Mike drained the last of his coffee, never realizing it had grown cold. So Tom Weston was another of

Becky's many conquests? Wasn't any man safe from her wiles?

"Becky's the spittin' image of her ma. Maybe even a mite prettier." Hannah's face had taken on a faraway look. "You see it was her ma, Amanda, that Ben really wanted to marry. But Amanda only had eyes for Matt Brantford, so Ben being the gentleman stepped aside. Ben never did stop caring for her. I think he still loved her until the day she died. That's part of the reason he won't stand to hear anyone speak ill of Becky." An incredible sadness showed on the kindly features.

Mike reached out to cover her work-roughened hand. "Ben's a wise man, Hannah. He knows beauty is more than skin deep. It's you he loves."

Hannah's eyes were misty as she met the dark blue ones gazing into hers with understanding. "Lord! What must you think of me? A crazy old lady jealous of a dead woman and her daughter?"

"I think you're a treasure, Hannah Sloane." Mike applied gentle pressure to the hand beneath his. "What more could a man ask for than to spend his life beside a woman who loves him as much as you love Ben."

What more indeed, he asked himself.

Lady daintily picked her way along the narrow path that followed the meandering creek. It was late afternoon yet the blazing August sun still beat down mercilessly. Becky was not immune to its searing rays. Tendrils of dark gold hair escaped the knot at the back of her head to form damp ringlets at her temples and the nape of her neck. Her skin felt dewy with perspiration, molding the thin cotton shirt and camisole to her ripe curves. After a day spent in the saddle, checking the farm, she was hot, sticky, and tired.

At last the creek widened to form a shoulder-deep basin. Becky nudged the mare forward to slake its thirst. The leather creaked in protest as she shifted her weight in the saddle to ease the ache in her back and the stiffness in her shoulders. Shoving back her hat, she wiped her brow with the back of her hand. Not even as a youngster had the pool looked so inviting.

Becky tied the horse to a sapling and sat down at the water's edge. She tugged off her boots and stockings and let her bare feet dangle in the crystal clear pool. A sigh of pure pleasure escaped. This is absolute bliss, she thought.

Planting her palms on the grassy bank, she leaned back, eyes half-closed, and lazily surveyed the tranquil setting. Time had not disturbed her favorite childhood haunt. Nearby, weeping willows trailed graceful drooping branches to touch and mingle with the tall grass. The hum of insects and chattering birds were the only sounds to be heard.

Becky kicked her foot and watched the ripples fan outward. The shimmering water beckoned her to plumb its cool depths. Why not? Becky glanced around. She was alone. Brewster had ridden off in the direction of town to enjoy a cold beer at the Satin Slipper. It was suppertime. No youngster was likely to wander by. Why not? she asked again.

It felt deliciously decadent to strip off her clothing and plunge naked into the sparkling water. She surfaced to dive even deeper, swimming like a minnow along the sandy bottom. Tiring of this, she rose again and turned to float on her back. She shut her eyes and let the water gently cradle her body. Her hair streamed about her head like a giant golden fan; the water felt like silk against her bare skin. Refreshed and invigorated, Becky turned over with a splash and swam toward shore.

Her gaze shifted from the pile of hastily discarded clothes to the man standing next to them. Damn! She floundered in midstroke. Why did Mike have to happen by? With his thumbs hooked in his belt and hat pulled low over his eyes, he looked as though he planned to stay indefinitely.

Becky's feet groped for and found the pool's bottom. Only her head and the top of her shoulders were exposed to the insolent perusal of her unexpected visitor.

"How long have you been watching?" she demanded angrily.

"Long enough," came the laconic reply.

"Well, go away!"

"Why should I?"

"Because that would be the decent thing for a gentleman to do under these circumstances."

"But I never claimed to be a gentleman, just as you never claimed to be a lady."

Becky was seething. "You're enjoying this, aren't you?"

"View's excellent." Mike squatted at the edge of the pond and plucked a blade of grass which he put between his teeth. "And bound to get better," he added.

Becky glared at him, but he seemed impervious to the venom directed his way. He was determined to humiliate her. For all he cared, she could stay in the water until she shriveled up like a raisin. Or she could expose herself to his leering gaze. Well, Becky wasn't about to let him have the last laugh.

"Frank, darling, over here!" She waved and called out, her mind seizing the first idea to present itself.

Instantly, Mike's head turned to meet the object of her attention.

Becky used that moment to dive. Resurfacing at the edge of the pool, she wrapped both hands around his booted foot and tugged with all her might. Mike lost his footing on the water-slicked grass and tumbled fully clothed into the water.

Becky didn't stick around to savor her victory. She scrambled out of the water, scooped up the bundle of clothes, and beat a hasty retreat to the spot where her horse was tied. Close at her heels was the sound of sloshing footsteps. She was torn with indecision. Reason urged her to flee for her life, while modesty insisted she not imitate Lady Godiva. The latter won.

The delicate batiste camisole balked at being drawn over moisture-beaded flesh. It twisted into a tight roll of fabric just above her full breasts and refused to budge. The sloshing grew louder and then ceased. Becky dared a look over her shoulder.

A grim-faced Mike stared down at her. Clutching her clothes to her chest, she reluctantly turned toward him. His hair was plastered to his skull like an ebony cap, his shirt and pants were sopping wet, his boots resembled overflowing vases complete with trailing fronds of greenery.

Her lips twitched with amusement. It was his hat, however, that proved her undoing. From a distance, Becky saw his hat slowly circling the swimming hole like a ship without a sail. Emerald eyes sparkling, she burst out laughing.

"You think this is funny, do you?" he thundered.

"Oh, Mike, if you could only see yourself." She stifled a giggle. "I'm sorry, but you picked the wrong time to lose your sense of humor." Becky tried again to tug the chemise into place with one hand while holding the rest of her garments in the other.

Mike took the small bundle of clothes and tossed them aside. Then he reached out and jerked off the chemise and let it fall to the ground. "I want your full attention when I talk to you," he grated.

"Stop behaving like a boor." Becky refused to be intimidated. "So you got a little wet. Well, it serves you right!" She spun away, a wet mane of hair flying behind her.

Mike caught it as easily as he might a pesky insect. "You think I got what I deserved, do you? Now it's time you get what you deserve." He coiled the dripping tresses around his closed fist and reeled her in like a fish caught on a hook.

It was useless to struggle unless she wanted her hair pulled out by the roots. His firm grip forced her around. A final twist of the hair around his wrist pulled her head back. Their eyes locked. Anger flaming in the dark blue depths was being doused by a more potent element—desire. His hold tightened convulsively. Her body arched, pressing against his. Becky shuddered at the powerful reaction invoked by overheated flesh and waterlogged clothing. The very air seemed to sizzle from their contact.

Holding her head immobile with one hand, Mike slowly trailed his other down her spine. He cupped her rounded buttocks, then pulled her hips against the hard bulge of his manhood.

Becky's eyelids fluttered shut. Ignoring the painful

hold on her hair, she moved her head from side to side. "No," she whispered. "No, don't . . ." A traitorous tide of passion threatened to drown her.

"Oh, yes," he breathed. His mouth covered hers, ruthlessly plundering its sweetness. There was no tenderness in his kiss, but a raging hunger only she could satisfy. His lips moved against hers, his tongue thrusting inside her mouth with fierce need.

Becky was incapable of holding back. She responded with every fiber of her being. Only with Mike did she feel truly alive and vibrant.

Mike dragged his mouth from hers and stared down into her passion-clouded eyes. "God help me, but I want you."

As though she weighed no more than a feather, he scooped her up in his arms. Determined strides carried him to the site where an ancient willow dipped its branches to the ground. Mike pushed aside the boughs until they parted like a lacy green curtain, admitting them to a secluded bower. He placed Becky on a bed of sweet-smelling grass. His eyes pinioned her to the ground, warning her not to move. His gaze never wavered from her face as he stripped off his wet clothes and let them fall in a careless heap. He lay down next to her, half-turning so one leg was thrown over hers. He began kissing her again, stoking fires that already burned brightly. His hands played over her body, working magic with their deft touch, seeking and finding all the places that heightened erotic pleasure.

Becky's breathing came in short, uneven gasps. She moaned, tossing her head from side to side. Impatiently, her hands moved up and down his hard muscled back, clutching his flesh so desperately she was unaware of the crescent-shaped gouges her nails made in the bronzed skin. His mouth suckled a rose-tipped nipple and then moved downward, lower and lower.

"Michael." It was a sob, an invocation, a plea to end this sweet torture.

But perversity goaded him on. Becky was quivering with her need for him when he poised above her and buried his manhood deep inside her. Each thrust sent her spiraling closer and closer to the heavens, until together their passion burst in a shower of a million glittering stars.

Subtly as a wisp of smoke wafted on a summer's breeze, the present returned to clear focus. Becky's head was nestled on Mike's shoulder, her hand rested on the mat of dark hair covering his chest. A dreamy smile played around her mouth. Somewhere above, a bird cried out and the branches rustled from its sudden movement. Becky looked upward and watched the shifting shadows of gold and green created by the slanted rays of sunlight piercing the leafy arbor.

Tentatively she reached out to stroke Mike's scarred cheek. "What is this special something between us, Michael? Is it magic or madness?"

When he didn't answer, she propped herself on one elbow and peered down at his face. His gaze was fixed on a point high above their heads.

With gentle pressure, she turned his face toward hers. The frost in his eyes chilled her to the marrow.

"It doesn't take fancy words to describe what's between us. Lust is as good a word as any."

His callous pronouncement was like a knife in her heart. It turned something beautiful and rare into something ugly. Stubborn pride refused to let him see how much he had hurt her.

Becky rose to her feet and casually tossed the chaotic mass of damp ringlets over her shoulder. "Lust, it must be. Leave it to a man not to mince words. Thank you for a delightful demonstration, Mr. Ryan. I can see why you've earned your reputation with the girls at the Satin Slipper."

There was a slight pause before he spoke. "My pleasure, Mrs. Foster."

Painfully conscious of the man behind the screen of swaying boughs, Becky quickly donned her clothes and rode off without a backward glance.

Chapter Nine

"WHERE WERE YOU THURSDAY?"

"Thursday?"

"Yeah, Thursday," Frank repeated impatiently. "I came by on the way from Mill Valley, but you weren't home. I waited as long as I could. When you didn't show up, I left."

A warm flush suffused her cheeks. Becky could account for every minute. That was the afternoon Mike had made love to her down by the creek. No, love had little to do with what took place. She mustn't forget that. It had been lust, only lust, the uncontrollable carnal urge that had swept away her willpower, her pride, her morals. Thank goodness Frank had left before she had gotten back. How could she have explained her wild disheveled appearance, her emotional turmoil?

"I spent most of Thursday with Brewster checking grazing land in the south pasture. I also checked to see if he had repaired some fences like I asked before I went away." Her tone was calm and matter-of-fact.

"If you can't depend on Brewster, hire somebody else."

"I can depend on him!" Becky hotly defended her bandy-legged foreman. "You're forgetting the farm is my responsibility. Not Brewster's."

"That's the whole problem in a nutshell."

"What is that supposed to mean?" she asked in a tight voice.

"Running a farm is a man's job. A woman's place is in the home."

Becky rolled her eyes heavenward and prayed for forebearance. "Since I don't have a family, I hardly see where I'm neglecting my duties."

"You're missing my point," Frank persisted. "A woman isn't as capable as a man for that kind of work. Women are the weaker sex, physically and mentally."

"Is that right?" Becky's irritation mounted. "I hardly consider myself weak. What I may lack in brawn, I make up for in brains and common sense. The farm is showing a nice profit, and Adam is more than satisfied with the results."

"There you go. You just proved my point. You're getting all emotional, a typical female reaction." He gave her a long considering glance. "Promise not to fly off the handle if I tell you something for your own good?"

"By all means, please do." The chill in her voice could have put frost on a pumpkin.

"Running this place is making you far too independent. That isn't a very ladylike quality. What you need is a husband."

Becky was too incensed over his derogatory comments about her femininity to pay any heed to his last statement. Of all the unmitigated gall! What colossal nerve! Not only did he insult her gender, but her intelligence as well. Before the evening ended, she vowed, he would eat his words.

After riding more than a mile in stiff silence, Frank asked, "You're not mad, are you?"

She purposely widened her eyes. "Frank," she said in mock dismay, "how could such a thought even cross your mind?"

"That's my girl," he said, beaming his approval.

They pulled into the winding drive of the Connolly place. It took all Frank's concentration to maneuver the buggy through the maze of conveyances that littered the farmyard.

"I haven't seen a crowd this size since the fair," he remarked after tying the buggy beneath a shaggy maple. Hands at her waist, he swung Becky down from the high seat. His eyes fastened on the view of her rounded breasts afforded by the décolletage of the ice-blue satin gown. His face grew slack while his dark eyes glazed with fevered brilliance.

"Marshal!" A woman's voice trilled from behind. "Isn't this a grand night for a party?"

Frank dropped his hands from Becky's waist and dragged his gaze from her bosom. A horse-faced matron dressed in puce green taffeta rustled up to them. A younger replica followed in her wake.

"Mrs. Bundy. Agnes." Frank greeted them. "Yes, indeed. Tonight is a fine night for a celebration."

The older of the pair turned to Becky. Her sharp gaze traveled from the cluster of amber curls high atop her head and cascading down her back to the tips of her satin slippers. Her lips curved in a malicious smile. "Gracious, Becky. It's a good thing you brought a shawl. You could catch your death in that dress."

The spinster daughter snickered at her mother's catty remark, but Becky ignored the girl. "How kind of you to be so concerned about my health, Mrs. Bundy. Perhaps you're right. I do detect a certain coolness."

Maude Bundy's mouth tightened and she turned her attention back to the marshal. "I've been told Nate Gibson is bringing his fiddle. I'm too old, but my Agnes just loves to dance. Maybe later you could show us old folks a step or two."

Agnes tittered behind a gloved hand and shot the lawman a coy glance.

"Of course." Frank's response lacked enthusiasm.

"Good! We'll see you later, marshal." Maude gave him a long-toothed smile. "Come along, Agnes." Mrs. Bundy bustled off in the direction of a recent widower with Agnes quietly following like an obedient puppy.

"Can that girl talk?" Frank shook his head in disgust. "All I've ever heard her do is giggle."

"Well, you'll find out whether she can talk when you dance with her later." Becky smiled. "If I were the jealous type, I'd be worried. I get the distinct impression Maude Bundy looks on you as a candidate for son-in-law."

139

Frank failed to find humor in the situation. "If that's what she has in mind, she's in for a big disappointment. I have very definite ideas of the kind of wife I want. Believe me, she's nothing like Agnes Bundy." He took Becky's arm and steered her toward the festivities.

It was still early yet, and most people were milling about the yard. Later, after sunset, they would congregate in the barn for dancing. For the time being, however, they were content to socialize.

Jeff Shields, the clerk from the general store, approached. "Evening, marshal. Mrs. Foster." Nervously he cleared his throat and blurted, "Gee, Mrs. Foster, you're beautiful."

"Why thank you, Jeff. What a lovely compliment."

Bright red crept upward from his starched collar to the tips of his ears. "I brought you some punch," he said holding out a cup. "It's awful good."

"How thoughtful." Becky rewarded him with a dazzling smile, causing the young clerk to swallow convulsively.

Frank shifted his weight from one leg to the other. "I'm surprised Mr. Curtis could spare you time from the store."

"We close early on Saturdays," the youth replied absently, his eyes glued to Becky. Wiping sweaty palms on his pants, he drew a deep breath and plunged ahead. "I was just wondering, Mrs. Foster, if you would save a dance for me?"

"I'd be delighted to."

"Gee, you will?" He couldn't believe his good fortune. "That's great! I'll see you afterward then." He backed away only to be brought up short against a table laden with pastries. "Excuse me," he mumbled. Realizing his mistake, his blush deepened to the roots of his blond hair. He flashed a weak smile in Becky's direction and retreated to the safety of a crowd of young people.

Frank gave a dry unpleasant laugh. "You may not be the jealous type, but I am. It's a good thing your young admirer is still wet behind the ears."

Becky found his possessive attitude nervewracking. The situation was beginning to get out of hand. Soon, very soon, she would have to set things straight. The difficult part would be to do so in such a fashion as not to incur his wrath. She had worked too hard, sacrificed too much, to make Frank an enemy.

Taking a sip of punch, Becky discovered it was quite delicious and quickly drained the cup. It didn't remain empty for long before someone pressed another in her hand, often with an extravagant compliment. In spite of her misgivings about Frank, her spirits lifted, and then took flight. Before long Becky was having a marvelous time. With her face animated, her eyes aglow, her infectious laughter ringing out, she flirted shamelessly with every man present be they eight or eighty.

Her beauty drew as many envious glances from the ladies as it did admiring ones from the men. Those less blessed than she gossiped among themselves, finding fault with her sunstreaked hair and the pale gold hue of her skin. No true lady, they clucked their tongues, would allow the sun to tint their skin that disgusting color.

"A real lady like my Agnes," Maude Bundy was quick to point out, "takes great pains to preserve her milky-white complexion. And isn't the cut of Becky Foster's dress scandalous?"

Over the sea of faces, Becky spied Ben and Hannah talking with friends. She caught Ben's eye and answered his quizzical frown with a sunny smile. The first strains from a fiddle carried into the twilight. Of one accord, people began moving toward the barn.

The spotless condition of the barn attested to weeks of preparation. The center of the floor had been cleared for dancing. Bales of hay along its sides formed low benches on which to sit. In one corner, Nate Gibson stood with several other men, one with a harmonica, another with a concertina. The newlyweds stood greeting guests just inside the wide double doors.

"Let's congratulate the bride and groom," Becky suggested.

"Might as well get it over with."

The couple looked so frightfully young and vulnerable, yet brimming with optimism about their future, that Becky felt her heart constrict. She was a hopeless romantic, another trait Frank would fault.

"Mary." Becky placed a light kiss on the girl's cheek. "You look positively radiant. You make a beautiful bride."

"Thank you, Mrs. Foster," she said shyly. The proud and happy bridegroom looked on with an ear-to-ear grin.

Frank added a perfunctory congratulations and shook hands with the groom. Others were waiting to wish the couple well, so Frank and Becky moved on. The musicians struck up a lively Virginia reel and the celebration began in earnest.

"Mrs. Foster," Frank said with a stiff bow. "May I have the pleasure of this dance?"

Becky's foot was already tapping to the rhythm. "I thought you'd never ask."

Frank's arm rode at her waist as they joined the fast-stepping dancers. Though Frank proved a proficient, if uninspired dancer, he seemed relieved when the next tune had a slower tempo.

Not more than a minute passed when Pete Mitchell tapped Frank's shoulder. "Mind if I cut in, boss?"

Frank glared at the red-haired deputy in annoyance, but relinquished Becky without an argument.

"Don't look like Frank was none too happy 'bout me cuttin' in. Can't say that I blame him. But if I had a little filly like you, I wouldn't give you up without a fight."

"I can see why you're considered a ladies' man, Mr. Mitchell."

He grinned boldly. "Mr. Mitchell is a bit formal between friends. Call me Pete. I've had my eye on you for some time. You're cool and ladylike on the outside. I have a hunch, underneath, there's a hot-blooded woman. I like 'em all fire and ice."

Becky stiffened and drew back, but his grip tightened, and he swirled her into the thick of the dancing. "Don't get all huffy. I meant it as a compliment."

For the first time since she had known him, Becky looked at Pete closely. The light blue eyes staring back at her were filled with a cunning that had gone unnoticed until now. He seemed to read her thoughts.

"Don't mean to boast, but I'm a lot smarter than folks give me credit for. Not that I care, mind you. Sometimes it works to my advantage. I like to sit back and take things in. A man can learn a lot that way, if you get my drift. Take you and Mike Ryan for instance."

Becky's mouth went dry. "I don't know what you're talking about."

Pete chuckled. "I couldn't help but see how he watches you when he thinks no one's looking. He eats you up with his eyes. What's going on between you two?"

"Nothing! Don't be absurd!" Becky tried to pull away, but his meaty hand bit into her waist.

"You're getting all riled up over nothing. Your secret is safe with me. Just be nice and I'll keep my mouth shut."

"There is no secret." She spat the denial.

"Sure," he said, grinning knowingly. "Reason I cut in is I thought it high time I let you know that when you're tired of Denby and Ryan, old Pete is available. I come with a long list of satisfied customers."

Becky couldn't believe her ears. "Don't hold your breath," she hissed, bringing the heel of her foot down on his arch. At Pete's gasp of pain, she jerked free and left him standing alone in the midst of swirling couples.

Darting a furtive glance to see who might have witnessed his comeuppance, Pete strode from the floor. His ruddy face was redder than usual and his pale eyes held a dangerous glint. The bitch! Who the hell did she think she was to treat him like dirt. No one, but no one, got away with that.

The encounter with Pete left Becky seething. It had been worse than finding a viper nesting in a flower bed. What she needed was another glass of Emma Connolly's punch to soothe her jangled nerves.

"Nicely done, Rebecca." Maggie Nelson applauded as Becky reached for the drink. "You certainly managed to bring the deputy down a peg."

"He had it coming," Becky said, turning toward the dowager. The amused expression on the woman's face told Becky she had witnessed the exchange with lively interest.

"No doubt. I've seen him in action. He struts his prowess with the ladies like a bantam rooster."

The comparison brought a smile to Becky's lips. "I think our rooster just had his wings clipped."

"Knowing Pete, they'll grow back soon enough."

Becky drained the contents of her glass and refilled it from a cut-glass bowl. "I seem to have developed an unquenchable thirst tonight."

The older woman gave a dry chuckle. "You and everyone else, it seems."

Jeff Shields came up to claim the next dance. After Jeff, Becky lost track of her numerous partners. Frank finally gave up his attempt to monopolize her time and sulked from the sidelines.

Perspiration beaded the forehead of Chester Rollins, her current partner. Taking pity on the man, Becky favored him with an apologetic smile. "I don't know how you keep up this pace, Mr. Rollins. As for myself, I need a chance to catch my breath."

"Certainly, certainly." The man was only too happy to oblige. Seeing Ben Sloane off to one side, Chester led Becky over to him, then making his excuses, left Becky in Ben's capable hands.

Becky tilted her head to one side and studied her old friend. "You look unusually somber tonight. This is a celebration, not a funeral," she scolded. "Don't be a stick in the mud." She caught hold of his hand

and tugged playfully. "Come on, Ben. Dance with me?"

His face creased in a grin though he resisted her efforts to pull him onto the dance floor. "You're in an exceptionally cheerful mood, honey."

"There's nothing wrong with having fun," she retorted saucily. "I've heard you say that hundreds of times."

Ben's dark brows drew together. "Have you been sampling Emma Connolly's punch?"

Becky nodded, feeling guilty for no apparent reason.

"I should have guessed." Ben's deep voice rumbled with laughter. "Emma's secret ingredient is rum—lots of it."

"Oh," Becky said in a small voice.

"Just take it easy on the punch for the rest of the evening," Ben cautioned. "You'll need a clear head later on."

Becky murmured her agreement. After the festivities ended, she and Ben were to meet a fugitive and take him north to Potterville. This time she had informed Ben she was going with him the entire way. Mike wasn't to be involved. In fact, he was to know nothing of the plan.

"Mike!" Ben called out, catching sight of his foreman. "You're just the one I'm looking for. Becky's in the mood to dance. Do an old man a favor and take my place."

Ben, Becky groaned silently, why are you doing this to me?

Turning, Becky watched Mike draw nearer. He presented a striking figure in an impeccably tailored suit of black broadcloth and a scarlet brocade waistcoat. The set expression on his face told her he didn't relish the prospect of dancing any more than she did.

"Perhaps the lady would rather choose her own partners," Mike told Ben.

"Nonsense! Becky never doubts my good judgment," Ben said, placing a firm hand at the small of their backs and giving them a gentle shove in the direction of the dance floor.

"Men don't look this grim on their way to a firing squad," Becky quipped.

"An appropriate analogy."

Mike drew her into his arms and they began to slowly circle the floor. In spite of being a large man, he moved with natural grace. Knowing full well she wasn't his choice as a partner didn't diminish the joy of being in his arms. Anxious to know if he was at all affected by her nearness, she glanced at his face. It was aloof and remote. His indifference was more difficult to deal with than his anger. Becky's earlier gaiety faded, replaced by aching sadness.

"Frank looked happier when he was dancing with Agnes Bundy," she observed with a trace of wistfulness.

"Let's set the record straight. I'm not doing this because I want to. I'm doing it to please Ben. All he's done lately is talk about how much he hates to see us at each other's throats."

"I see." Becky pinned a smile on her face as they whirled past Ben who watched them with a benevolent grin. "Then for Ben's sake can't you pretend for a few minutes that we're not enemies?"

"I've never been good at make-believe."

"Do you dislike me so much you can't bear to look at me?" The words were wrung from her heart.

Mike steeled himself against her pleading voice. He wanted to tell her, yes, he did dislike her, even came close to hating her at times. She was everything he wanted and couldn't have. But mostly he hated himself. He couldn't stop wanting her.

"This dance is mine, Ryan," Frank's slurred voice cut in.

"The lady is yours for the taking, marshal."

Becky gasped at the harsh reply. Before she could find a rebuttal, Mike melted into the crowd.

"Ryan acted like he was glad to see me."

"Yes, he did." Becky swallowed the knot in her throat. "It would seem I'm not his type."

Frank pulled her closer than propriety deemed acceptable. "Well, you're mine," he whispered thickly.

Whiskey fumes filled her nostrils. Frank had been imbibing in something more potent than Emma Connolly's punch. His foot trounced on her slipper-shod foot, and Becky winced. She was happy when the music ended.

"Ladies and gentlemen," Will Connolly called out and raised his arms for silence. "We have a special musical treat in store for you. Maude Bundy and her charming daughter, Agnes, have generously offered to grace this occasion with a duet. With a little persuasion, they may even favor us with an encore."

"There's no way in hell I'm going to stick around for this," Frank whispered. "I've got some unfinished business to attend to. You wait here." He shouldered his way through the crowd.

After listening to the opening bars of a favorite ballad being ruined by quavering sopranos, Becky realized Frank had made a wise decision. She had no greater desire to listen than he had. Unnoticed she edged to the back of the crowd and slipped out the opened doors. She found herself in an apple orchard adjacent to the barn.

The color of her gown blended with the silvery moonlight giving her a wraithlike appearance as she wandered in and out among the trees. The evening was not turning out as she had imagined. First there had been the disquieting incident with Pete, leaving her uneasy over his reference to her and Mike. The episode with Mike hadn't helped either. Any secret hope she might have harbored for a relationship was doomed; the situation had deteriorated beyond redemption. If only she could accept that and not feel the ripping pain each time she thought of what might have been. Her sigh was a lonely sound in the summer night.

Twigs snapped beneath heavy footsteps. Becky stood still as a statue and waited.

"Becky!" Frank's voice rang out. "You out here? Speak up!"

Becky turned toward the voice. "Here I am," she said quietly.

"I thought I told you to wait inside. I've been lookin' all over for you. Lucky for me, Ryan saw you duck out here."

"I needed a breath of fresh air."

He smiled down on her, and for some unexplained reason it made her more uneasy than his usual criticism.

"Actually I'm glad you came outdoors. There's something I've been wanting to say, and I'd rather do it in private."

There were only vestiges of his earlier inebriation.

149

Becky wondered what could have happened to shock him into sobriety. Strains of music drifted out to them, and Becky realized how truly alone they were.

"Can't whatever you have to tell me be said while we're dancing?" she suggested hopefully.

He smiled. "What I have to say can best be said from right here." He clamped his hands on her bare shoulders. "Becky, I did a lot of thinking while you were gone. I discovered that there's a lot of truth to the old saying about absence making the heart grow fonder. I decided you'd make me a good wife. Will you marry me?"

Becky stared at him in consternation. She should have guessed what he was leading up to. She should have been ready with an answer. "Frank . . . I . . . I don't know what to say."

"That's easy. Say yes."

"This is so unexpected. I need time to think," she stalled.

"I hoped we might make a grand announcement tonight." He sounded disappointed. "Just don't keep me dangling too long, I'm not a patient man."

He crushed her to him in a rough embrace. His mouth, fierce and demanding, moved over hers until Becky felt her supply of oxygen cut off. She pushed against his chest, but his hold only tightened. Tomorrow, she knew there would be purple bruises where his fingers dug into her flesh.

From the darkness, a man loudly cleared his throat. Frank's head jerked up in surprise.

"Sorry to break up this tender little scene," Mike drawled silkily before stepping out of the shadows.

Frank released Becky and drew back. "Ryan! What

150

the hell are you doing out here? Can't you see you're interrupting?"

In the narrow swath of moonlight, Mike's mouth twisted into the mocking slant Becky had come to despise and fear. "Your deputy's been searching all over for you. Said it was urgent. He spread the word that if anyone saw you, to have you meet him back in town pronto."

Frank swore under his breath and shook his head. "Becky, I hate like the devil to run off, but I have to go. It sounds important."

"Certainly, I understand," she said, her thoughts on Frank's proposal and Mike's interruption and not the fact that something must be up to pull Frank away from her now.

"Go ahead," Mike urged. "I'll see Mrs. Foster back to the party safely."

"You take the buggy," Frank told Becky. "It would only slow me down. I'll borrow one of Will's horses." Then he was gone.

"I admire his dedication to duty," Mike said dryly. "Under the same circumstances, I don't think I would have had his willpower." He came toward her slowly.

Becky found herself incapable of moving. As though in a hypnotic trance, she watched him advance. Her brain was numb, thought was difficult, and speech was impossible. The play of moonlight and shadow made Mike's scar-ravaged face both fascinating and sinister. Unsure of his mood, Becky ran the tip of her tongue over her lips. His indigo gaze followed the movement.

"Have you been here long?" Becky found her voice at last.

"Long enough to know congratulations are in order."

"I really should return to the party."

Mike braced his arms against the tree trunk on either side of her head. "There's no need to rush." The faint scent of sandalwood pervaded the air. "How long are you going to keep the marshal waiting in suspense?"

"Mike, I don't . . ."

"You're right. It isn't any of my business. I called you a witch once." His voice was low and husky, his words seductive. "I was wrong. Witches are ugly old crones covered with warts. You're far too beautiful to ever be called a witch. Yet, witch you must be for you've cast your spell over me."

Just as you've done to me, Becky thought. She longed to throw her arms around his neck and be held against his chest where she could feel the heavy beating of his heart. Caution held her back. Did a note of cynicism underlie the flowery compliments?

"If we don't get back, people will talk." Her voice was thready.

Mike ignored the feeble protest. "Denby didn't tell you that moonlight becomes you. It makes your hair gleam like molten gold." His hand burrowed beneath the luxurious torrent of curls.

Don't be fooled by eloquent flattery, Becky told herself. He doesn't care a fig about you and don't forget it. Strong fingers played lightly up and down the back of her neck. Tiny jolts of electricity ran down her spine and radiated along nerve endings until even her toes tingled. Break away and run before it's too late, her mind flashed the warning. But it was already too late. Her eyes closed.

"Denby didn't say how your eyes have a luminous glow that makes the moon dull in comparison." Mike kissed her eyelids, his lips no more than a whisper on the delicate skin.

A soft sigh escaped her parted lips.

Mike's head lowered until his warm breath mingled with hers. "Did Denby ever mention that your mouth tastes sweeter than wild honey? A man can drink deeply, yet come away craving more." His lips moved over hers, gentle, coaxing. His tongue slid past her teeth, seeking out and savoring its honeyed essence as though unable to drink its fill. When at last he dragged his mouth from hers, it was to rain light kisses down the slim column of her throat.

"Michael," she shuddered and pressed her back against the rough bark. She felt her fears and reservations being swept away.

Mike's fingers slipped inside the low-cut bodice to fondle the soft mounds of her breasts. "Your beauty is what legends are made of, and wars are fought for," he murmured.

Mike felt Becky tremble. She was a prize ready for the taking. The fact gave him grim pleasure. Like a besotted lovesick fool, he dared to dream she might care for him. But dreams shatter under the harsh glare of reality. He had watched her all evening, couldn't seem to take his eyes off her. He had seen the way she laughed, and the way she flirted. And he had seen the way the men responded. No, she didn't care about him—any man would do.

"You may be a beauty, lady, but you're no challenge," he sneered, moving away so abruptly Becky pressed her palms against the tree for support. "You're nothing but a cheap little tramp. I just had to find out once and for all how easily you traded your body for sweet talk and a few stolen kisses. Go back to Denby. I don't want you."

Becky held her hand against her mouth to smother the sobs that threatened to escape. With tear-filled eyes, she watched him stalk away.

Chapter Ten

THE THROBBING IN HER TEMPLES WAS LIKE HORSE'S hooves pounding against hard ground. Perhaps a cup of tea would tame the pain into a simple ache. Mechanically, Becky moved about the kitchen, lighting a small fire, putting the kettle on to boil, and setting out a cup and saucer. On impulse, she set out a second cup in case Ben wanted to join her before they began the night's journey.

When she had returned to the party earlier, there had been no sign of Ben or Hannah. Fortunately, there had been no sign of Mike either. Becky had pleaded a headache and left.

Mike's cruelty had occupied her thoughts during the ride home. Never had she been so humiliated. He had called her a tramp. Judging from her wanton behavior, she could understand why. Provided she could find the words to explain, would Mike believe that no one, not even David, had been able to ignite such a burning desire? Probably not, Becky thought sorrowfully.

Greater than the humiliation was the hurt. Knowing how easily Mike assumed the worst of her, how little regard he had for her feelings, was like a rapier thrust into her heart. When had she started caring so much?

The tea helped ease the headache, but didn't lift her spirits. Moodily, Becky stared into the dregs at the bottom of the cup. If she truly had magical powers, she would be able to read tea leaves. She wondered what the future held in store. The cup slipped from her fingers with a clatter. She didn't want to know, she realized. She would learn all too soon.

Becky was rinsing her cup at the sink when she heard a sharp rap on the door. She answered it fully expecting to find Ben. Her smile of welcome vanished when she found Mike instead.

"Mike," she stammered. "What are you doing here? I was expecting . . ."

"Your lover?"

"What do you want?"

"Can I come in, or are you going to keep me standing out here?"

Becky reluctantly stepped aside and allowed him entrance. His gaze swept around the room before resting on the unused cup on the table. The expression on his face told her he had found her guilty as charged.

Pain radiated up her arm. Becky looked down and was surprised to find herself clutching the door handle so fiercely that her knuckles were blanched and the tendons were raised cords. She released her death grip with slow deliberation and closed the door.

Mike seemed unable to meet her gaze. For the first time since meeting him, he had lost his usual self-assurance. It wasn't a mere apology that brought him here at this hour, Becky knew with a flash of insight. "Something is wrong. I can feel it."

He fixed his gaze somewhere near her left ear. "I don't know how to say this . . ."

Becky's hand flew to her throat. A shiver whispered down her spine. She felt as though a cat had walked over her grave. She had heard the expression for years, but until this moment never truly appreciated the meaning.

"It's Ben, isn't it?" she asked through numb lips.

"Ben isn't well." Mike chose his words with care. "We think it might be his heart."

Her eyes were enormous in a distraught face. The room tilted beneath her feet before righting itself. Becky grabbed the back of a chair to steady her reeling world. "How bad is it? He isn't . . . ?" She couldn't voice her greatest fear.

"Don't worry, he's alive. He gave us a good scare, but he seemed a bit better before I left."

"Thank God," she breathed, closing her eyes.

"You'd best sit down," Mike ordered. "You look awfully pale."

Becky didn't argue. Her legs were jelly as she sank into the nearest chair.

Mike regarded her with calm detachment. "You could use a drink. Do you keep anything stronger than tea around this place?"

"Over there." Becky indicated a cupboard in one corner.

Mike rummaged inside until he found a bottle of brandy. Splashing some into a teacup, he handed it to her.

Her hands shook so much the brandy threatened to spill over the rim of the cup and stain the satin folds of her gown. Realizing her predicament, Mike took pity. Taking the cup, he held it to her lips.

"Drink!" he ordered in a tone that forbid argument. "All of it."

Becky did as she was told. The liquor burned her throat and seared the pit of her stomach. Though her eyes were watery, her brain began to function in a rational manner.

"Sorry," Mike said gruffly. "I didn't mean to give you such a shock. I just didn't know an easy way to break the news."

"What happened?"

"Ben complained of indigestion, so we left the wedding early." Mike shoved his hands into his pockets and gave a tired sigh. "By the time we got home, he had broken out in a cold sweat and complained about a heavy feeling in his chest. Doc Nolan came by and gave him something to make him sleep."

Becky carefully set the cup on the table. "It was kind of you to come and tell me."

"That was Ben's idea. I tried to explain it could wait until morning, but he insisted it had to be tonight. Rather than upset him, I didn't argue. Hope I didn't interrupt any plans."

"Plans?" she echoed. *Plans!* Concern for Ben had driven all else from her mind. Could she manage without him? It was possible, she knew, but dangerous. An alarming number of slavecatchers patrolled the road after nightfall. Adam had frightened her with countless stories of their brutality. These men were bullies who preyed on the weak and helpless, greedy for bounty money and with little respect for human life. They wouldn't hesitate to challenge a lone youth, maybe rough him up, and then ransack the wagon. They were experts on ferreting out hiding places. However, these bullies might have second thoughts about meddling with a man and his son on their way to market with a load of produce.

Besides, Becky admitted, she was tired of working at cross purposes with Mike. He was as trustworthy as they come. It no longer seemed a good idea to keep him in the dark about her involvement. He had to be told. Yet she had given her word, and she never broke a promise. Tomorrow, she decided, she would go to Ben and ask him to release her from her vow. But that was tomorrow, and she needed Mike's help tonight.

"Mike, wait!" she called out. He was already at the door by the time she reached him. "Please don't go," she said, placing her hand on his sleeve. "I need your help."

"Are you sure it's *my* help you need?" he asked sardonically, as he plucked her hand from his arm as though it were a loathsome insect and let it drop.

Becky ignored the rebuff. "You were right. I was waiting for someone, but it wasn't Frank. It was Ben."

A dark brow shot upward. "You expect me to believe that?"

Becky felt a moment's doubt. Perhaps it hadn't

159

been prudent to ask for Mike's help. She should have realized he would pose questions she wasn't ready, or able, to answer. But once uttered, the words couldn't be taken back. "Just hear me out," she forged ahead.

Mike nodded, albeit reluctantly.

Nervously Becky ran the tip of her tongue over her lower lip. "Ben and I were supposed to meet a fugitive down by Willow Creek and take him to Potterville."

She might as well have declared her intention to walk on the moon. Under different circumstances, the look of disbelief on Mike's face would have been comical. Now, instead of laughter, she wanted to stomp her foot in frustration. "I realize this must sound farfetched," she said in a tight voice.

"That's an understatement." Mike shook his head. "Why should I believe you?"

"Why would Ben, as sick as he is, insist you come here tonight? Do you think he'd ask that of you if it wasn't important? Ben thought I might need help."

"And do you?"

"Yes," she said simply.

The skepticism was still on his face. "What if I refuse?"

"Then I'll just have to do the best I can without you," she replied with quiet dignity. "It's late, and I still have to change clothes. Think it over. If you're not here when I come downstairs, I'll understand." With a swish of satin, Becky left him to ponder his decision.

Becky began pulling hairpins from her elaborate coiffure as she walked up the stairs. A shake of her head brought dark gold curls tumbling around her shoulders. The hooks of her gown were unfastened by the time she reached her room and the costly garment was flung across the foot of the bed. Stepping out of her petticoats, Becky walked to the bureau and pulled out Adam's castoff trousers and shirt from the bottom drawer. After donning these, she gathered her hair at the top of her head and twisted it neatly into a knot. A wide-brimmed hat completed her transformation; she looked like a boy. Before slinging a jacket over her shoulder, she patted its pocket to make certain the whistle was tucked safely inside. The whole time she wondered if Mike would still be waiting when she went downstairs.

Less than ten minutes later, she stopped just inside the kitchen. Mike was seated at the table having a cup of tea. "I wasn't sure you would still be here." She sounded breathless.

"I stayed to call your bluff." Mike's gaze raked her from hat to boot. Surprise gave way to anger. He bounded to his feet and strode over to confront her. "What the hell do you think you're doing? This isn't a masquerade party you're going to. It's serious business."

"I'm well aware of that."

He glared down at her as though he'd like to shake some sense into her. "Maybe you look at this as fun and excitement, an adventure of some sort. Well it isn't a game! If we get caught, your pretty little hide is in this as deep as mine. It could mean heavy fines—or prison."

"If you're trying to scare me, save your breath."

"Of all the stubborn, muleheaded females." Mike combed his fingers through his hair. "Look," he said, trying again to make her see reason, "ever since I came to town I've heard you agree with Denby's pro-slavery notions. Why get involved in something you obviously don't believe in? Why take the risk?"

Becky spread her hands in a helpless gesture. "I know you must have a dozen questions. For now just think of me as doing this for Ben's sake. He's been like a father to me. It's little enough to do in return."

That was something Mike could accept. "All right," he agreed, knowing Ben was the rare man who inspired that kind of loyalty.

"We're wasting time. Let's go." Turning down the wick of the lamp, Becky led the way out of the darkened house. "I see you brought the wagon. We can take it as far as the cabin and leave it there. We'll go the rest of the way on foot." Her manner was brisk and businesslike, leaving no doubt who was in charge. "There's a large boulder about ten feet from the creek. That's where we wait until we hear the signal from our passenger."

Mike climbed into the driver's seat. "You lost me. What kind of a signal are you talking about?"

"When we hear the cry of a whippoorwill, we're to return the call twice. That lets the fugitive know it's safe to come out of hiding."

Mike snapped the reins, and the wagon sped down the drive and out onto the main road. "I sure hope you're better at birdcalls than I am."

Becky laughed softly. "I brought this along for added insurance." She showed him the slender wooden whistle, then slipped it back into her pocket.

"Ben must be in his dotage to trust you with so much information. It must be quite a temptation not to tell Denby."

Becky bit her tongue to keep back a retort. Neither spoke for the remainder of the ride.

"Leave the wagon here," Becky instructed as they neared the shed adjacent to the cabin.

"Whatever you say. You're the boss."

Becky was out of the wagon and was heading for the dense cover of woods before Mike was able to secure it. But he was quickly behind her. "It's as black as pitch. Don't you need a lantern?"

"Shh." She held her finger to her lips and spoke in a hushed voice. "I have eyes like a cat. Just keep quiet and follow me."

Soundlessly as a wood sprite, Becky wove in and out of oak, ash, elm, and maple, pausing from time to time to listen. The tall timbers assumed spectral shapes in the shafts of moonlight that pierced the thick foliage. The woods had an alien feel, making the skin at the nape of her neck prickle. She gnawed her lower lip. Something was wrong, she could feel it. Becky was tempted to confide her unnamed fears to Mike, but a quick glance at his set features lent little encouragement.

At last she stopped and pointed to a huge boulder at the edge of the trees not far from the bank of the stream. Mike nodded and followed her to crouch in its shadow. Seconds crawled into minutes. Five. Ten. With each one, Becky's tension mounted until her nerves were strung taut as piano wires about to snap. This was the moment she always feared—when careful plans were most apt to go awry. After the final signal, for a few precious moments, the fugitive would be exposed and vulnerable.

Becky strained her ears, but quiet was all around. Once she thought she heard a faint rustling from the opposite bank of the creek. Probably a small animal foraging for food, she assumed. Then thick heavy silence smothered all further sound in its dank folds.

The answer came to her with a jolt. Suddenly she realized what was amiss. All the usual nocturnal sounds were absent. Not even the screech owl made its presence known. Becky half-turned to Mike, her lips parted to speak when the whippoorwill sounded its mournful cry.

"I saw something move!" a strange voice rang out. "Over there!"

Becky started to rise, only to have Mike haul her down behind the boulder's protection.

"There he goes!" Denby barked. "After him!"

Footsteps crashed through the brush and splashed along the bank of the stream.

"He's getting away!" Pete Mitchell yelled.

Guns spit orange tongues of flame as bullets exploded. One bullet whined as it ricocheted off the rock in front of them. The sound of a hefty mass being slammed into the earth was followed by a moment of silence.

Becky clamped her hands over her ears and squeezed her eyes shut. Burying her head in Mike's shoulder, she futilely tried to block out that her greatest fear was becoming a reality. Though she shivered as if with ague, no comforting arms encircled her.

"Hey, Mitchell, you shot him deader than a door-nail," the stranger protested. "I told you guys I wanted him alive. There's no market for haulin' in a dead nigger."

"That's your problem," Pete snapped.

"Stop bickering!" Frank ordered. "Let's load this carcass and take him into town."

"If I'm lucky, maybe I can still collect part of the reward," the stranger said hopefully. "Mr. Parkins might want to use this runaway's hide as a warning to others who might get the itch to take off."

After the three left with their burden, Becky let her hands drop from her ears and awkwardly scrambled to her feet. Her legs were stiff and cramped, but she barely noticed their discomfort. Tears she didn't remember shedding glistened on her cheeks, and she wiped them away with the back of her hand. She was conscious of Mike next to her, but didn't dare look at him. Her emotions were too fragile. Keeping her mind a blank, she retraced her way through the woods, propelled more by instinct than conscious effort.

The swaying motion of the wagon eventually penetrated her stupor. Becky's mind began to work frantically. A list of unanswered questions chanted through her brain. How could this have happened? Who was the stranger? A slavecatcher? Willow Creek was miles long and tortuous. How did they know the precise spot to wait? Why did Pete have to kill the man?

With a start, Becky realized the wagon had stopped. Turning, she found Mike watching her, his eyes narrowed and searching. "That poor man," she murmured. "He never had a chance."

"No. He didn't." It was an accusation.

Mike's tone wounded her. She searched his face. A cold forbidding mask had settled over his features. The events of that night weighed heavily on her mind. "It couldn't have been coincidence. Someone had to tell those men when and where." She spoke as much to herself as she did to him.

"Funny. The same thought occurred to me."

"Who . . . ?"

"Stop playing games! I'm not stupid." He bit out each word. "You're clever, lady. The tears were a nice touch, but I've got it all figured out. Don't you think you should go inside and get ready for your lover? Denby is bound to be along as soon as he finishes his filthy business. Then the two of you can gloat over your victory."

Her eyes wide with disbelief, Becky stared at him. This couldn't be happening; Mike couldn't be serious. Surely he didn't think she would lead an innocent man into a baited trap! "Mike, you're wrong! It's not the way it looks. Why would I have asked you . . ." she began, trying to make him understand.

"Get out of here," he snarled before she could finish. "The sight of you sickens me."

Becky scrambled down from the wagon, nearly falling in her haste. She looked up at him, hurt and despair rendering her speechless.

The moonlight etched harsh planes on Mike's scarred face, and his eyes gleamed with obsidian brilliance. "You betrayed Ben's trust." His words flayed her like a whip. "Earlier this evening I called you a tramp. Well, you're a traitor as well. Because of you a man died. I hope you can live with that on your conscience." He slapped the reins and the wagon shot down the drive.

Her shoulders slumping in defeat, Becky stood rooted to the spot long after Mike had disappeared from view. With a sound that started as a sigh, but ended as a sob, she wheeled around and ran into the house and up the stairs. Face down on the bed, she abandoned herself to horrible racking sobs that convulsed her body.

Mike's face loomed above her, dark and accusing. "Liar! Traitor! Tramp!" he intoned. "Because of you a man died!"

"No, no," Becky whimpered. "It isn't true. It wasn't my fault." The sound of her protests brought her awake from a fitful sleep.

She sat up in bed and buried her head in her hands. The nightmare had brought the disastrous events of the previous night rushing back. Mike was right, she admitted dully. It was her fault, only not in the way he imagined. Her ploy had proved a monumental failure. At the crucial moment, Frank hadn't confided in her at all, but kept his plans secret. She should have probed deeper and discovered what urgent business called him from her side shortly after proposing marriage. If only she hadn't been so preoccupied with personal matters.

"Oh, Mike," she moaned softly. "Will you ever understand?" Tears began to well again, and she steeled herself against the ache in her heart.

In the endless hours before dawn, Becky had confronted a truth she had been too frightened to face in daylight. She loved Mike. It was so simple she wondered why she hadn't realized it sooner. Her attraction to him involved not merely her senses, but her soul. Her feelings for him were deep and irrevocable, as basic as food and water, as vital as fire and wind, as inevitable as night follows day. Once there had been a possibility that her love might be returned. Was there still? Though Becky was doubtful, she wasn't ready to accept the fact it might be too late. "There has to be a way," she whispered. "There just has to be."

Then it came to her. Ben was the key. Once Ben realized Frank was no longer important to their plans, and once he realized how much she loved Mike, he would agree to tell Mike the truth. After everything that had happened, Mike would never believe her, *but he would believe Ben*. Mike had to be convinced she was innocent of the heinous crime he'd accused her of.

Becky jumped off the bed. She needed to see Ben. He would know what to say to make things better. Hadn't he always been there when she needed him?

She stubbornly refused to dwell on the fact that Ben might be seriously ill. Surely he would be fine this morning, she reasoned. Last night Mike had said Ben was already beginning to look better. Ben would be just fine, she told herself repeatedly as she washed and dressed. Hannah would be in her glory fussing over him. More than likely, she already had a pot of chicken soup simmering on the stove.

Half an hour later, Becky threw Lady's reins over the hitching post near the Sloanes' back door. The house wore a subdued air in direct contrast to the bright summer day. When no one answered her knock, Becky peeked into the kitchen window. There was no sign of anyone stirring, not even the familiar coffeepot was in evidence. Perhaps Hannah had sat all night with Ben and was catching up on lost sleep, Becky reasoned. It might be best if she came back later. She turned to leave when the door opened.

"Come in," Mike said hoarsely. If he was surprised to see her, he didn't show it.

With legs that felt like wooden stilts, Becky entered the kitchen and perched stiffly on the edge of a chair. Her gaze fastened on Mike's face. It was drawn and haggard, covered with dark stubble. His black curls were tousled as though raked through countless times by anxious fingers. But it was his eyes, red-rimmed and filled with pain, that made her heart trip with fear.

"Ben died an hour ago."

Becky didn't move a muscle. Not even a blink of an eyelash betrayed her inner anguish. Mike expected hysteria, not the icy calm that encased her emotions. He watched uneasily. Her face was void of color except for violet smudges of fatigue beneath her eyes. She held her hands tightly clenched in her lap, mute testimony of the battle she waged for self-control.

"How is Hannah?" Becky finally asked, her voice strained.

"I'm not sure." Mike went to a cupboard and pulled out a bottle of bourbon. He poured himself a generous measure and frowned into the amber liquid. "She might be in shock. All she does is sit at the bedside and stare into space. She hasn't even cried."

Becky slowly rose to her feet. "I'll go to her." She stopped in the doorway. "Mike, I'm sorry. I know how much you cared for Ben."

Mike drained his glass and poured another. When he looked up, Becky was gone. She was a mystery. A contradiction. Strength when he expected weakness. And once he'd watched her shed tears at a time of rejoicing. She bewildered him, kept him off balance. One minute he wanted to strangle her, the next make love to her. He might hate her on a Monday only to admire her on Tuesday. Maybe Ben with his simple homespun wisdom could explain her behavior and his confusion. But it was too late now. Ben was dead. Mike took another long drink.

Becky stood unnoticed just inside the bedroom. Ben lay in the center of the four-poster bed covered with a patchwork quilt. Death had erased lines of worry and fatigue from his weathered face. In repose, his mouth was curved in a half-smile of contentment, as though he enjoyed a pleasant dream. Afraid that if she looked at him any longer her veneer of composure would shatter into a million splinters, Becky turned to the bereft figure seated alongside the bed in a straight-backed chair.

Guided by instinct, Becky knelt before the woman. Hannah's faded blue eyes held a faraway look. Overnight her face was seamed with a network of fine wrinkles. Becky's heart constricted with sympathy. Taking Hannah's cold work-roughened hands in hers, Becky held them until her warmth penetrated their chill. Gradually the glassiness disappeared from Hannah's eyes and they focused and cleared. She looked at Becky's upturned face.

"I'm glad you're here, child," Hannah murmured. "Did you know Ben . . . ?" her voice cracked.

Becky's eyes held hers. "Yes, I know," she said softly. "He's gone, Hannah, and it hurts. It hurts terribly." She swallowed hard. "I loved him too."

Hannah's control crumbled, and her eyes flooded with tears. Loud choking cries escaped at last, filling the room with their tortured sound. Becky wrapped

170

her arms around Hannah and rocked back and forth, crooning unintelligible words of comfort until the sobs finally ceased. She led the exhausted woman into a spare bedroom, and after covering her with a light blanket, quietly left the room, closing the door behind her.

Slowly Becky walked downstairs. When she reached the lower landing, she paused with one hand on the banister and listened. The house was still, deathly still. She moved down the narrow hallway toward the kitchen. The door to Ben's study was ajar. Becky reached for the knob intending to pull the door shut, but instead she was drawn inside. The room looked like Ben had just left and would return at any moment. The rolltop desk was piled with its usual clutter of papers and journals. Becky smiled sadly, recalling how Ben always carried on after one of Hannah's cleaning sprees. Can't find a damn thing on a neat desk, he'd fume, his dark shaggy brows nearly meeting in a frown. Becky was impelled deeper into the room.

Another object caught her attention. Ben's favorite brierwood pipe lay undisturbed on an opened book, probably where he had left it the night before. Tears blurred her vision. Blindly, Becky reached out and her fingers curled around satiny wood worn smooth by years of use. She clutched the pipe to her breast. Head bent, her tears ran unchecked down her face.

A slight noise from behind made her whirl around. Mike's tall form filled the doorway.

"Go away," she begged and turned her back to him. She wanted to be left alone with her grief. Tears continued to rain down her cheeks. Becky groped in the pocket of her skirt for a handkerchief, then remembered she had given it to Hannah. To no avail, she tried to brush the tears away with her fingertips.

Instead of leaving, Mike came closer. Placing his hands on her shoulders, he turned her around. With a light pressure of his thumbs beneath her chin, he tilted her face up to his.

Becky felt like a small child craving love and reassurance. Her lower lip quivered. "Hold me, Mike. Please." Then she was in his arms and nothing in the world mattered. She felt safe, comforted, cherished. Hostilities were forgotten. Her arms twined around his neck, her face burrowed into his broad chest. Becky cried out her grief.

Mike buried his face in her sweet-smelling hair and held Becky as though he'd never let her go. His compassion cushioned her sorrow, and his strength absorbed her tremors. When her sobs subsided, he stepped back and once more tilted her face up to his. Tenderly he wiped the wetness from her face. Unshed tears clung like crystal beads to the tips of her spiky lashes. Lowering his head, his lips lightly brushed the moistness from her eyelids. A sigh escaped. Her fingers dove into Mike's thick ebony curls forcing his lips to meet hers. Greedy for the sweet solace his kiss promised, her mouth opened under his. The salty taste of her own tears reminded her of the sorrow that shadowed this moment of stolen bliss.

Becky wanted the kiss to go on forever, to be held in his embrace for eternity. She didn't want to think, to feel, to hurt. She only wanted the peace and oblivion Mike could offer.

Mike seemed to share her need, for even after the kiss ended he held her close. "I wanted to hold you like this the last time we were in this room," he confessed, his warm breath feathering her temple.

"But we argued instead."

"And that upset Ben. It was the only time I saw him lose his temper."

An unpleasant thought scurried through Becky's mind. If Ben were upset by a single argument, how would he have reacted to events of the previous night? News of that magnitude could have proved fatal. What had Mike told Ben? Dear Lord! She could never forgive herself if she were even remotely responsible for Ben's death.

"Mike, I have to know," Becky pulled away. "Did you tell Ben what happened last night?" Sick with dismay, she watched while his features hardened into a mask of contempt, his eyes glittering with anger.

"Why you conniving little bitch!" he snarled. "So that's all you wanted. All you were interested in is finding out how much Ben knew of your treachery. You can't stand the thought your sterling image might be tarnished. Well," he continued, ignoring her stricken look, "you can rest easy. Ben died never realizing what a traitorous she-devil you really are." He turned on his heel and stalked out of the room.

A minute later Becky heard the kitchen door slam. She slumped into Ben's chair. The situation was hopeless. Ben was dead and with him died any chance of Mike ever learning the truth. He would always believe she had betrayed the trust of her oldest and dearest friend. And because of that betrayal, a life had been lost.

Becky's gaze dropped to her lap where one hand still held Ben's pipe. She stared at it dry-eyed. There were no tears left; they had all been spent.

Chapter Eleven

THE FUNERAL HAD BEEN A WEEK AGO. BECKY PAUSED AT the Sloanes' back steps and looked around. Marigolds still formed a bright border along the base of the porch. The rocking chair sat in its usual place. The same calico curtains fluttered at the kitchen window. How was it, Becky reflected, that nothing looked different, yet everything had changed? She squared her shoulders and marched up the steps.

"Come in, child." Hannah's voice drifted through the screen door before Becky had a chance to knock. "I just took a pan of apple turnovers out of the oven."

"Why do you think I'm here?" Becky asked with a

smile as she entered the kitchen. "I could smell them baking a mile down the road."

"Have a seat. I'll put on some coffee."

While Hannah was busy grinding coffee beans and measuring them into an enameled pot, Becky had a chance to study her. Though Hannah's dress hung loosely on her large frame, and her facial bones were more pronounced, her movements were sure and purposeful. Hannah would be all right, Becky decided. She was a survivor.

Soon the smell of freshly brewed coffee mingled with those of cinnamon and apple. Hannah placed a turnover surrounded by a moat of thick cream in front of Becky and after pouring two mugs of coffee sat down across from her.

"There's a nip in the air," Hannah remarked. "Some say there's going to be an early winter."

"On the way over, I noticed a few branches on the sugar maples are starting to turn color." Becky took a bite of the pastry. "Umm," she sighed. "This is delicious. I can never get crust this flaky."

"These were always . . ." Hannah faltered and recovered, "Ben's favorite."

Becky stopped eating, her fork poised in midair. "Hannah, I'm sorry. I meant to come by sooner. I really did, but . . ."

"No need to fret, it's just as well. I needed some time alone to get used to Ben being gone."

Becky began to eat again though the rich dessert had lost its earlier appeal. The conversation between the two women proceeded with an odd series of starts and stops before dwindling into an uncomfortable silence. Becky attributed Hannah's uncharacteristic behavior to her recent bereavement.

"Hannah," Becky said gently. "I can see something is bothering you. Is it Ben?"

Hannah's face was troubled as she met Becky's gaze. "Honey, I hope you know me well enough to realize I'd never hurt you."

Becky nodded, more than a little puzzled by Hannah's strange statement.

Hannah rose ponderously. "Ben left something with me that he wanted you to have." She left the kitchen and returned a minute later with an envelope yellowed with age.

When Becky made no move to take it, Hannah laid it on the table between them. Hannah slowly slid it across the checkered cloth toward Becky, her forehead grooved with lines of worry.

For a long moment, Becky stared at the envelope, her hands clenched tightly in her lap. The color drained from her face. "I don't understand," she said faintly. "This is my mother's handwriting."

"I know, child. Read the letter."

Becky's hand trembled as she took out the sheets of parchment. She had the strange sensation she stood on the brink of a precipice and was about to hurtle off the edge into space. Drawing a steadying breath, she began to read.

My darling Rebecca,

I realize now that I shall never recover from my illness. There are certain facts regarding yourself that you are entitled to know. How I hoped to be able to tell you these as one woman to another. But that is impossible. Each time I gaze into your lovely face I am reminded you are still an innocent in so many ways. I beg

177

of you, when you learn my secret, not to judge me
too harshly. Judge me with the heart of a woman,
with understanding and forgiveness. Ben Sloane, who
you always regarded as a dear friend, is in reality your
father.

The writing blurred as Becky's mind struggled to
comprehend its meaning. Becky shook her head to
clear the confusion and reread her mother's words.
Ben was her father?

"How can this be?" she asked, unaware she had
spoken aloud.

"Go ahead, child, finish the letter."

The letter went on to explain how following an
argument, Matthew Brantford had left his wife and
small son. Amanda had no idea when, or if, Matt
would return. It seemed only natural to turn to their
longtime friend, Ben Sloane, for comfort and advice.
Months passed. Amanda fell hopelessly in love with
Ben and learned he returned her feelings. She and
Ben planned to go to Texas or California and begin a
new life together. Then Matthew returned.

Amanda was immune to his charm and turned a
deaf ear to his apologies. Careful not to mention Ben,
Amanda informed Matthew of her intentions to leave.
He was furious. Not even the thought of imminent
scandal could dissuade her. But Matthew knew her
weakness. If Amanda insisted on leaving, he wouldn't
stand in her way, but she would never again see her
son, he warned. Knowing Matthew would make good
his threat, Amanda abandoned her plans.

Shortly afterward, she realized she was pregnant
with Ben's child. Matthew had no reason to suspect
otherwise, so Amanda let him continue to believe he

was the father. Meanwhile Ben surprised everyone by his sudden marriage to Hannah Baldwin. It wasn't until Amanda was dying that she confessed the truth to Ben.

Anger, confusion, love, pain, joy. A host of conflicting emotions churned inside of Becky and flickered across her face.

"Your ma left it up to Ben when to give you her letter," Hannah remarked quietly.

"All those years," Becky shook her head sadly. "Why did he wait so long? Was he ashamed to admit he was my father?"

"Honey, in all the time we were married, I never knew Ben to be a coward, but he'd break out in a sweat each time he thought about giving you Amanda's letter."

"But . . . why would Ben be afraid to tell me?" she asked in a choked voice.

Hannah picked her words with care. "Ben was worried that your feelings for him might change. He didn't want to lose your trust—or your respect."

Becky sprang from the chair and began to pace the length of the kitchen. "I'm so mixed up. I don't know what to think, what to feel. I don't even know who I am," she ended with a strangled laugh.

Hannah came over and clumsily patted Becky's shoulder. "I hated to be the one to tell you all this, but I figured you had a right to know."

"I'm not blaming you, Hannah." She managed a weak smile. "Now I'm the one who needs to be alone to sort things out. I'll be back another time." Becky turned and ran from the house.

She flew down the steps and collided with a rock-solid mass.

Hands fastened on her upper arms like steel bands. "Didn't your mother ever tell you to watch where you're going?" Mike asked roughly, not releasing her.

Becky blinked back a haze of tears clouding her vision. "There are a great many things my mother neglected to tell me." She made no effort to hide her bitterness.

If she hadn't been upset, she would have seen concern in the sapphire gaze. "Are you sure you're all right?"

"I'm fine, wonderful, never better." A note of hysteria crept into her voice.

"Liar," he rebuked her gently. "You're shaking like a leaf." He had tried so hard to hate her, but all he could think of at this moment was gathering Becky in his arms. She seemed so vulnerable and in desperate need of protection. But she wasn't his to protect. She belonged to Denby.

"Mike? That you out there?" Hannah called from inside the house.

Becky used that instant to wrench free from Mike's grip, mount Lady, and gallop off.

Mike stared after her until she disappeared from view. Upon entering the kitchen, he glanced at the untouched mugs of coffee and partially eaten turnover and the yellow sheets of paper spread on the checkered cloth.

"I literally ran into Becky a minute ago," he ventured. "Did you two have an argument?"

"Poor child," Hannah said worriedly. "Hope I didn't go and do the wrong thing."

Mike sat in the chair Becky had recently occupied and drummed his fingers on the tabletop, making the

SWEET POSSESSION

parchment rustle. "Whatever happened has to do with this letter, doesn't it?"

Hannah nodded. "It's from Becky's ma."

Mike kept silent, not wanting to pry, yet curious.

After Hannah cleared the dishes from the table, she sat down heavily. "Maybe I should have waited a bit. Maybe it was too much of a shock coming so soon after Ben's passing."

"Once Becky calms down, she'll realize you meant well."

"Wish I could be sure of that." Hannah was doubtful. "Becky was pretty upset hearing how Ben was really her pa."

Mike gave a low whistle. "No wonder she acted strangely."

"Oh my land!" Her hand flew to her mouth when she realized what she had done. "It isn't my place to go telling. Promise me you won't ever repeat this to anyone."

"Don't worry the secret is safe. So Ben was Becky's father?" Mike couldn't believe his ears.

Hannah nodded as she picked up the sheets of paper and stuffed them back in the envelope. "Becky and Ben have always been close, but until this afternoon she thought of Matthew Brantford as being her pa."

The missing piece of a puzzle fell neatly into place. Becky was Ben's flesh and blood. Seen in that light, it wasn't surprising that Ben had been blind to her faults and invested trust where it wasn't deserved. In Ben's eyes, Becky could do no wrong. Ben had deliberately turned his back on her true character. Finding out Ben was her father had no doubt come as a shock to

181

Becky, Mike surmised, but like a cat she was sure to land on her feet.

Both horse and rider were exhausted by the time they reached the grassy knoll. Becky let the mare drink from a shallow stream and tied her to a sapling. Sprawling in the deep grass, she laid with her arms folded behind her head, staring at the sky. She tried to keep her mind blank, to postpone facing the facts of her parentage. Just as fleecy clouds drifted lazily across the azure surface, so did memories drift across her consciousness. Her mother. Ben. Matthew Brantford.

Ben—gentle, wise, compassionate. Matthew—quick to criticize, slow to praise. Her mother—her smile rarely lighting her eyes. No, Becky finally acknowledged, she couldn't condemn her mother for being ruled by her heart. How could she when she knew only too well how easy it was to yield to the magic only a special man could create? Her mother had asked for forgiveness, but there was nothing to forgive. Becky's only regret was that she hadn't learned the truth earlier. She wished with all her heart she could have told Ben how proud she was to be his daughter.

Becky threw herself into the business of running a farm. She wanted no spare time to grieve over Ben, or to brood over Mike. Fall was a hectic season. Even with a relatively small herd of cattle such as Becky managed, there were countless details to attend to. Agreements had to be reached with local farmers to purchase surplus grain for winter feed. Extra hands needed to be hired to assist Brewster with the actual roundup. Last, but not least, arrangements had to be made to send the cattle to market. In previous years, the Brantford and Sloane farms had joined forces. The combined herds were driven along the same trails to a mutually agreed-on market.

One evening Becky curled in the corner of the library sofa flipping through the pages of a farm journal. An article extolling the merits of a recently built stockyard in St. Louis caught her attention. It sparked an idea. The remainder of the evening was spent poring over railroad timetables and scribbling notes on a pad. Her calculations complete, Becky sat back with a satisfied grin. Early the next morning she rode over to see Hannah.

Hannah listened patiently while Becky outlined her plan. "I don't know, Becky." She shook her head. "Ben was always the one to make these decisions."

"I know, Hannah," Becky leaned forward in her eagerness, "but can't you see it's a good idea? I'm positive it will work."

"Maybe." Hannah was cautious. "Tell you what. Go talk to Mike. If you can convince him, then it's all right with me."

Becky stifled a groan. Mike was the last person she wanted to see, much less talk to. "It might be better if you talked with him. Mike and I always rub each other the wrong way."

"Then it's high time you two set things straight." Hannah practically shoved her out the door.

Becky found Mike in the tack room. After a cursory glance, he resumed work on the bridle he was mending.

"Hannah said I might find you here," Becky ventured.

He continued to ignore her.

"You could at least be civil."

"What for?"

Becky could see Mike was determined to be difficult. "Look, I'm not here for another sparring match. I have a business proposition for you."

"Well? I don't have all day," Mike said, not looking up.

Becky lowered her gaze and found herself mesmerized by the strong slender fingers skillfully working the leather. They had played their skill upon her body in such a fashion that even now she burned at the memory. His hands stilled. Becky's eyes flew upward and caught Mike watching her with an intensity that made her fear he could read her mind. The thought brought a rush of color to her cheeks.

Becky cleared her throat. "In the past, both farms have cooperated at fall roundup," she began. "This year I'd like to do things differently. I've already explained my idea to Hannah, but she said the final decision was up to you. I would like to send the cattle to the stockyard in St. Louis by rail. There's a brand new line that goes straight through. I've read that the market is better there. We ought to get top dollar for our herds."

"What do you stand to gain from this?"

Becky frowned, not sure what he meant by the blunt question. Then her enthusiasm took over. She held up her hand and began ticking off the merits on her fingers. "First of all, our herds will reach their destination when the market is at its peak. Secondly, without the rigors of the long drive, the cattle will be in prime condition. Last of all, we'll need fewer hands which will offset the cost of shipping."

"You've got this all figured out, don't you?" Mike stood and tossed the bridle aside. "Let me rephrase the question. What's in this for you?"

"I don't know what you mean." Becky had the distinct impression that whatever it was she wouldn't like it.

"Who owns the Brantford farm, Becky?" he mused out loud. "You, or your brother?"

"That's none of your business." She flared at the sensitive subject.

"Come on, Becky," he coaxed. "Who does it belong to?"

Her soft mouth set in a mutinous line, Becky crossed her arms over her chest and glared at him, refusing to answer his question.

"Of course," he shrugged, "if you don't want to tell there are other ways of finding out."

"Adam! It belongs to Adam."

"I thought so."

In short agitated steps, Becky crossed the tack room, pausing at one end to run her hand over the smooth leather of a saddle. "Willing the farm to Adam was father's way of exacting revenge on children who disappointed him in his lifetime."

"Leaving someone a place the size of yours is hardly my idea of revenge," he observed dryly.

Becky gave a short humorless laugh. "That's exactly what father wanted people to think. Adam always hated the farm. Even as a boy he dreamed of leaving Oak Ridge and living in a big city. Father knew I loved the place as much as Adam detested it. When mother died, father and I argued. The next day I left for Boston. That was the final straw. Father decided the farm would never be mine even though I could easily afford it with the money David left me."

"What's stopping you?"

"Father's will." The words tasted like gall. "There was a clause stipulating Adam can only sell or will the property to a male family member. If these conditions aren't met, the land will revert to a distant cousin in Pennsylvania. Father made sure Adam was saddled with a burden he didn't want . . . and I will always want something I can't have."

"I see." Mike towered over her, his eyes glinting with the hardness of twin sapphires. "So you'll settle for Ben's property instead."

"You know! Hannah told you Ben was my father!"

"She didn't intend to." Mike quickly rose to the woman's defense. "She was upset after you left, and it slipped out. Hannah might be gullible, but I can see through you. You can't wait to get your greedy hands on Ben's land. Already you're trying to impress Hannah with how capable you are. Gradually you'll take over more and more of the responsibilities. Hannah will want to do the right thing and since you're Ben's only heir . . ."

Mike never finished the sentence. With blood roaring in her ears and a scarlet haze obscuring her vision, Becky's fury erupted. She swung her closed fist and caught Mike on the jaw. When she drew back ready to strike another blow, he caught her wrist. The tip of her boot connected with his shin, bringing a moment of intense pleasure at his yelp of pain.

"You little devil!" Mike brought both of her wrists behind her back and pinned her against his large frame. "Settle down! I don't want to hurt you."

"Of all the vile, rotten, low-down, despicable," she raged, trying to land another blow with her boot.

"You might as well give up," Mike advised, holding her tighter. She reminded him of a wildcat, clawing, scratching, and mean as hell when riled.

"I've had enough of your insults. I refuse to stand by and listen to you attack my character. If I were a man . . ."

"If you were a man," Mike interrupted smoothly, "the first lesson you'd learn is to pick a fight with someone your own size. Not one a foot taller who outweighs you by nearly a hundred pounds."

Humor laced his voice, but it only fueled her anger. "If I were a man, you'd be sporting two black eyes."

The corners of Mike's mouth twitched. "I never would have guessed you'd turn out to be a scrapper. That was no ladylike slap. Your right hand really packs a wallop."

Her breath coming in short gasps, Becky ceased struggling and grew very still. For the first time, she was aware their bodies were locked together. Her head thrown back, she peered into his face and from his expression knew he was conscious of it too. Desire darkened his eyes to the color of purple ink. The hard bulge of his manhood pressed against her stomach, bringing forth a liquid warmth deep in her very core.

"No!" she cried out, denying her response. "Let me go!"

The iron grip on her wrists relaxed and he stepped back and stared at her for a long moment. "In answer to your proposal," he spoke at last. "I believe it is in my employer's best interest if I decline your offer."

"I hate you, Mike Ryan. You turn everything I do into something ugly."

"Go ahead, hate me all you want." Mike's voice was devoid of feeling. "There never was any love lost between us."

Mike picked up the bridle he had been mending and didn't watch her leave. Absently he rubbed his jaw and felt the swelling beneath the skin. Becky's anger had been genuine and potent, not something manufactured for his benefit. Try as he might, he couldn't dismiss the nagging suspicion he might be wrong about her wanting Ben's land. If he was wrong about that, he wondered, could he be wrong about other things as well?

Becky plucked a squash and balanced it on top of a basket already filled to overflowing. She stood, flexing cramped muscles, and looked around the garden. Soon it would be bare except for a few fat pumpkins left to ripen on the vine. Picking up the basket, she turned and started for the house. Halfway there, she paused and shaded her eyes against the glare of late afternoon sun. A wagon was coming up the drive. Oh Lord! she groaned, not company. Not today of all days. She must look a fright, with untidy strands of hair straggling down her back and wearing her faded blue calico. If only she could dart in the back door for a quick look in the mirror. But it was too late. One of the figures had spotted her and was frantically waving an arm.

Becky drew closer and stopped in her tracks. It couldn't be! But it was. The basket slipped from nerveless fingers sending vegetables scattering. "Adam!" she shrieked. Picking up her skirts in both hands and holding them above her knees, she sprinted toward the wagon.

Adam climbed down and caught her in outstretched arms. He lifted her off the ground and whirled her around until she was dizzy.

From his vantage point on the driver's seat, Mike watched the reunion with interest. In spite of being sired by different fathers, brother and sister bore a distinct family resemblance. Both possessed the same fair coloring and fine bone structure. But where Becky's features were delicate, Adam's were sharp planes and angles. His face could have been called aristocratic if it hadn't been for a slightly misshapen nose that looked as though it had once been broken. Instead of detracting from his appearance, the flaw gave him a rakish air. Adam's hair was several shades darker and his eyes more a grayish-green lacking the translucence of his sister's. Mike's first impression of the impeccably-clad stranger was that of a dandy, but the illusion was soon dispelled by Adam's unpretentious friendly manner. To his surprise, Mike liked the man. Under different circumstances, they might even have become friends.

"Stand back," Adam ordered. "Let me take a good look at you." He held Becky at arm's length while his gaze roved from her disheveled curls to the scuffed toes of her shoes before coming to rest on her smiling face and shining eyes. He shook his head in mock despair. "Mother tried so hard to make a lady out of you." He took a large linen square from a pocket and scrubbed a streak of grime from her cheek. "All that work," he said with an exaggerated sigh, "and you're still just a dirty-faced brat."

"And you're still the overbearing big brother," Becky laughed. "Why didn't you tell me you were coming?"

"What! Spoil the surprise?" Adam grinned broadly. "I wouldn't have missed the expression on your face for all the world."

Belatedly, Becky recalled seeing two men. Her gaze swung toward the wagon. Mike's eyes met hers. He greeted her look of dismay with a lopsided smile.

"Mike, forgive me." Adam remembered his manners. "In all the excitement, I nearly forgot about you."

"No need to apologize. I know only too well the effect your sister has on men."

Adam frowned before dismissing Mike's words and turned to his sister. "Mike just happened to be in town this afternoon. We talked a bit, and when he learned I was headed out this way, he offered me a lift."

"We never got around to introductions until we were almost out of town," Mike supplied.

"Too bad. If you had realized Adam was my brother, you probably would have let him walk."

"Becky!" Adam rebuked her, then faced Mike. "I hope you'll overlook my sister's bad manners and join us for supper. Becky is an excellent cook even on short notice."

Becky closed her eyes and offered a hasty prayer Mike would refuse. When she opened them again, she found Mike watching. He seemed to be enjoying her discomfiture. Becky raised her chin a notch and glared at him.

"If I accepted your offer, I'd be afraid your sister would season my dinner with arsenic," he said, a sardonic slant to his handsome mouth. "I appreciate the invitation, Adam, but Hannah will have supper waiting for me. Perhaps another time."

"Can't thank you enough for the ride." Adam reached up and shook Mike's hand after getting his bags from the back of the wagon. "Maybe you'll let me buy you a drink at the Satin Slipper some night."

"It's a deal," Mike agreed. With a nod in Becky's direction, he drove off.

"What was all that about?" Adam draped his arm over Becky's shoulders as they walked toward the house. "From your letters, I gathered you thought pretty highly of Mike Ryan, but from what I just saw, the two of you acted like sworn enemies."

"We don't get along. Is that a crime?"

"Don't be so touchy." Adam gave her shoulders an affectionate squeeze. "You can't blame a fellow for being curious."

Later that evening Adam's curiosity was appeased. He gradually wore down Becky's defenses and the whole story poured out. Becky carefully omitted mention of certain facts too personal, too intimate, to share with anyone. But Adam was a keen observer of human behavior.

"You're in love with Mike, aren't you?" he asked quietly.

A denial sprang to her lips, but was never uttered. She stared miserably at her hands. "Yes," she said in a small voice.

Adam covered her hands with his. "Would it help if I explained to Mike?"

"How I wish it were so simple." Becky summoned a tremulous smile. "I'd agree in a second if I thought there was a ghost of a chance. As far as Mike's concerned, you're virtually a stranger, and to make matters worse, my brother. Ben was my only hope." She swallowed a lump in her throat. "And he's gone."

191

"Your last letter hinted you had something important to tell me, but you didn't want to do it by mail. Care to talk about it?"

"Ben was my father," Becky said quickly, then held her breath and waited for Adam's reaction.

Swirling the brandy in his glass, Adam walked over to the window and stared into the darkness beyond.

"Don't ignore me." There was a ragged edge to her voice. "Say something."

"What do you want me to say?" he asked mildly. "This doesn't come as a shock. I suspected as much years ago. Don't forget little sister, I am five years older and wiser than you. I put certain clues together before mother died and drew my own conclusions."

"Why didn't you say something?"

"I could have been wrong. Besides," Adam shrugged, "it doesn't alter the way I feel about you."

Becky went to Adam, put her arms around him, and gave him a hug. "I'm glad you're here," she whispered.

Chapter Twelve

"YOU'RE BEING BULLHEADED," BECKY STORMED.

"I'm being practical," Adam insisted.

"We could easily triple our herd and still have land left to grow our own feed." Becky continued the argument that had started over breakfast. It was now early evening and they were on their way into town to enjoy dinner in the dining room of the town's only hotel, the Buckingham.

"I'm not disagreeing that your plan makes sense." Adam took a diplomatic tack. "Try to see things from my point of view. You're a beautiful young woman. Someday you'll remarry. When that time comes, I want you free to turn your back on the farm and leave. I don't want you so bogged down you might pass up a chance for happiness."

"But all that land is just going to waste." She shook her head sadly.

"Sorry. That's the way it has to be." Adam was unyielding. "If we did expand, I'd have too much invested to turn its management over to a stranger. Then if you left, I'd be obligated to return to Oak Ridge. I won't place myself in that position."

Becky was dejected and it showed.

"Tell you what," Adam said, trying to cheer her up. "Should you remarry and want to make the farm your home, I'll reconsider. I think I might have stumbled across a way to get around father's will—provided you remarry. Enough said." He held up his hand to stave off a barrage of questions. "I'm only here for another week. Let's not ruin it by arguing."

Becky managed a smile and murmured her agreement. Since she had no intention of marrying now or in the foreseeable future, why prolong the dispute?

"By the way," Adam flashed her a grin, "have I told you how glamorous you look this evening? You could put many a Creole lady to shame."

They had decided to make their excursion into town a festive occasion and had dressed in their best finery. Becky could have stepped from the pages of *Godey's Lady's Book* in her low-cut gown of claret-colored velvet. A short matching cape trimmed with ostrich feathers was draped around her shoulders. An osprey plume tucked into her high crown of curls added a further touch of elegance.

"Why thank you, kind sir." Her imitation of a simpering beauty was spoiled by a giggle. "You look quite debonair yourself." Adam did look particularly dashing in gray-and-white pinstriped trousers, charcoal frockcoat, and white ruffled shirt. A coral brocade waistcoat embroidered with tiny silver flowers provided a bright contrast.

"Remember when we were little and played dress up?"

"Of course." Becky laughed. "Remember the time you borrowed father's favorite pipe to blow soap bubbles?"

"It was a week before I was able to sit without a pillow," he chuckled.

Both made a concerted effort to put their differences aside, and by the time the buggy rolled into town they were in a lighthearted mood.

"Is it my imagination, or do the streets seem unusually busy tonight?" Adam asked as he maneuvered around yet another slow-moving vehicle.

"Something must be going on. People are usually home eating supper at this time."

"Let's find out what this is all about." Adam found a space to tie the buggy further down the street. He assisted his sister from the high seat, and they made their way down the boardwalk toward the general store.

Even before Adam pushed open its door, the rise and fall of angry voices rushed out to meet them. The store was filled to capacity. Becky and Adam squeezed inside and kept to the back of the crowd. The air was blue with cigar smoke and smelled of closely packed bodies. Becky noted she was one of only a few women present.

"What's going on?" Adam asked the man next to him.

"President Fillmore signed a new Fugitive Slave Law today."

Becky and Adam exchanged looks. She felt Adam's fingers dig into her waist, the only sign of his inner tension.

"Way I understand it," the store's proprietor complained, "if a fugitive already in custody tries to escape while I'm around, I can be forced to help in the recapture—whether I want to or not."

Becky stood on tiptoe and craned her neck.

"You got it, Wilbur," Frank answered loudly from his position in the front of the store.

An angry murmur rippled through the crowd.

"That right, marshal? You mean no matter what my feelings are about slavery, I'd still have to help?" another man asked.

"I'd hate like the devil to use force," Frank said, though his tone suggested otherwise. "But that's the way the law reads."

"What's this I hear about fines and jail terms?" Will Connolly demanded.

"Glad you brought that up," Frank commended. "Everyone listen, and listen good!" He waited for the talk to quiet down. "There's a thousand-dollar fine or six months in a federal prison, possibly both, for anyone violating the new law."

Indignant protests drowned out further comments. Becky felt anger and frustration knot in the pit of her stomach. A sidelong glance at Adam revealed his face clear of expression, but Becky knew under the bland surface his feelings echoed hers.

"My responsibilities as a lawman are greater than ever." Frank sounded more than a little pompous.

"Should a fugitive in my custody escape with or without my help, I'm accountable for the full value of that slave. I will not hesitate, friends, to see that any person caught breaking this law is punished to its fullest extent."

"I've heard enough," Adam said under his breath. "Let's get out of here."

Becky allowed Adam to propel her out of the store and down the street. Near the Buckingham, her feet lagged to a halt. "I seem to have lost my appetite somewhere between the fines and the federal prison. Can't we just go home?"

"I feel the same way you do, but it will look strange if we come into town all gussied up only to turn around and leave."

"I suppose you're right," Becky conceded.

Tall potted palms flanked either side of the two entrances of the small but genteel dining room. Every table save one was occupied. Becky and Adam made their way across the crowded room from the street entrance and reached it seconds before Mike Ryan and Margaret Nelson did from the lobby entrance. All four stopped, looking from one to the other in embarrassment.

Mike smiled at Adam and acquiesced defeat. "The best man won. The table is yours."

"Why not join us," Adam suggested. "Judging from how busy this place is, it could be a long wait."

"No, thank . . ." Mike started.

"We'd be delighted." Margaret Nelson overrode his objection.

Adam directed his considerable charm at the fashionably garbed matron in gray moire. "I don't believe we've met. I'm Adam Brantford. From my sister's description, you must be Margaret Nelson."

"How do you do, Mr. Brantford." The dowager scrutinized the leanly handsome man with interest.

"Please, my friends call me Adam," he said with a disarming smile.

The woman's cool manner thawed perceptibly. "Then Adam it is." She returned the smile. "Friends call me Maggie."

Becky resisted the temptation to roll her eyes heavenward. Adam had only met the woman two minutes ago and was already calling her Maggie. She, on the other hand, had known the widow three years and had never addressed her as other than Mrs. Nelson.

"Allow me," Adam said, holding out a chair for his newly found friend.

Tightlipped, Mike was left with little choice but to hold out the opposite chair for Becky. She swept past him without a word and accepted the proffered seat with a regal inclination of her head, causing the plume in her hair to tickle his chin.

Adam signaled the waiter and ordered bourbon for the men and sherry for the ladies. No sooner had the waiter departed when Maggie Nelson turned her attention on Becky. "You look exceptionally lovely this evening, Rebecca. Are you in town to celebrate?"

"Celebrate?"

"Why, yes. I should think you would be overjoyed that the new Fugitive Slave Law passed. In the store, I couldn't help noticing how you hung on to the marshal's every word as though your life depended on it. I was surprised you didn't stay long enough to join in the applause."

"Some situations require a great deal of self-control," Becky said with false sweetness.

The drinks arrived just then. To hide his amusement, Adam took a quick swallow of bourbon.

"How do you feel about the new law, Adam?" Maggie asked after sipping her sherry. "Are you and your sister always in complete accord?"

Adam threw back his head and laughed. "No." His eyes were alight with humor. "Matter of fact, Becky and I frequently disagree. To set the record straight," he sobered, "I'm against it all the way."

"I have the distinct impression it's going to prove unpopular with a great many people," Maggie observed dryly.

Following Adam's admission that he was opposed to the new legislation, he and Maggie seemed to have no problem finding subjects to discuss. Neither noticed the other two members of their party were unusually quiet.

Becky toyed with the stem of her sherry glass. She was furious with Adam for getting her into this awkward situation. He knew how she felt about Mike, yet had invited him to join them. Well, Becky told herself, she could handle it. She would be cool. She would be polite. Somehow, provided she didn't choke on her dinner, she would survive this evening.

Seated next to her, Mike wrestled problems of his own. Becky's nearness was distracting. She was a radiant jewel and difficult to ignore. Her hair shone topaz under the crystal chandelier. Her skin gleamed ivory above the ruby-red velvet. Her eyes had the sparkle of priceless emeralds. Was her character as many-faceted as her beauty? Once again, he wondered if he had judged her too harshly. What was she?

Devil? Or angel? Under the fan of her lashes, Becky stole a look at Mike and found him watching her. "You're staring, Mr. Ryan," she chided softly. "Is my face dirty?"

Mike's mouth quirked. He caught her chin in his strong fingers, turning her face first one way, then the other. "No, not a single smudge. You look damn beautiful, and you know it." The words were spoken softly, meant for her ears alone. His thumb traced small concentric circles on her skin.

Becky forgot her resolutions of a moment ago, forgot they were in a roomful of people, forgot to breathe. Her mind was wiped free of everything but Mike. She started to turn her head; she wanted to press a kiss in the palm of the hand that cupped her face.

"Stop fondling my fiancée!"

At Denby's loud command, activity in the dining room skidded to a halt. The cutlery ceased to rattle. Conversation dwindled to nothingness.

"I don't see a ring on the lady's finger," Mike said as he slowly lowered his hand.

"Ring or no ring, the lady is private property. No trespassers allowed!"

Mike rose to his feet.

The lawman mentally appraised Mike's size. It was formidable. Basically a coward, Denby sought refuge by flaunting his authority. "You better have listened good to what I said earlier. I meant it about throwing the book at anyone caught breaking the law. Soon as I hear of runaways passing through this neck of the woods, you're the first one I'll come looking for. I'd get a charge out of locking you up."

The venom in his voice turned Becky's blood to ice. The man was lethal. She hadn't realized it at first, but the danger was there, lurking below the surface.

Mike's hands bunched into fists. "I'd get a charge out of wiping that sanctimonious look off your face," he gritted between clenched teeth.

Denby knew he had pushed the man to his limit. When it came to brawn, he left that up to his deputy. As for himself, he preferred to control matters from the business end of a pistol. Yet he was aware the whole room eavesdropped collectively. He couldn't let people see him back down from a fight.

"All right, Ryan. Just remember there's a bunch of witnesses. Take a swing at me, and I'll arrest you for assaulting an officer of the law."

"Gentlemen, please," Adam intervened. "Surely this isn't the time or place to air your grievances. Becky is all set for a night out, but she's never been partial to boxing matches. You wouldn't want to ruin her evening, would you?"

"Mike," she pleaded. His forearm was like steel under her touch. No doubt Mike would be the winner in a fair fight, but she didn't trust Denby to fight fairly.

Ignoring her, Mike spoke to Adam. "I would never forgive myself for spoiling your sister's evening. I'm willing to postpone this to another time—provided the marshal is."

"Yeah, sure," Frank quickly agreed.

Business returned to normal in the dining room. Becky raised her glass and drank the sherry as though it were water.

"I'm disappointed in you, Becky," Frank said.

"You ought to be more careful about the company you keep."

"Don't blame me. It was Adam's fault," she said flippantly. "I haven't seen much of you lately." She smiled at him. "You must be busy."

"Not that busy," Frank grinned. "I was afraid your brother would be monopolizing most of your time."

The effects of the sherry hit Becky with a jolt, leaving her feeling reckless. She laughed softly, a teasing provocative sound. "I have the perfect remedy. Why don't you join us for dinner Saturday night. Afterward, I'll persuade Adam to make himself scarce so we can talk a bit."

A grin spread across Frank's face. "Wild horses couldn't keep me away." He walked away with a jaunty step.

Becky glanced around the table at her audience. Adam's scowl suggested she had taken leave of her senses. Margaret Nelson was thin-lipped and disapproving. Only Mike seemed amused by her performance. He raised his glass in a mock salute. To the perfect couple, his toast seemed to say.

Maggie Nelson cleared her throat. "Have any of you decided what to order? I'm famished."

The remainder of the evening passed in a blur. Becky pushed the food around on her plate and showed only a pretense of interest in the conversation. She was glad when the meal was over.

Always the gentleman, Adam helped Maggie settle the paisley shawl over her shoulders. With a sigh of resignation, Mike helped Becky with her wrap. She presented her back and he let the velvet folds swirl over her smooth satiny shoulders. A delicate sweet fragrance drifted up to him. His hands stilled while he tried to identify the scent. Reaching up to fasten the satin frogs at her throat, her fingers brushed his. She turned slowly to face him.

"Mike, I . . ." She wanted to tell him she hadn't meant to invite Denby. It had been an impulse, one she already regretted. She wanted to tell him he was the only one who mattered. But there was no warmth in the dark blue eyes staring down at her. "Never mind," she said, shaking her head sadly. "You wouldn't understand."

Somehow, she managed to smile woodenly at Margaret Nelson and bid a polite farewell. Then Adam's arm was at her waist, guiding her toward the buggy.

They were nearly home when Adam broke the silence. "Whatever possessed you to invite Denby for dinner Saturday? He's going to show up expecting you to set the wedding date."

"It was a stupid thing to do," she admitted with a weary sigh.

"Becky," Adam spoke with uncharacteristic urgency. "Leave Oak Ridge. Come to New Orleans with me."

"Oak Ridge is my home," she protested. "Why would I want to leave?"

"What's to keep you here?" he asked. "Until tonight I never appreciated what you were up against. You've alienated a lot of people by letting them think you share Denby's half-baked views. You are quite a convincing little actress, but your skill has cost you dearly."

"Don't treat me like a child, Adam. I knew from the beginning what I was getting into."

"Promise me you'll think it over. You don't have to give me your answer now. I plan to stop back in Oak Ridge after I finish my business in Chicago. We'll talk about it then."

"I'm touched by your concern, but I'm not going to let anyone or anything drive me from my home ever again."

Adam shook his head. "And you have the nerve to call me stubborn."

"Do me a favor? After dinner Saturday, please leave the house for awhile. I'm going to tell Frank I don't want to see him anymore. He expects me to marry him, Adam. Marriage? I can't stand the sight of him. Frank kept his plans a secret from me once and will again. I can't keep up the pretense any longer."

"Listen to a piece of brotherly advice," Adam counseled. "Denby has a lot of pride, let him down easy. Don't make him an enemy."

The walls reverberated from the slam of the door, then the house grew quiet. Except for the ticking of a grandfather clock, the room was still. Gradually, the rapid hammering of Becky's heart slowed to match the clock's steady cadence.

She huddled in a corner of the sofa, absently massaging her shoulders. Dark shadows heralded a bruise that would soon bear the contour of a man's fingers. Cool air assaulted her bare flesh where frayed edges of her bodice gaped open. She drew in a deep breath. In spite of the bruise, in spite of the torn gown, she was lucky. She had barely escaped being raped.

Frank had gone crazy when she refused to marry

him. He had raged at her, shouting obscenities. When she ordered him to leave, he shook her until she thought her neck would snap like a broken matchstick. The entire time, she was acutely aware that one wrong word, a single false move, would sever his minuscule strand of control. What had kept him from the final retaliation? she wondered. More than likely it had been the knowledge Adam could appear at any moment.

She clutched the remnants of her dress together and made her way up the stairs, her legs unsteady. She had to change into her dressing gown before Adam returned. He mustn't learn of the violent scene that had taken place in his absence.

Frank's final words rang in her ears: "If you tell your precious brother I laid a hand on you, you'll be sorry. If he comes looking for me, he'll never know what hit him."

Becky knew it wasn't an idle threat.

Light spilled through the windows of the Satin Slipper, forming gold rectangles in the dusty street. Raucous laughter nearly drowned out the tinny notes of a piano. Mike allowed the bright lights and loud noises to lure him inside.

Men were wedged shoulder-to-shoulder along the oak bar. In one corner of the saloon, a man in shirtsleeves, a detached look on his pockmarked face, let his fingers roam the keys of a battered piano. No one paid attention to either his music or its frequent lapses while he quenched his thirst from a foamy mug. Loretta Porter, part-owner of the Satin Slipper, and three other women circulated with trays of drinks, stopping often to flirt with the customers. With their brightly painted faces and gaudy dresses, they resembled exotic tropical birds.

Mike was elbowing his way toward the bar when a familiar voice called out.

It was Adam. He sat alone, a bottle of bourbon on the table in front of him. "Join me for a drink."

"Sure." Mike nodded, easing his large frame into a vacant chair.

Adam swiped a shotglass from a tray destined for another patron and filled it to the brim. He refilled his own and raised it in a toast. "Cheers."

Mike returned the toast and lounged back in the chair. "How long do you plan to stick around?"

"Another week at the most. I have business to attend to in Chicago, but I'll stop back here before I go on to New Orleans."

"I'm sure your sister will hate to see you leave." Mike idly scanned the busy saloon.

Adam leaned forward, arms resting on the table, and stared into his half-finished drink. "I'm trying to convince Becky she should return to New Orleans with me. Permanently."

"Oh." Mike tried to keep his tone noncommittal. "Rumor has it she's about to marry Denby."

"You don't strike me as the type to believe gossip," Adam observed quietly.

Mike took a sip of bourbon. "Normally, I don't."

"I'd feel better knowing you're keeping an eye on Becky for me."

Mike groaned inwardly. Keeping an eye on her was easy, it was keeping his hands off her that was hard. Invariably one led to the other. He shifted his weight.

"Your sister strikes me as the type who can look out for herself."

"Sometimes she's too independent for her own good."

Mike gave a derisive laugh. "Becky has the unique talent of bewitching men who are usually sensible and levelheaded. Once under her spell, they're ready to ride to her rescue like knights of old, willing to defend her honor with their dying breaths."

Adam wasn't offended by Mike's remark. "Did it ever occur to you," he said mildly, "some men are better judges of character than others?"

The two men regarded each other across the space of the table. Mike felt a twinge of guilt and looked away. After all, he reasoned, it wasn't fair to hold Adam liable for the sins of his sister. "Don't worry about Becky. If it makes you feel better I'll look in on her every now and then."

"Thanks, Mike. I can't tell you how much I appreciate that." Adam rose to his feet. "I better be going. The bottle's paid for. Enjoy it." He flashed an easy grin and strolled out of the saloon.

Mike scowled into his glass. Damn! Why did he get the feeling he had just been had?

"If looks could kill, honey, someone would keel over."

Mike glanced into fever-bright eyes set in the garishly rouged face of Loretta Porter.

"Mind if I join you?" The woman's cherry red lips were fixed in a smile. She didn't wait for an answer.

"Suit yourself." Mike shrugged.

Loretta helped herself to the bourbon. "I saw you talkin' to Adam Brantford. He a friend of yours?"

"More of an acquaintance."

"Me and Adam's father used to be close friends. Very close friends if you get my drift," she said with a broad wink. "Adam's not a bit like his old man. Country life was never good enough for his lordship." Loretta poured another drink. "I might not cotton to Adam, but his sister's the one I really can't stomach."

The malice in the woman's voice came as a surprise. "I wouldn't think you two knew each other."

"I know her better than most folks," she boasted, her words beginning to slur. "Everybody thinks she's such a lady with her fine airs and fancy clothes. Little miss sweet and innocent. Hah! That's a laugh."

"Look, I'm really not interested in gossip." Mike started to get up, but she grabbed his arm and pulled him back down.

"This is fact, honey. I'm talkin' fact." Her large breasts threatened to spill out of the purple satin confines of her gown as she leaned toward him. "I was just a kid when I first started here. Prettiest thing around in those days. Matt Brantford used to come by real regular to see me. His wife was still alive back then, but was sickly."

"I don't see what this has to do with Becky," Mike said, immediately regretting the use of her nickname.

"So it's Becky, is it?" Loretta pounced on the slip. "Maybe you know her better than I do," she said with a bawdy laugh. "Now where was I? Oh, yeah, I remember. I was about to tell you about the night Matt's wife died. Matt was with me when Becky came looking for him. She stormed right into my room and found me and her pa in bed. Didn't shock her one little bit. Didn't even bat an eye." Loretta set her empty glass down with a thud. "She ignored me like I was dirt, then laid into her pa for not being there while her ma was dyin'.

"Becky poisoned her pa's mind against me. Things were never the same after that. Pretty soon, Matt stopped coming by altogether. Hadn't been for Becky, Matt would have married me. Then I'd be a fine lady with money, clothes, and a big house."

"I've heard enough." Mike was appalled he had listened to even a small portion of the woman's drunken ramblings. Only a morbid curiosity about Becky had induced him to stay.

Loretta wasn't finished. "Notice the way she's got Denby eating out of the palm of her hand. I watched a lot of others try and fail. Believe me, honey, that girl knows all the tricks to pleasin' a man."

As Mike stalked out, Loretta's heavy-lidded eyes boldly measured the width of his broad shoulders. Leave it to Becky Foster to latch onto the best, Loretta thought, emptying the bottle.

Chapter Thirteen

HER EMBROIDERY FORGOTTEN IN HER LAP, BECKY STARED unseeingly into leaping orange flames. Time had passed slowly since Adam's departure. She missed his ready smile, his quick wit, his easy companionship. In spite of her earlier protests, the idea of returning with him to New Orleans was sorely tempting. For that Frank Denby was responsible.

He had promptly spread malicious lies. Abetted by Jed Rawlins's loose tongue, these lies spread like wildfire. Rumor had it that Frank, tired of Becky's constant badgering to marry her, had severed the relationship. On trips into town, Becky was subjected

210

to countless snickers and sly nudges. Though she tried to ignore them, she found the situation intolerable. She picked up her handiwork and viciously jabbed the needle through a French knot, pricking her finger in the process.

"Drat!" she muttered. A loud knocking at the back of the house provided a timely excuse to fling the offending square of linen aside. Sucking her injured fingertip, she hurried to answer the impatient summons.

"Open up, Becky. It's Mike. I need to talk with you."

As she tugged at the latch, her heart hammered with a wild hope he had come to resolve their difficulties. The moment he stepped inside she realized she was foolishly mistaken. One glance at his cold implacable expression doused the tiny spark that had flickered ever so bravely.

Tossing an amber cloud of silken curls over her shoulder, she tried to mask her disappointment. "Is this a social call, or business?"

Mike shifted his weight, suddenly ill at ease. "You don't owe me anything, but I've come to ask a favor."

"One born of desperation?"

"You're not going to make this easy, are you?" A muscle twitched in his jaw as he struggled to control his temper. "I'll get down on my knees if that's what it takes."

Becky pulled the lapels of her dressing gown closer together and pretended to consider the idea. "The notion appeals to me, but in the interest of saving time just state why you're here."

"Tom Weston asked me to look in on Sally and little Jamie while he was away. I stopped by tonight and found Jamie sick. Sally is frantic. She said Doc Nolan was by earlier, but the boy has gotten worse since. Doc isn't expected back for some time. I thought you might know what to do." He jammed his hands deep into pockets. "I hope you won't let our past differences influence your decision." The last came out sounding rehearsed.

"Mike Ryan, I swear I never met another soul who could make me this angry," Becky raged. "Do you honestly think I would refuse to help a sick child? Do you see me as some kind of monster? Why is it you're always willing to believe the worst of me?" Her voice choked.

"Becky . . ."

"Never mind." She brushed aside his effort to explain. "Make yourself useful while I get dressed. Saddle my horse."

When Mike returned, Becky had already changed clothes and was busy collecting supplies and stuffing them into a leather satchel. "Tell me everything you know about Jamie's illness," she said, disappearing into the pantry.

Mike dragged his fingers through his hair. "Sally said it started out with a cold. Now he's flushed, feverish, and his breathing is coming hard."

"Does he have a cough?" Becky reappeared with two glass-stoppered bottles.

"I don't remember Sally mentioning any cough." He nodded at the bottles. "What are those for?"

"One is camphor, the other cottonseed oil. When mixed together, they form a paste. It helps loosen chest congestion." The bottles were added to her bag, and the bag snapped shut. Taking a woolen cape from a hook near the door, Becky announced she was ready.

Sally Weston came out to greet them, her china blue eyes worried. "Oh, Mrs. Foster, I'm so glad to see you. I was afraid you might not come. Mike said not to worry, that you'd be happy to help. He told me you know as much about medicine as Doc."

Becky shot a surprised glance at Mike. "I appreciate Mr. Ryan's vote of confidence, but I'm not a doctor. I'll do whatever I can for Jamie," she added, seeing the woman's distress. "Why don't you let me take a look at him?"

Sally led Becky up a narrow flight of stairs. "I was so relieved when Mike came by. He's been a good friend. I was a little jittery when Tom first invited him over because of his scar and all, but once you get to know him he's really a very nice man," Sally babbled nervously. "This here is Jamie's room."

The sound of ragged uneven breathing filled the small room. Jamie lay listless, his cheeks flushed an unhealthy pink. Becky wasn't surprised to find his forehead hot and dry beneath her practiced touch.

"Jamie, hon, this is Mrs. Foster," Sally explained to her son. "Uncle Mike brought her to make you better."

The little boy nodded drowsily before his slight body was caught in a spasm of dry rasping coughs. When they subsided, Becky bent and placed her ear to the boy's chest. With each labored breath, she could hear a faint bubbling sound.

She straightened and saw Mike watching from the doorway. "We're going to need a lot of hot water." He nodded and disappeared. Sally was dispatched to

213

find extra blankets and quilts while Becky took off her cape and rolled up her sleeves.

When Mike returned, Becky had him move a pine dresser next to the bed. Under Becky's direction, the three improvised a makeshift tent over the head of the bed. A kettle of steaming water was placed nearby where the boy could inhale its moist vapor. Becky poured gumlike camphor into a shallow dish and added a small amount of oil. A strong pungent odor was released, burning their throats and stinging their eyes.

"Jamie, I'm going to rub some medicine on your chest and wrap this flannel around it to keep you warm. That's a good boy," she praised when the child docilely submitted to her ministrations. She supported his head and had him swallow a concoction of honey, lemon, and whiskey. Closing his eyes, the boy drifted into a fitful sleep.

Hours passed. Mike stayed in the background, his presence unobtrusive but comforting. He chopped firewood, pumped water, and made sure there was a constant supply of steamy water. Becky found herself thinking how very easy it would be to lean on his quiet strength.

Shared hours of waiting and worrying eroded the younger woman's reserve. "I have a confession to make," Sally said, tucking a wisp of blonde hair behind her ear. "Until tonight I never liked you very much. Everyone around here still remembers you and Tom used to be sweethearts. You're always dressed so pretty, and you're . . ." she groped for the right word ". . . worldly. Yes, that's it. You're worldly. Next to you, I feel like a plain little farmgirl who's never been away from Indiana."

It was ironic Sally should envy her. "Do you know how I see myself?" Becky asked with a rueful smile. Blue eyes rounded in curiosity to meet hers. "I see myself as a plain little farmgirl who has been out of Indiana. Clothes and travel are poor substitutes for what I want most. I'd give them up in a minute to have the things you take for granted—a loving husband and a family."

Sally stared at her, pondering what she had just heard. "You really mean that, don't you?" she said at last.

Becky didn't have to say anything. The look on her face said it all.

A renewed bout of coughing brought a stop to further confidences. This time there was a difference. The congestion was looser and the fever had broken.

"Jamie is going to be fine," Becky reported to the anxious mother. "Why don't you close your eyes and get some rest? I'll stay until he doesn't need me any longer."

A short time later Mike brought up another steaming kettle to replace the cooler one. Becky stood and smoothed her wrinkled skirt. "We won't need any more after this."

Setting down the water, his glance shifted from mother to child, who were both sound asleep, then settled on Becky. "How's the boy?"

"He's all right." Becky was suddenly conscious of her bedraggled state. In addition to her rumpled skirt, the humid room had wilted her blouse and twisted escaping tendrils of hair into ringlets along her brow and temples. She raised her chin and defied Mike to comment on her appearance.

To her amazement, Mike reached out to cup her

face in his hands. His thumbs lightly traced the violet smudges of fatigue beneath her eyes. "You look exhausted," he said quietly. "Turn around. No arguments," he added when he saw she was about to protest.

Rhythmically he massaged the tense muscles at the base of her neck and slowly worked his way down her spine. He kneaded the stiffness until it became buttery soft and supple beneath his touch.

Becky closed her eyes. A throaty purr of satisfaction escaped. Her weariness dissolved in a puddle of contentment.

"Better?" His breath tickled her ear.

"Hmmm. It feels absolutely delicious."

He turned her around to face him. Lazily, Becky opened her eyes to find him staring at her mouth. "Delicious," he repeated as his lips covered hers, tasting, lingering, savoring. "Sweet, very, very sweet."

Then he was gone.

Becky stood statue-still. Her bemused glance swept the room. Jamie and Sally slept undisturbed. Becky's hand flew to her mouth, touching it in wonder. Mike's kiss had been so unexpected, his touch as soft as the wings of a dove. Had it been real, or a figment of her imagination? Whatever, it was "such stuff as dreams are made on," Becky thought as she smiled to herself, recalling a line from Shakespeare.

At last the accounts balanced. Becky replaced the pen in the inkwell at the same time as pounding started at the back of the house. Instantly she smoothed an already flawless golden coil at the nape of her neck. Mike? A whole week had passed since the night spent nursing Jamie Weston. A week spent on tenterhooks, waiting and wondering when she would next see him. She wanted to race to the door, but forced herself to walk.

The knock was repeated, louder, more impatient. She threw open the door and found herself face to face with Frank Denby.

"You!" she gasped. "What do you want?"

"Disappointed? Expecting someone else?"

"That's none of your business." Becky would have slammed and bolted the door if his booted foot hadn't been firmly planted between door and sill.

"All I'm asking is five minutes of your time. That can't be too much to spare an old friend, can it?"

"Friend!" Her voice rose. "After that last time, you call yourself friend? And what about the malicious gossip you spread?"

"C'mon, Becky, don't act this way," he cajoled. "Can you blame me? After all, a man has his reputation to protect. How much respect would I have in this town if word got around you turned me down?"

Becky didn't care to debate the issue. "State your business and leave."

Frank's mouth set in a grim line. "I came to apologize. I behaved like a rat. I'm sorry."

Becky looked at him long and hard. If anything, the lawman seemed more uneasy than sincere.

"Can you forgive and forget?" He gave her a sheepish grin.

"I'll try," she agreed. "It's over and done with. Let's put it behind us."

"Good! Wish we could have a cup of coffee and talk

a spell, but I can't. Pete and I are about to spring a trap. Catch ourselves an abolitionist." He turned to leave.

"Don't rush off." Becky was on the porch, questioning him. "What kind of trap are you talking about? Who is this abolitionist?" She gave a small laugh. "You know how curious I am. I'll never be able to sleep not knowing what's going on."

He considered it for a moment, then shrugged. "I suppose it won't hurt. By tomorrow everyone will find out anyway."

"Well . . ."

Frank seemed to enjoy playing cat-and-mouse. "Mike Ryan." He grinned. "I'm finally going to have that bastard right where I want him."

Becky's fingers curled around the porch rail. "It isn't a crime to be an abolitionist." It took an effort to keep her voice calm, her tone impersonal.

"It is if they help slaves escape."

"Wouldn't you have to prove it first? A judge isn't going to convict a man on hearsay."

"That's why we set a trap," Frank explained patiently. "Pete is putting the finishing touches to it this very minute. By the time we're done, we'll have enough proof to make a saint look guilty."

"Maybe I'm not very bright, but I don't see how you're going to connect Mike with the underground railroad."

"Ryan's going to put himself in our hands like a present on Christmas morning," Frank boasted.

Becky's grip on the wooden rail tightened. "Can you tell me about it, or is it a secret?" she asked, praying he would say more.

"We sent Ryan a phony message to meet a runaway

at the abandoned cabin by Willow Creek. He'll be there waiting, only we'll show up instead. That'll be all the proof I need."

"How clever," Becky mumbled. If she knew Mike at all, he was already at the cabin. She had to warn him!

Frank took out his pocketwatch and squinted to make out the time. "It's getting late. Got to go."

Becky waited until he mounted his horse and rode out of sight. Snatching her cape from inside the door, she sped down the steps and across the yard toward the woods where she dodged around a massive syca-more. Her feet found the narrow path, the shortcut between her home and the cabin. Nature seemed to conspire that night to impede her progress. Branches and bushes pulled at her cloak while roots and twigs tried to entangle her feet. Every minute, every second was valuable. Ignoring the stitch in her side, she raced on. Breathless, Becky pushed open the cabin door and slipped inside.

Mike's mouth gaped in astonishment. His hands froze in the act of shuffling his ever-present deck of cards.

"I was afraid I'd be too late," she panted.

"Too late," he thundered. "What the hell are you doing here?"

"I came to warn you. You've got to get out of here. It's a trap. Frank will be here any minute. He wants to arrest you." The words tumbled out, nearly incoher-ent in their haste to be said.

"It's you and Denby again, is it?" Mike shuffled and reshuffled the worn deck. "I thought that was over. So much for rumors."

Becky couldn't believe it. He should be fleeing for

his life, yet he wasn't budging. Instead he sat playing cards like he had all the time in the world. "Mike, listen to me," she said, trying again to convince him. "It's a trap! We have to get out of here."

His reply was a harsh grating laugh as he methodically placed the cards in a familiar configuration.

"What are you doing?" Becky cried. She ran to the table and began picking up the cards faster than he could put them down. "There isn't time to explain. Trust me."

"Name one reason why I should?" The coldness in his eyes impaled her.

The door crashed open on its hinges. Becky whirled toward the sound. Her heart nearly stopped at the sight of two gun barrels leveled at her. She was vaguely aware of a chair scraping the planked floor behind her.

"Hold it!" Denby stepped inside. "Don't move or I'll put a bullet through your head."

"Didn't I tell you Becky would hightail it to Ryan the minute you left?" Pete bragged, following behind the marshal.

"Keep 'em covered," Frank growled at his deputy. He lowered his gun and advanced on Becky. Involuntarily she retreated until she was brought up short by the edge of the table.

"Slut!" His arm sliced through the air to crack against the side of her face.

Becky staggered under the blow, tasting the saltiness of her own blood. Pain exploded in her head like a shower of stars. She blinked back a haze of tears in time to see Frank's arm raised to strike again.

"Hit her once more, and you'll regret it the rest of your life."

Even to Becky's fear-fogged mind, Mike's threat sounded deadly.

"Leave her be," Pete concurred. "Townfolk would be more likely to send her off with their blessing and string you up for beating a lady."

Frank lowered his arm, and Becky slowly let out her breath.

"What gives you the right to break in here like this?" Mike's tone blended authority and outrage.

The lawmen exchanged looks. "Come off it, Ryan," Pete snapped. "We know what you're up to."

"Don't try to fool us. You're here to meet a runaway. We know you're part of the underground railroad so don't deny it. We have proof," Frank said hotly.

"What are you talking about?"

"We found a rowboat hidden by the creek along with a feed sack stuffed with food. And this." Pete took a sheet of folded paper from a vest pocket. "This here is a handbill describing a certain Moses Edwards, property of Mr. Leon Edwards of Biloxi. A telegram from Mr. Edwards will verify his slave Moses ran away and was last seen headed for Indiana."

"So what? I don't see what any of this has to do with Mrs. Foster or myself."

"If you're not waiting for Moses, why are you here?" Frank challenged.

"I hardly think what the lady and I do is anyone's business but ours."

Pete's eyes narrowed in suspicion. "Dammit, Ryan. Are you implying what I think?"

"You're the ladies' man, Mitchell," Mike jeered. "Do I have to spell it out for you?"

"Are you saying you and Becky are lovers?" Frank

was having a hard time reconciling the fact Becky would reject his advances, but welcome Mike Ryan's.

"It's true, Frank." Becky's voice was filled with quiet conviction. "Mike and I have been lovers since last spring."

"You cheap little tramp!" Frank's grip tightened on the butt of his gun. "You kept me at arm's length while you were sneaking around behind my back."

"Simmer down, Frank. They're lying through their teeth." Pete motioned with the barrel of his gun. "I want a word with you in private, Frank. I got an idea."

While the two conferred in hushed tones, Becky edged around the table to stand beside Mike. Ignoring the firearms pointed in their direction, he took out a handkerchief and dabbed the trickle of blood at the corner of her mouth. Becky's smile of gratitude was rewarded by the warm glow of approval on Mike's rugged face.

Both marshal and deputy were grinning broadly when the conference ended. Pete swaggered toward them. "Since you claim to be lovers, we're going to make it all nice and legal. Call it a favor. I happen to know a justice of the peace who would be happy to perform a wedding tonight."

Stunned, Becky stared at the pair. Mike stood next to her in wooden silence.

"What'll it be, folks?" Pete chortled. "A short term in jail or a life sentence?"

"Let's get a move on." Frank jerked his head toward the door. "Don't try anything dumb, Ryan, or the lady is liable to get hurt."

Outside, Pete brought three horses forward.

"Looks like the bride gets to ride with me." He swung into the saddle and pulled Becky up behind him.

They made a strange procession with Pete and Becky in the lead, followed closely by Mike, with Frank bringing up the rear. The only witness to their journey was a boldfaced hunter's moon.

This can't be happening, Becky kept telling herself. If I close my eyes and count to ten, I'll wake up. She squeezed her eyes shut, counted to twenty for good measure, and opened them. Pete Mitchell's plaid wool jacket was no dream.

Actually the situation was almost funny. Almost. Instead of an irate father, she was being brought to the altar by an irate suitor. She tamped down a wild impulse to laugh. This is no time for hysterics, she cautioned. Marrying a man at gunpoint is no joking matter.

The miles were gobbled up by galloping hooves. When the group reached a small house near the village limits of Mill Valley, Pete reined to a halt. A sign swinging from a post in the front yard proclaimed the residence of Amos Gribbs, Justice of the Peace.

"This is your last chance, Becky. Speak up and we'll let you off the hook. Of course," Frank grinned, "we can't be that lenient with your friend here."

Becky risked a glance at Mike. He met her look, his expression stony as though he half-expected her to gain freedom at the cost of his. Mike's chestnut gelding danced restlessly, sensing its rider's tension.

"C'mon, Becky," Pete coaxed. "Tell us the truth, and we'll let you go."

The man was arrogant and needed to be put in his place. "I do have a confession to make, Pete." Becky smiled innocently. "Given a choice, I'd have chosen a prettier bridesmaid."

Pete uttered a savage curse while the corners of Mike's mouth curved in a smile.

"Do you, Michael Sean Ryan, take this woman . . ."

The ceremony began. A feeling of unreality settled over Becky. She felt detached, a spectator at her own wedding. All her attention was fixed on the official holding a worn black book. Details assumed unnatural clarity. The gravy stain on his shiny broadcloth suit. The haphazard way his shirt was buttoned over a striped nightshirt.

"I do," Mike responded in his rich baritone.

"Do you, Rebecca Anne Foster, take . . ."

What did she know about this man? He was an enigma in many ways. Sometimes cruel, often tender. She knew she loved him. Given time he might come to love her in return. Perhaps this strange quirk of fate might prove a blessing in disguise.

Becky became aware that Amos Gribbs's dry monotone had ceased. Everyone was staring at her expectantly. Everyone except Mike who stared at a point above the official's head. With a start, she realized what was amiss.

"I do," she pledged softly.

"You may place the ring on the bride's finger," Amos Gribbs yawned.

Frank and Pete glanced from one to the other. "This was so sudden and all . . ." Pete mumbled.

"I guess a couple can be just as married without a ring," the official conceded, more concerned about getting back to bed. "I now pronounce you man and wife. You may kiss the bride."

Becky lifted her face to Mike's and was disappointed at the chaste kiss he brushed across her lips.

Pete caught Becky in a rough embrace and kissed her greedily while Frank sulked in a corner.

"Ease up, Mitchell." The hard edge of Mike's voice brought Pete's head up with a snap. "That's no way to act around a jealous husband." Though the deputy glowered at Mike, he released Becky without argument.

After fixing their signatures to the register, the four left the official to resume his interrupted slumber. Pete indicated Becky was to ride with him, but Mike was adamant.

"My wife rides with me."

Becky grabbed his outstretched hand and was pulled up behind him. *My wife,* she repeated silently. It sounded like music.

It was well after midnight when they arrived at Becky's doorstep. Out of the corner of her eye, Becky caught the glint of silver as moonlight reflected on metal. Gunmetal! Her eyes rounded in fear at the sight of a pistol aimed at her heart. Reflexively, her hands tightened at Mike's waist. He glanced over his shoulder and saw the reason for her fear.

"Are you going to shoot us, Mitchell? Don't you want any witnesses to your stupidity?"

"You're the one who's stupid if you think I don't know what you're up to. You got hitched to avoid jail. I'm going to see that you stay married."

"I've about had it with your bright ideas, Pete."

Frank leaned on the pommel of his saddle and gave his deputy a look of derision.

"It would be easy for you to sneak an annulment," Pete persisted. "No one would be the wiser. All you'd have to do is claim you never slept together. Well I'm appointing myself your guardian angel. I'm going to stick around and make sure you lovebirds enjoy a honeymoon." His jarring laughter rang out.

"I have to hand it to you, Pete," Frank said with grudging admiration, "until tonight I never appreciated the devious way your mind works. Stay as long as you like. I'll stable the horses, then head back to town."

Humiliation scorched Becky's cheeks as she swung down from behind Mike. Head high, spine stiff, she marched into the house not turning to see who followed, or who stayed behind. The lamp, its wick low but still burning, sat on the kitchen table, mute testimony to her haste. Picking it up, she climbed the stairs, pausing just outside her bedroom door.

"You two won't be needing this." Pete grabbed the lamp. "It's always more fun in the dark. Course, I've never had such quality merchandise." His lewd laughter followed them into the darkened room.

Her nocturnal instincts guiding her, Becky walked to the rosewood dresser where she struck a match and lit a candle. Lacking the courage to face Mike just yet, she unfastened her cape, folded it neatly, and draped it over the back of a chair. The entire time she was painfully aware of Mike, silent and watchful. She had no idea what his thoughts were. She was almost afraid to find out. Anger? Frustration? Surely this situation must go against his grain. If the finger of blame were to be pointed, it would be at her. From their very first meeting, she had deliberately schemed to embroil him in her plans. She walked across the room and gathered the drapes in both hands. After jerking them shut, she slowly turned.

Mike was watching, as she knew he would be. "I'm sorry." She drew in a shaky breath. "This is all my fault. I never should have involved you."

His brows knit in confusion. "How is any of this your fault?"

"I can't believe I was so gullible," she berated herself. "I walked right into their trap and dragged you in even deeper. I should have realized Frank didn't come by to apologize."

Mike rubbed the back of his neck as though that would erase his confusion. Dammit! He hadn't expected an apology. Neither had he expected her to go through with the shoddy little ceremony. The whole time he had been certain she would back down. In fact, he had been braced for it. The lady was unpredictable. That was the one thing he could be sure of.

"Don't blame yourself." A smile warmed his eyes. "If I hadn't been so determined to play cards, we could have gotten away with time to spare. You risked everything to warn me. I'm grateful."

"Then you're not angry?" she asked hopefully.

"No, not angry." He dragged his fingers through his hair. "I only wish I understood you better. They gave you every chance to avoid a wedding. I kept expecting you to tell Denby what he wanted to hear. But you didn't. Why, Becky?" The question was wrung from his heart. "I have to know why."

Mike deserved all the answers, needed to hear the details from the very beginning. But not tonight.

Tonight was special—their wedding night. Becky didn't want to waste it. They had been given the special gift of time. There would be a dozen tomorrows.

"Tomorrow, Michael," she said, her voice ripe with promise. "All your questions will be answered."

"Tomorrow." He gave a small nod of agreement.

The low timbre of his voice sent a flush of anticipation coursing through her veins. Her heart thudded in her ears.

Mike raised his hand and lightly grazed the knuckles across her cheek. "Does it still hurt?"

"I'm fine," Becky returned throatily. "Now."

Mike cupped her face in his hands, staring into dark green depths as welcoming and mysterious as a primal forest. The world ceased to exist for them. Time hung suspended; a single dewdrop poised on a blade of grass.

"Tonight is ours, love," he whispered, reaching behind her to pull the hairpins from the sedate coil one by one, letting them fall to the floor. His fingers combed through her silky tresses until they were a shimmering torrent of molten gold around her shoulders. "There, that's how I like it best."

Becky was helpless to control the furiously bounding pulse beneath the fingertips that rested lightly on either side of her neck.

The knowledge that his touch could invoke such a response gave Mike immense pleasure. "I've often dreamed of a night spent making love to you slowly, ever so slowly. I need you, Becky, in every way a man can need a woman. I want to feel you quiver, to hear you sigh my name, to taste every inch of your delectable body."

Already Becky was quivering, her body aching for his. What he planned was torture, but a torture so exquisite she had no will to resist. "I'm yours, Michael, only yours."

"I could wake and find this a dream. If so, it will be one to remember." With unhurried ease, his hands left her throat and trailed down her breastbone to unbutton the tiny pearl buttons of her shirt. The waist of her skirt was unhooked. The material slipped down her hips to fall at her feet. Mike's eyes devoured her beauty. Sweeping her into his arms, he carried her to the bed.

Becky gazed into his passion-darkened face. Awed at his intensity, part of her exulted in being the cause of such powerful emotion.

His gaze drank in her full breasts straining against a gossamer camisole, then wandered downward. Lace-trimmed drawers of fine cotton were cinched around a narrow waist with blue satin ribbon. The dusky triangle at the juncture of her legs was clearly visible beneath sheer fabric.

Watching his eyes darken to the color of a midnight sky, Becky felt a hot surge of pleasure rush through her.

Reluctantly, Mike dragged his gaze to follow a slender thigh and graceful calf. His brows knit in a frown.

"What is it?" Becky whispered, not wanting him to find anything about her displeasing.

"Boots, love. You're still wearing them." He tugged one off, then the other, letting them drop with a thud. "I want to see all of you right down to your baby toes," he said as he supported the arch of her foot in his palm, pretending to study it critically.

Becky wondered hazily if this was how Cinderella felt while the handsome prince appraised her foot for the fabled glass slipper.

"Beautiful." Mike brushed a kiss across its dainty arch. Becky felt the tingle all the way up her spine.

He pulled his attention upward. Catching the end of ribbon threaded through the top of her camisole, he exerted gentle pressure until the bow slipped from its knot. "I want nothing to separate us." He did the same with the bow of her drawers. Where the material gaped, he planted a kiss on the satiny smooth skin.

A low moan of delight escaped her parted lips.

Her undergarments removed and cast aside, Mike's eyes traveled her length. Arrayed only in the mellow glow of a single flickering candle, Becky felt neither shame nor embarrassment under his bold perusal, only a radiant joy at being this very special man's woman.

"My memory did you a disservice," he murmured with velvety huskiness. "You're more beautiful than I remembered."

He was about to lower himself next to her, and Becky held up her hand to forestall him. "Nothing between us, Michael." Pulling herself into a sitting position, she unbuttoned his shirt with the same infuriating slowness with which he had unbuttoned hers. Emerald eyes locked with those of sapphire. "No scraps of fabric to separate us. No more secrets."

When Mike's clothes joined hers, their bodies came together in mutual celebration. His tongue invaded her mouth, and she gladly surrendered to its gentle plunder. Sensitive fingers explored every nuance of her slender form, committing to memory each swell and hollow. Her skin burned with feverish heat wherever he touched until her entire body was engulfed in raging heat.

"Michael," she half-sobbed when his mouth left hers.

"Ah, sweet witch, you'll never know what pleasure it gives me to hear my name on your lips." His mouth blazed a moist trail down her neck and across each breast. A sucking motion tugged an already turgid nipple past the roughened edge of teeth.

Speared by a stab of intense pleasure, Becky gasped. She thought she would go mad when he repeated the passionate assault at her other breast.

His mouth left the full globes to taste as promised every inch of her, intimately learning secret flavors.

Tossing her head from side to side, she writhed beneath him. Every nerve in her body was finely attuned to his touch.

"Open your eyes, love. Look at me."

Eyelids heavily weighted, Becky struggled to obey the urgent command.

Mike parted her thighs and thrust his manhood deep within her. The tempo built with each stroke.

Already heightened senses continued to soar making her cry out, "Michael, I need . . . I love . . ."

Her final words were lost in a glorious shattering crescendo.

Chapter Fourteen

HE WAS SPLENDID; HE WAS MAGNIFICENT—AND HE WAS hers! Becky smiled. Her finger idly traced the diagonal swath that marred one side of Mike's face. The raised surface was shiny and smooth while the edges were reddened, puckered. On either side of the scar, she felt the rough uneven ridge of cheekbone. Her smile faded. The offending blow had shattered the underlying bone as well as branding flesh. She had meant it when she said she wanted no secrets between them. *Someday, Michael, she vowed silently, I'll know the secrets about your scar. But I can be patient.*

Her lips curved again. Last night she had been his

woman. This morning she would be his wife. Careful not to awaken him, Becky eased out of bed. Dressing quickly, she slipped out of the room, nearly stumbling over Pete Mitchell sprawled like a hibernating bear in the middle of the hall. She skirted around him and went downstairs.

As she prepared breakfast, her fragile bubble of happiness was pricked by doubt. Marriage was more than a night of lovemaking. It was a lifetime commitment. She didn't want Mike to feel trapped and resent her. If Mike wanted his freedom, she wouldn't stand in the way, even if it meant he would take her heart with him.

"If you're fixin' eggs make mine fried."

Becky glanced over her shoulder to find Pete lounging against the doorjamb. "You've overstayed your welcome. Get out!"

His ruddy face split into a wide grin. "Is that any way to treat a guest?" His eyes roamed over her insolently. "It's amazing how sound carries in a house. Shame you and me never got together. We'd make quite a team."

Becky's cheeks flamed at the thought of his ear pressed to the bedroom door. "If you don't leave this minute, I'll have my husband throw you out bodily!"

"You heard my wife!"

Pete swung around. Mike was halfway down the stairs and rapidly closing the gap between them. Pete retreated into the kitchen. "All right. I'm goin', I'm goin'." The slam of the kitchen door echoed after him.

Pete's expression at finding Mike ready to evict him by the scruff of his neck struck Becky as funny. The sound of her laughter was contagious. Still buttoning

233

his shirt, Mike strolled into the kitchen where his deep rumbling laughter mingled with hers. Their merriment gradually subsided, leaving a strained silence. She turned back to the stove and poked at a piece of sizzling bacon. Out of the corner of her eye, she saw him pour a cup of coffee from the metal pot and heard the scrape of a chair.

Knowing there would be no peace of mind until certain issues were resolved, Becky set the platter of food on the warming rack. "Mike . . .?" she began as she slowly approached the table.

He stopped stirring his coffee.

"I know most marriages don't start out as ours did." Nervously, she ran her hands down the sides of her apron. "No longer is anyone making threats or pointing a gun. If you don't want to stay married, I'll understand."

"If that's the way you want it." His tone was flat, emotionless.

"Stop twisting my words!" Becky wanted to scream in frustration. Instead she gripped the back of a chair until her knuckles whitened. "I made my choice last night, but I'm trying to be fair. I don't want you to feel trapped. It's not too late to leave. No hard feelings."

A thick fringe of dark lashes veiled his thoughts. With the tip of his spoon, he outlined the checked squares of the tablecloth. "What about you? You have more at stake than I. Are you ready to pretend we fell so madly in love that we eloped?"

"Yes."

Mike's eyes opened wide at the prompt response. He shook his head in wonder. Someday, he vowed, before he reached a ripe old age, he would figure out the workings of this woman's mind. In the meantime, he wouldn't question Providence. Humor tugged the corners of his mouth into a smile. "Well, Mrs. Ryan, for better or worse, you've got yourself a husband."

Becky's deathgrip on the back of the chair relaxed. Her answering smile was radiant.

How could Becky imagine marriage to her might be a hardship, Mike marveled. She was everything he had ever dreamed of in a wife, and more. Much more. But what did she get in return? Since the accident, he was no prize to look at. Surely Becky deserved the same fair play.

"You gave me a choice. Now I'm giving you one."

"This sounds ominous." Becky tried to laugh away a nibble of fear.

"If you would prefer separate bedrooms, I won't object."

Becky mimicked his earlier indifference. "If that's what you want," she shrugged.

Mike's fist crashed down on the table, making the dishes rattle. "No, dammit! That's not what I want."

The laughter dancing in her eyes stopped him. Mike grinned somewhat sheepishly, realizing their earlier conversation had reversed.

"It's a bit late for separate bedrooms, don't you think?" she teased, then grew serious. "I never planned for us to become lovers. Call it fate, or destiny. Whatever the name, I have no regrets. I hope you don't either."

"Nary a single one." He caught her hand and stroked the place where a wedding band belonged.

The smell of scorching food broke the spell.

"My muffins!" Becky tore her hand free and ran to the stove.

Bran muffins spicy with cinnamon and apple were rescued in the nick of time. Mike did justice to the hearty breakfast Becky had prepared while she ate sparingly, her mind elsewhere.

"News of our marriage is going to create quite a stir." She watched Mike reach for another muffin. "I wish we could be so convincing that Pete and Frank will look like village idiots if they even think of mentioning their suspicions."

"Your wish is my command." Mike's blue eyes twinkled. "Between the two of us, I think we can pull it off. Shall we start by convincing Hannah that we're a case of true love?"

"That's a wonderful idea," Becky agreed enthusiastically. "Mike?" She caught her lower lip between her teeth.

"Out with it, love."

"It will seem strange if you continue to work for Hannah. Would you work here instead? I'm sure Brewster won't mind switching places. Besides," she said, laughing, "I think he's sweet on Hannah."

Mike swallowed the rest of his coffee. A smile hovered in his eyes. "I like the way your mind works, Rebecca Ryan. You'd make a great general."

Hannah was midway across the yard headed for the bunkhouse when Mike and Becky rode up. "Mornin'," she sang out cheerfully. "Mike, you had me worried," she scolded. "It ain't like you to miss breakfast. I was afraid you mighta took sick."

"Sorry, Hannah. I didn't mean to worry you." Mike swung down from the saddle.

"No harm done. You must of got an early start and

met up with Becky. Odd seein' the two of you together without hearin' you argue."

Mike and Becky exchanged looks. Dismounting, Becky gathered her courage. "Mike and I have something we'd like to tell you." The rest of the announcement was caught behind paralyzed vocal cords.

"Go ahead, child. Don't be afraid to tell me bad news."

Becky cleared her throat. "It isn't bad news." She felt like a young girl about to confess her elopement to an unsuspecting parent. "Mike and I were married last night by a justice of the peace in Mill Valley."

The admission spilled out so quickly the words ran together. It took Hannah a moment to sort through the jumbled sentence. "Married?" Her jaw dropped open. She stared from one to the other, certain she had misunderstood. "Why I never knew you two even liked one another. Married! I can't believe my ears."

Mike stepped closer to Becky and put his arms around her shoulders. "I know it's sudden." He flashed a boyish grin. "I only convinced Becky to marry me last night. If she had time to think it over, I was afraid she'd change her mind."

It seemed perfectly natural for Becky to put her arm around his waist. "Don't believe it, Hannah." She laughed up at him. "If I hadn't been the one to force the issue, he never would have proposed."

Hannah's faded blue eyes misted at the sight of the smiling young couple. "If Ben were only here," she said, her voice cracking. She came forward in a rush and enfolded them in an exuberant hug. "I never would have guessed it, but seein' you now, well, you're just perfect for each other." She dabbed at her eyes with the corner of her apron. "This calls for a celebration. Come with me."

Mike and Becky followed Hannah into the parlor where they toasted the future with elderberry wine in Hannah's best glasses. Before they left, they reached an agreement whereby Mike would move his things to the Brantford farm and Brewster would work for Hannah. Hannah poured another glass of wine. Smiling to herself, she wondered how she could have been so blind. Why, the two hadn't been able to take their eyes off each other. Anybody could see they were crazy in love.

Dinner was over and the dishes were done. There were no more chores, no more excuses. It was time to end the secrecy. It was also a time of uncertainty. If she bared her soul, would Mike believe her? Everything she was about to tell him would contradict what he thought to be true.

Mike watched as Becky paced the length of the library. Halting before a sideboard, she opened a crystal decanter and poured a generous amount of brandy into a snifter. She hesitated, then poured a second. Wordlessly, she handed one to Mike. Walking over to the fireplace, she stared into the amber liquid. Fool's courage, her father called it. It was aptly named, she thought, taking a sip.

"You'll never know how many times I've rehearsed what I'd say in this situation. Now that it's actually here, I don't know where to start."

"Just say what you have to say."

Her gaze met his without wavering. "I've been involved in the underground railroad for nearly two years," she said quietly.

"You what?" Mike bounded to his feet.

"It's true."

"Why didn't you tell me this before?"

"I wanted to, but couldn't." Her eyes unconsciously pleaded for understanding. "Adam feared for my safety. He made Ben and me swear never to tell another soul, or he'd stop sending passengers by this route."

"Adam is in this, too?" At Becky's nod, Mike took a large gulp of brandy. "Perhaps you'd better start at the very beginning." He lowered himself to the sofa.

Becky, pacing as she talked, spared herself no pain. Upon her return to Oak Ridge after the deaths of David and her infant daughter, she often had trouble sleeping. Many times she would hear Adam coming and going at odd hours of the night. She decided to follow him. What she discovered proved a turning point. Thereafter, she became as active in the abolition movement as he. When Adam decided to make his home in New Orleans, Becky continued the effort in Oak Ridge. Adam would let her know by means of coded telegrams when to expect a shipment. No one ever questioned their frequent messages.

"How does Denby figure into this?" Mike asked when she reached the end of her narrative.

"It all started quite innocently. He invited me to a church social," Becky said with a half-laugh. "It was obvious he was interested in seeing more of me."

"What about you? Were you interested in him?" He hated himself, but had to ask.

Becky stopped pacing. "I was never interested in Frank Denby."

He set the snifter down and leaned forward intently. "Then why did you encourage him?"

"Adam and Ben were against it at the onset, but I convinced them that a friendship with the local marshal would be useful. No one would connect me with abolition activities if they thought I shared Frank's views. And," she made an expansive gesture with her glass, "in case of trouble, I hoped Frank would confide in me so that I could warn Ben."

Head to one side, he regarded her through narrowed eyes. "If you didn't tip Denby off about the fugitive at Willow Creek, who did?"

Becky wearily sank into a wingbacked chair. She had known it would all boil down to this one final question. "I have no proof," she sighed. "Only a theory."

"I'm a good listener," he reminded her.

"In the past, slavecatchers in hot pursuit lost their victims at that particular spot. This one wasn't about to let another bounty slip away. When he lost his prey, he contacted local officials and set a trap."

"I see," Mike said quietly.

Silence flowed between them, stranding them on opposite banks of a widening gap. When Becky could stand the tension no longer, she made her excuses and fled to the privacy of their bedroom.

Mike watched hungry flames consume a stout log. Good Lord! Was it possible he had been wrong about Becky all these months? Everything she said tonight rang true. He groaned, dragging his hand through his hair, and recalled the night at Willow Creek. He had called her a traitor, accused her of causing a man's death. If she was telling the truth, and he no longer had reason to doubt her, he qualified as a prize idiot.

After only one night, the bedroom seemed lonely without Mike. Becky sat in front of the vanity, pulling a brush through her hair in long slow strokes. Her reflected image stared back solemnly. She had pinned such high hopes on tonight, and all for naught. Anger, even disbelief, would have been easier to contend with than the damning silence.

Mike watched unobtrusively from the shadowed hallway. Her beauty was gut-wrenching. Her long, gold hair spilled down her back. The expression on her delicate oval face was pensive, vulnerable. It brought out a fierce protective instinct in him.

A slight movement, or perhaps a sixth sense, alerted her to his presence. Their eyes met in the mirror.

"Until tonight, I never realized the many times I complicated your life. You deserve an apology."

Carefully placing the silver hairbrush on the vanity, Becky rose and went to him. "I don't want your apology. I want your trust."

Mike searched her upturned face. Eyes like clear cool pools tempted him to submerge himself in their depths, to explore their hidden mysteries. "Becky." His voice was thick. He reached deep into a pocket and brought out a wide gold band. "It belonged to my mother. I'd like you to have it."

She blinked rapidly to stem a sudden flood of tears.

"It would mean a great deal to me if you would wear my ring. You're my wife, and I want everyone to know. If you'd rather, I'll buy you a new one," he offered.

Becky shook her head. "I would be honored to wear your mother's ring," she said softly.

He caught her left hand and slipped the ring on the third finger. "I now pronounce us man and wife." He smiled. The warmth in his eyes melted any lingering doubts about their future.

"Oh, yes, Michael," she cried, throwing her arms around his neck. "Yes, yes, yes."

Chapter Fifteen

FRIDAY WAS THE DAY SET ASIDE FOR TRIPS INTO TOWN. Although Becky was reluctant to have the outside world intrude, the weekly excursion would mark their debut into the community as a married couple.

Heads turned as they progressed down Main Street. Blatant curiosity overruled good manners. Becky couldn't suppress a smile at the stir of interest.

"An audience this size deserves a performance worth watching, don't you think?" Her eyes were alight with mischief.

Mike concurred with a wicked grin. "Keep looking

at me that way, and I'll give the good citizens enough gossip to keep tongues wagging for a year." No sooner had the words left his mouth when they were accosted by Maude Bundy. Agnes, as usual, trailed at her heels.

"Is it true?" The buxom matron dispensed with formalities. "It's all over town you eloped!"

"You heard correctly." Becky tucked her hand in the crook of Mike's arm.

"How romantic," the woman cooed. "You look especially fit this morning, Rebecca. I've always admired your tiny waist." Her eyes lingered on Becky's midsection. "I was saying to my Agnes just the other day that it's a shame about a waistline. It's the first thing to go once a woman is in a family way."

Agnes twittered nervously behind one hand.

"Congratulations." Maude sailed off with Agnes following in her wake.

Mike shook his head. "Does that girl ever talk?"

"Does she ever have a chance?"

He chuckled. "Was I imagining things, or did that woman imply what I think she did?"

Becky nodded grimly. "Next time we meet, she'll probably tackle me with a tape measure."

Giving her hand a reassuring squeeze, he bent his head to hers. "Our public is getting impatient," he said in a low voice. "Are you ready to run the gauntlet?"

"As ready as I'll ever be." Her grip on his arm tightened.

They made a striking couple as they strolled down the walk, stopping frequently to chat with well-wishers. They parted company as planned, Becky in one direction to telegraph Adam, Mike in another to attend to an errand at the blacksmith's.

When Becky finished sending the wireless, she proceeded to the general store. The clerk paused in the act of measuring flour, his freckled face wreathed in a grin. "Mornin', Mrs. Foster. Be right with you."

"Good morning, Jeff." She ran her hand over a bolt of fabric displayed on a counter. "By the way, it's no longer Mrs. Foster. I'm Mrs. Ryan now."

"So, it is true."

Margaret Nelson's voice swept over Becky like a cold wind. Turning around, she found disapproval etched in every line of the woman's face. "Yes, Mike and I were married by a justice of the peace."

"I hoped the rumor was false, but I realize that was wishful thinking on my part. We need to talk."

"Perhaps another time," Becky demurred. "I told Mike I would meet him here."

"Jeff," Maggie addressed the gawking young man. "Tell Mr. Ryan that Rebecca and I are having tea at the Buckingham." She turned and marched out of the store.

It was pointless to protest. With a sigh of resignation, Becky handed her list to Jeff, then followed Maggie's ramrod stiff form.

The dowager chose a corner table and waited until tea had been served before beginning her attack. "Your marriage was quite sudden."

"Yes, it was."

Becky's calm further annoyed the woman. "Mike and I have become quite good friends since he arrived in town. News of his marriage came as a shock, although not nearly so much as his choice of a wife."

"Or as disappointing?"

"Precisely." Margaret pursed her lips. "For the life of me, I don't see what you find in common."

Becky shrugged. "A case of opposites attracting?"

"Don't be flippant with me, young lady," she retorted sharply. Making a steeple of her fingers, she regarded Becky thoughtfully. "It's possible Mike was flattered by your attention. You're very pretty. However, I should think he would realize beauty is only skin deep."

"Did you invite me here to listen to insults?"

Irritation flitted across the woman's features. "I thought you might be interested in hearing the rumors circulating about you."

"Not particularly," Becky replied before taking a sip of tea, wishing Mike would come to her rescue. "But since you seem so determined, let's get this over with."

"Some say you've been seeing Mike behind Denby's back. You found out you're pregnant with Mike's child and had to marry."

"Is that what you think?"

"No. I'm more inclined to go along with the other school of thought."

"Which is?"

"When Denby refused to be led to the altar, you latched onto the first available male. Mike happened to be around at an inopportune time."

Both rumors were so far from the truth they were ridiculous. Her lips twitched in amusement. Judging from the disapproving look on the older woman's face, she knew that once again her sense of the absurd had landed her in trouble.

"I fail to see the humor in any of this," Margaret bristled.

"As for the first rumor," Becky replied evenly, "anyone who can count to nine will find they were mistaken. Since you claim to know Mike so well, I should think you better than anybody would realize how preposterous the second theory is."

"You're speaking in riddles."

"I shouldn't have to tell you what an exceptional man Mike is. When the opportunity to marry him presented itself, I grabbed it with both hands."

"Ha!" Maggie snorted in disbelief. Her gray eyes were colder than the Atlantic on a winter's day. "The truth as I see it, Rebecca, is that you'll give Mike nothing but heartache. You'll use him, hurt him, and cast him aside. We do agree on one point, however. He is an exceptional man. He deserves better than the likes of you."

Becky was stunned by the vitriolic attack. Looking up, she saw Mike crossing the dining room in long strides. She fought the urge to hurl herself into his arms.

"Mike, you ought to be ashamed of yourself," Maggie scolded as soon as he was within earshot. "You ran off and got married without even so much as a hint."

"Sorry about the oversight, Maggie," he grinned unabashedly. "Thought that was what eloping was all about."

She rose to her feet, her tea untouched, and picked up her reticule. "You can get back in my good graces if you and your lovely wife will be my guests for dinner tomorrow night."

"We'd be happy to." Pleased by the invitation, he failed to notice the sly cunning in the woman's flint-gray eyes.

"You look a lamb being led to slaughter."

"Stagefright."

Mike frowned. "You really are nervous about tonight, aren't you?"

"I know it's silly," Becky tried to laugh at her fear. "But Margaret Nelson has never been exactly subtle in her dislike for me."

"Give Maggie a chance. Once she knows you better, she'll come around. I did." He drew a smile from her. "Would it make you feel better if I told you how beautiful you look?"

She laughed outright at his lecherous ogling. "Why thank you, sir. You are a most thoughtful and gallant gentleman." She adopted the melodious tone of a southern belle.

That voice. The dulcet drawl triggered a memory. He had heard it before. But where? Then it came to him. The widow at the railroad station. Impossible! He had seen Becky board a train for Chicago with his own eyes.

Beside him, Becky tensed as he reined to a stop before Margaret Nelson's home. Designed in the neo-Grecian style of architecture, its uncluttered lines and four symmetrical pillars reflected the owner's classic taste. Mike assisted Becky from the buggy and followed her trim form. A black velvet cloak flowed around her. The sight was disturbingly familiar.

She had nearly reached the porch when she realized Mike was no longer behind her. Glancing over her shoulder, Becky found him standing stock-still in the middle of the flagstone pathway. "You look as though you've seen a ghost."

"I think I have," he remarked cryptically. "For a minute you reminded me of a woman I saw once in Indianapolis at a railroad station. She was a brave tragic figure on her way north to stay with relatives accompanied by her servants."

Becky froze, her eyes wide and watchful.

Mike sauntered toward her. "This woman was recently widowed. Her husband, if I recall, had been thrown from his horse when it stepped into a gopher hole during a fox hunt." He raised his arm to knock on the door. "What was his name?" he puzzled.

"Beauregard," she answered absently as the door swung open.

"So it was you!"

Mutely, Becky stared at him, aware of his anger, mystified as to its cause.

"My, my, don't tell me you two are having a lover's spat?" Maggie asked with feigned concern. "Is the honeymoon over so soon?"

"No argument," Mike replied easily, "just a discussion that will have to be postponed until later."

"I see," Maggie said, smiling. She knew an argument when she saw one. Even without her interference, the marriage was doomed.

Taking Becky's wrap, she ushered them into a dining room resplendent with Brussels lace, bone china, and leaded crystal. While Maybelle Harris, Maggie's cook-housekeeper, served an excellent dinner, Maggie kept the conversation flowing. When dinner was over, she suggested they retire to the parlor for dessert.

"Mike, would you be a dear and get my shawl for me? I believe I left it in the bedroom."

"Certainly." Mike left in search of the shawl.

Maggie seated herself on a damask sofa while Becky sat on the opposite loveseat. She poured from a sterling tea service and handed Becky a fragile cup. "I understand your first husband was a member of one of Boston's leading families."

"David was the grandson of Jeremiah Foster who founded a prosperous mercantile business."

"Life in Oak Ridge must be quite dull in comparison," she commiserated, pouring herself tea and adding lemon. "Boston is so cosmopolitan. Pity it's having such problems."

"Problems?"

"The immigration trouble, dear. The city is being virtually overrun by boatloads of shiftless Irish immigrants. They're content to live in waterfront shacks. All they seem to know is drinking and brawling." She shuddered in apparent distaste. "They'll be the ruination of a fine city." She sat back, teacup in hand, and waited for Becky's agreement.

"I beg to differ with you." Becky's hand trembled from the force of her anger. She carefully set the cup down lest she spill its contents. "That is the most outrageous remark I have ever heard."

"I beg your pardon?" Maggie was aghast.

"The people you loosely term *shiftless Irish* are hardworking, honest, generous to a fault. My best friend immigrated from Dublin. At great risk to her own health, she nursed me through typhoid. I owe her my life." Becky stood, her hands curled into tight balls at her side. "I mean no disrespect, Mrs. Nelson,

250

but I cannot in good conscience sit by while you disabuse people I have a great admiration for."

"Bravo," Mike applauded from the opened doorway behind her.

Becky glanced from his thunderous expression to the older woman's stricken one. Margaret actually seemed to shrivel from the heated anger directed at her. Becky felt a moment's compassion. She knew from experience what it was like to be the target of Mike's black rage.

"You owe my wife an apology."

"Mike, I only wanted to show you the kind of woman you married. She's not good enough. You'll get hurt."

"I already know the kind of woman she is," he said, his tone uncompromising. "An apology, Maggie."

"I don't understand any of this." Becky looked from one to the other, conscious of the duel of wills being waged.

Mike's gaze rested on her briefly. "Maggie set a trap, but you failed to take the bait." He flung the shawl over the back of a chair. "Maggie and I are both part of Boston's *shiftless Irish*. She deliberately tried to lead you into making derogatory remarks— knowing full well I'd overhear them."

Maggie slowly drew herself up. "It's true. I wanted to expose you for the shallow-minded creature I believe you to be. I took a gamble and lost. You won, Rebecca."

"You're wrong, Mrs. Nelson," Becky said quietly. "We all lost."

"Perhaps you're right, Rebecca," she conceded wearily. "Whatever my motives, it was uncalled for.

251

You are a guest in my home, and the wife of a dear friend. My behavior was inexcusable."

"We'll be going now." Mike's hand at Becky's waist urged her toward the door. Maggie didn't try to dissuade them.

Just before the buggy lurched forward, Becky looked at the woman framed in the lighted doorway. Margaret Nelson's proud carriage slumped dispiritedly; her skin resembled fine parchment. Perhaps it was a trick of the lighting, but she seemed to have aged dramatically in a short span of time. For Becky, the formidable dowager ceased to exist. In her place was a lonely old woman.

Neither Becky nor Mike spoke more than a few words on the way home. After helping Becky alight, Mike stabled the horses. Leaving a lamp burning, Becky went upstairs, changed into an apricot-colored nightgown, and waited. When there were no footfalls on the stairs, she decided to investigate. She found Mike in the library where a single log blazed in the hearth. Seated on the sofa, his chin resting on his hands, he didn't look up at her entrance.

"I always prided myself on being a good judge of a man's character. But I swear, I'll never understand the way a woman's mind works."

Becky perched on the arm of the sofa. "Is that what's bothering you?" Her hands began to play along the tight ridge of muscle spanning his shoulders. "Care to talk about it?"

"I've never been so confounded by anyone in my life as I have been by you," he sighed. "It took me until tonight to figure out you were the widow at the train station."

"You were angry, weren't you?" Becky could feel his muscles knot in response to her question.

"You're damn right I was! All I could think of was the danger you were in. How could Ben ask you to take such a risk?"

"He didn't." Her breath was a warm breeze behind his ear. "It was all my idea."

"Figures," he said with a short laugh. "Seems like I underestimated you, and overestimated Maggie. I still can't believe she'd pull a stunt like she did tonight."

"Michael?" Becky purred, feeling taut muscles grow lax beneath her touch. Bending forward, she playfully nipped his earlobe.

"Lady," he growled, "you drive me to distraction." An abrupt twisting maneuver brought her tumbling into his lap. Her nightgown rode high on her thigh. Mike's eyes roamed the path his hand soon followed. "I can't tell where the silk ends and your skin begins," he murmured.

"Mmm, Michael?"

All coherent thought fled as his lips crushed hers.

Later, their bodies entwined, they lay before the dying embers. Becky finally remembered what she had started to ask. "Would you mind very much if I invited Maggie for dinner one night soon?" She sensed rather than saw his frown.

"After the way she treated you, why?"

"Because I think your friendship deserves a second chance." Becky turned to stare into the ruggedly carved face so close to her own. Eyes that appeared indigo in the waning light mirrored his conflict. Reaching up, she stroked his cheek.

He caught her hand and pressed a kiss in the palm. "If that's what you want."

She laughed deep in her throat. "That's only the beginning of what I want," she said, rolling on top of him so that the peaks of her breasts teased his chest.

He chuckled. "Whoever said the way to a man's heart was through his stomach?"

Chapter Sixteen

"HE LOVES ME. HE LOVES ME NOT," BECKY SAID UNDER her breath, seething. She vented her frustration on the hapless mound of bread dough, slamming it against the floury surface, then vigorously kneading it with both hands. It had been weeks, three to be exact, since the wedding. Not once had the word love crossed Mike's lips.

Why wasn't loving him enough? Why was it so important he love her in return? She craved more than his body's passion. She wanted his heart and soul as well. Hypocrite, a small voice at the back of her mind accused. Though she had said *I love you* a thousand times, she had yet to say the words out loud. Whenever they threatened to burst forth, she swallowed them back. She rationalized that she didn't want Mike to think her a clinging female. Truth is, she was afraid her declaration would upset the delicate status quo. What if Mike told her it was desire, not love, that he felt?

Becky straightened and pushed aside a strand of hair with the back of her hand. The skin at the nape of her neck prickled with the uncomfortable sensation of being watched. She whirled around. Her hand flew to her throat. A man lounged in the doorway behind her.

"My, ain't this a homey sight?" he smirked, relishing her fright.

"You startled me," Becky managed to gasp.

"Good!" The smirk spread into a grin. "I was afraid you might have a squeaky floorboard to ruin my surprise."

"What do you want?" Her heart pumped so furiously it threatened to crack her ribs. Fear brought an acrid taste to her mouth.

"Thought you and me could work out a deal."

"What kind of deal?"

"I came by the other day, but nobody was home. I took it on myself to do a little snooping. Guess what I found?" He reached into a pocket and pulled out a slender wooden cylinder.

Becky stared transfixed. It was the whippoorwill whistle.

"Familiar?" He produced an identical one from another pocket. "Got this one off a dead nigger. Quite a coincidence."

"That's all it is. It doesn't prove a thing."

"It's all the proof I need. You're up to your ears in trouble along with that husband of yours. Sure would hate to see a pretty little thing like you rottin' away in a stinkin' cell. Federal jails are the worst sort. Full of rats, roaches, lice. Food no better than hog slop. Don't think you'd wish that on an enemy, much less someone you're married to." He started toward her. "That's where our deal comes in."

Becky retreated a step only to have the table halt her retreat.

He chuckled at her plight. "Here's my idea. I been thinking maybe you and me could get together real friendly like every now and then. No one would ever know. In return, I keep my mouth shut."

Becky began to inch around the table. If she could reach the door, she might have a chance.

"Where you think you're goin'?" He sounded amused. "Ain't a soul around."

"I'm not afraid of you." The tremor in her voice betrayed her brave words.

"Nothin' to be afraid of—unless you cross me," he warned. "So what's your answer?"

"Your proof would never hold up in a court." She called his bluff. "I won't play the whore for you."

Becky was nearly around the table. Before she could take one full step, he lunged at her, catching the sleeve of her dress and tearing it at the seam. Her hand groped along the table behind her back for something, anything, she could defend herself with. Her fingers curled around the mound of dough. Without thinking, she flung it in his face. His hold loosened, and she wrenched free.

He recovered with amazing speed. She was less

than three feet from the door when his long arm shot out catching the folds of her skirt. "Oh, no," he snarled. "You're not getting away from me." He pulled on the muslin, reeling her in as effortlessly as a fish on a hook.

Becky dug in her heels, pitching her weight forward. She would not give up without a struggle. Her captor laughed at her futile attempt to pit her strength against his. He liked a challenge.

Rapidly losing ground, Becky spied the earthenware bowl she had used to mix the dough. Grabbing it with both hands, she twisted about, hurling it at his head. He ducked. The bowl shattered against the wall, sending a spray of fine white flour into the air and over the floor.

"You sure are awful sassy," he growled, hauling her against him with a rough jerk that tore the skirt from the bodice. His grip on her shoulders was painful. "I'm tired of you lookin' down your nose at me." He spun her around. "It's time you were taught a lesson."

Becky renewed a struggle born of desperation. He laughed when she tried to rake his face with her nails. A cry of pain escaped as he captured her wrists and twisted her arms behind her back. He exerted pressure until her body arched against him, the contact bringing an avid expression to his face. Remembering a trick Adam had taught her, Becky brought up her knee and aimed for his groin. He sidestepped adroitly. The blow was deflected by the fleshy portion of his thigh.

He released her arms to grab the front of her dress in a large fist. With calculated brutality, he brought the back of his hand across her face. Through a haze of pain, she looked up to see his arm poised to strike another blow. Drawing the last of her reserves, she shoved at his chest. Losing her footing on the flour-slick floor, her feet flew out from under her. She fell backward, her head striking the cast-iron cookstove with a sickening thud. A blinding explosion of light splintered into a million glittering shards that slowly faded into impenetrable blackness. Becky embraced the dark well of peace—and safety.

It was late afternoon when Mike chanced upon Maggie Nelson headed in the same direction. He slowed the gait of his mount to match that of her buggy.

"You may find this difficult to believe," she said, "but I was just on my way to your place."

"Is that right?" He was skeptical. Becky, he knew, had extended dinner invitations on two separate occasions. Each time her effort had been rebuffed. "What brought on this change of heart?"

"I'm not very proud of myself, Mike. I've been behaving like a child. Rebecca, on the other hand, has been more than generous. It's high time I try to make amends." She gave him a small smile. "Can you forgive a misguided old woman?"

"We'll say no more." Mike grinned. "Becky will be happy to see you. She's been after me for weeks to set things right."

"Has she now?" Maggie looked pleased.

"Stay for supper. Adam's due any day now so Becky's been cooking up a storm."

"I don't want to impose."

Mike laughed. "Knowing Becky, she'll insist. I've learned never to argue with her once her mind is made up."

Upon arriving home, Mike looped the reins around a post and helped Maggie from the buggy. He glanced at the back door expecting to see Becky come out to welcome their guest. Strange, he thought, surely she must have heard them ride up. Concern outweighed courtesy. Forgetting Maggie, he bounded up the steps and pushed open the door. He stopped short. The kitchen was a shambles. It looked like a battleground littered with bits of broken crockery, shreds of clothing, and strewn with a white powdery film.

"Oh, my God! Becky!"

"Mike! What is it?" Maggie picked up her skirts and rushed to his side.

They gazed in horror at Becky's still form, sprawled like a broken discarded doll on the kitchen floor.

Mike crossed the room to kneel at her side. It seemed like an eternity before he was able to detect the shallow rise and fall of her chest and locate a feeble pulse. His hands trembled as he gently examined her for injuries. He found a large raised knot at the back of her head.

"Is she . . . ?"

"She's alive," emotion clogged his throat, ". . . barely."

Tenderly, Mike lifted Becky, cradling her in his arms, and carried her upstairs where he placed her on the bed. Maggie was shocked by his pallor. She always thought of him as invincible, a pillar of strength. Now he seemed shaken to his very foundation.

"Go into town and get Doc." She took command. "Hurry!"

There was no need to mention haste. Mike rode like a man possessed. His gelding was lathered with sweat when he brought up the reins before a neat frame house. Vaulting from the saddle, he raced up the walk and pounded with his fist on the door.

"Becky's hurt!" he shouted the instant a small bearded man with wiry salt-and-pepper hair opened the door. "Quick! She needs you."

"Simmer down, son," the doctor spoke with infuriating calm. "Let me fetch my bag."

"At first I thought she was dead." Mike shuddered, remembering that terrible moment. "Maggie and I found her unconscious with a lump the size of a goose egg at the back of her head, and her clothes half-ripped off. She might have been raped too."

"I'll tend to Becky." Doc placed his hand comfortingly on Mike's shoulder. "You'd best report this to the marshal."

Mike felt torn. He wanted to be with Becky, yet Doc's advice was sound. Reluctantly, he nodded his agreement.

The marshal's office was empty. After asking around, Mike found Pete Mitchell at the bar of the Satin Slipper. "Where's Denby?" he asked without preamble.

The deputy gazed back through bleary eyes. "At the court house in Indianapolis." The last word was slurred almost beyond recognition.

"You're drunk!"

"Damn right." Pete sloshed more whiskey into his glass. "And goin' to get drunker."

"I'll talk to you when you sober up." Mike turned on his heel and stalked out.

Doc Nolan was still with Becky when Mike returned home. He prowled the downstairs hallway like a caged

261

beast. At last, he heard Doc's tread on the stairs. Mike was waiting at the bottom step, one question on his mind. "Is she going to be all right?"

"Don't suppose you have a shot of whiskey handy?" Doc parried.

With an effort, Mike pulled himself together and led the way into the library. He poured a generous amount of liquor into a glass and handed it to the doctor.

"Not for me, son." Doc shook his head. "Myself, I never touch spirits. You looked like you could use a stiff drink." He nodded his approval when Mike complied. "Now about your wife. Becky's still unconscious and shows no sign of coming out of it just yet. From what Maggie tells me, she must have landed pretty hard against the stove. Might have cracked her skull. Nothing much to do, but wait and see."

"Wait? How long?"

"No way of telling." Doc stroked his beard thoughtfully. "Could be tonight, could be tomorrow, could be . . ." He shrugged.

"Never?" It was no more than a whisper.

Doc's look of sympathy said it all. Mike turned away. He walked to the fireplace and stared at ashes in a cold hearth. Bleak and lifeless, they symbolized what life would be like without Becky to share it.

Doc cleared his throat. "Becky wasn't raped. Maggie found a telegram under the front door. That's probably what saved her. Whoever delivered it most likely scared off her attacker." He picked up his bag. "I'll drop by tomorrow."

Mike trudged up the steps. With a heavy heart, he pushed open the bedroom door. A lamp burned low, casting its mellow light on the unmoving form on the bed. Becky's hair flowed across the pillow like a skein of bronze silk. Lashes like sable fans rested on her pale cheeks. She could have been asleep. Mike's chest constricted. An agonized moan broke from his lips.

"You mustn't give up hope." Maggie slipped her arm around his waist. "Becky's young and strong. She'll come through this. You'll see."

"She has to, Maggie. I can't bear the thought of losing her."

Mike drew a chair alongside the bed. He covered Becky's small cool hand with his large calloused one, as though the mere touch could impart a measure of strength. Maggie swallowed the lump in her throat and quietly left the room.

He was sitting just as she had left him when Maggie returned later with a tray. "No arguments. I brought you a bite to eat. Making yourself sick isn't going to help Rebecca."

Mike reluctantly left the bedside to clear a space on a small table for the tray. Maggie looked on approvingly as Mike downed a slice of meat and wedge of cheese on a thick slab of bread. As soon as he finished eating, he returned to his chair. Maggie removed the tray and came back a short while later. She sat in the shadows, an unopened book in her lap.

The clock chimed midnight. Mike uncoiled his large frame and stretched stiff muscles. "She hasn't so much as blinked," he said softly. "I've never felt so helpless."

Maggie came to stand next to him. "You love her very much, don't you?"

Mike exhaled a shaky breath. "Until tonight, I never realized how much. The worst part is, she doesn't even know it."

"What are you saying?" Maggie asked sharply.

Rubbing the back of his neck, Mike stared up at the ceiling. "The circumstances surrounding our marriage were a bit . . . unusual."

"In what way?"

Mike gave a short bitter laugh. "We literally had a shotgun wedding with Denby and Mitchell at the business end of the guns. It's a long story," he said with a crooked smile. "Care to hear it?"

"Why not?" she smiled in return. "I've got all night."

After eliciting her promise not to disclose what he was about to tell her, Mike told Maggie the whole story. It was a revelation. Never once had Maggie seen through Becky's guise. When Mike finished, her attitude had undergone a complete reversal. She viewed Becky with newfound respect and admiration, realizing she had done the girl a grave injustice. Mike was not the only one with things left unsaid. She prayed it wasn't too late.

A dismal November dawn brought no change in Becky's condition. Mike maintained his vigil, not leaving to sleep, eating little of what Maggie brought on a tray. Doc Nolan stopped by as promised, but offered scant encouragement. Adam was due to arrive that afternoon. Ironically, the lifesaving telegram had been from him.

Becky was reluctant to leave the dark silent sanctuary. There was pain on the other side. Slowly she turned her head. The pain was excruciating, the slightest movement was torture. Exerting every ounce of willpower, she opened her eyes. A man sat slumped in a chair next to the bed, sound asleep. His face was a smudged charcoal sketch of bearded stubble and lines of fatigue. She blinked to clear the image, and a soft moan escaped from the effort. The light was so harsh.

"Becky!" The man was instantly awake and bending over her. "Becky, love, open your eyes. Tell me I'm not dreaming." His voice was hoarse, raspy.

She tried to ignore the pounding inside her head. Opening her eyes again, she found herself staring into blue depths, red-rimmed with worry, and darkly circled from lack of sleep. Eyes with a silvery film that even to her hazy state of mind looked like tears.

Becky ran the tip of her tongue over her lips and found them as cottony dry as the inside of her mouth. "So thirsty," she whispered.

Pouring a glass of water from a pitcher near the bed, Mike raised her shoulders and held the glass to her lips. After she had drained it, he carefully lowered her to the pillow.

"My head, my whole body hurts. Was there an accident?"

"Don't you remember?" The words were torn from him.

"I'm afraid not," she sighed. "Are we related?"

Her eyes drifted closed; she failed to see anguish distort the man's strong features.

"Becky doesn't remember me. She even asked if Maggie was her mother. Hannah's been by since the accident. She was very upset when Becky didn't recognize her. She said she'll come by daily to see if Maggie needs help." Mike glanced anxiously at Adam. It didn't seem fair to dump all this on him minutes after his arrival, but it couldn't be helped. "Doc called it amnesia. Said it could last a day, a week, or indefinitely."

Adam walked to the sideboard and poured himself a drink. "Are you telling me everything?"

"There is a temporary complication." Mike shifted uncomfortably. "It's her eyesight."

"She isn't blind?" Adam paled visibly. The hand holding the drink trembled.

"No, not that." Mike hastened to reassure him. "Besides everything looking blurry, Becky sees double. Doc had to bandage her eyes to prevent strain that would make her headaches worse. It should only be a day or two before her vision is back to normal."

Adam sank down heavily on the sofa. "Who would do such a thing? I'd like to kill the bastard."

"First person I thought of was Denby." Mike sagged next to him and rubbed the bridge of his nose between thumb and forefinger to relieve the dull ache.

"Denby." Adam spat the name with loathing. "He was furious when Becky turned down his proposal. But I never thought he would go this far."

"Pete claims Denby is in Indianapolis. But who's to say Denby didn't stop here on his way out of town. It was useless talking to Mitchell. Last I heard he was sleeping off a record drunk."

Adam took a long look at his new brother-in-law. "You need sleep, man. You're dead on your feet. I'll look after Becky."

"You'll have to fend off Maggie first," Mike chuckled tiredly, getting to his feet. "She's adopted all of us. I'm afraid she's here for the duration."

"Did I hear my name?" Maggie asked from the

doorway. She came forward and gave Adam a hug. "Mike, upstairs to bed with you. I'll tend to things."

He didn't stick around to argue.

Adam clasped the older woman's hand. "We're very grateful for your kindness."

"Pshaw!" She brushed aside his gratitude. "I nearly forgot how good it feels to be useful."

Chapter Seventeen

MIKE SLEPT AROUND THE CLOCK AND WOKE FEELING drugged and disoriented. Slowly he became aware that he was lying on a bed in a guest room, fully clothed except for his boots. A light quilt had been spread over him. Thoughts of Becky cleared the mists from his mind.

Tossing the quilt aside, he swung his long legs over the edge of the mattress. He rubbed his jaw and noted it felt like sandpaper. Getting to his feet, he grimaced at his reflection in the small mirror hanging above a chest of drawers. He looked like a trail bum with two days' growth of beard, tousled hair, and wrinkled clothes. Before he went to Becky, he needed to bathe and shave.

He hesitated outside Becky's closed door, wondering whether he should indulge in one quick peek to assure himself she was all right. While he stood debating, the door opened and Maggie came out.

"Well, it's about time. Adam and I were beginning to wonder when you would wake up."

Mike managed a lopsided grin and ran his hands through his disheveled hair. "How is she?"

"She's drifting off to sleep again. Why don't you get cleaned up and have something to eat? By then, she ought to be awake."

What Maggie said made sense, yet Mike couldn't resist the opportunity. Easing the door a crack, he looked inside. Nothing had changed. A bandage still covered Becky's eyes. The quiet rise and fall of breathing was her only movement. A small hand rested on the counterpane. A wide circlet of gold on her third finger gleamed dully in the lamplight. Mike quietly closed the door, his concern obvious to the woman who observed with a sad smile.

In the kitchen, Adam looked up from a huge piece of apple pie. "It's about time," he said, unknowingly repeating Maggie's greeting.

"You and Maggie are beginning to sound alike," Mike replied easily. "Is this a conspiracy?"

Maggie bustled to the stove. "I have water heating for your bath, then I'll fix your supper."

After a shave, bath, and clean clothes, Mike felt like his old self again. Maggie watched approvingly as he dug into a platter of scrambled eggs, slices of smoked ham, and biscuits dripping with honey. "Doc was by this afternoon," she said, pouring coffee.

"According to him, Becky's doing fine. He said it's to be expected for her to tire easily and have headaches."

"What about her eyesight?"

"Doc thinks the bandage can probably come off tomorrow. If not, the day after."

"Does Becky remember what happened?"

Maggie shook her head. "Not a thing. It upsets her, but she tries not to show it. She's not eating enough to keep a bird alive. Maybe she'll drink some juice if you coax her."

"After you see Becky, join me for a brandy. There's something I'd like to discuss." Adam's expression gave no clue to his thoughts.

"Sure." Mike shrugged. He couldn't help but wonder how much Becky had told her brother about the circumstances surrounding their marriage. Did Adam resent Mike as a brother-in-law? After all, it was one thing to share a drink with a man, another to have him part of the family.

Taking the stairs two at a time, Mike pushed open the bedroom door and found Becky in the center of the bed, propped up by pillows. At first he thought she must be sleeping. He half-turned to go when she turned toward him.

"Who's there?" A thread of fear wove through her voice.

"It's me, love. Mike." He approached the bed and gingerly perched on its edge. "How are you feeling?"

"Much better, thank you."

So proper. It pained him to think that by a single act they had become polite strangers. "Is your headache still bothering you?"

"Some. But not like yesterday."

"Maggie said Doc might take the bandages off your eyes tomorrow."

"Good!" Becky replied with a show of spirit. "If he doesn't, I will."

Mike's mood lightened for the first time in days. "You'll do nothing of the sort," he said, smiling. "I'm going to make sure you follow Doc's orders to the letter."

Becky wrinkled her nose in disgust. "Everyone is determined to tell me what I can and cannot do. Please don't say it's for my own good. If I hear that one more time, I'll scream. And," she added, "that will make my headache worse."

Mike chuckled softly. "Maggie's worried about you wasting away. She told me I was to make sure you drank this. Behave yourself and don't argue with me."

"If you insist," she sighed, struggling to raise herself on one elbow.

"Here, let me." Mike started to help her.

"I can do it myself." She was determined not to ask for assistance. Lying on her side, leaning on one elbow, she held out her hand. Mike pressed the glass into her palm, his fingers curling around hers as he guided it to her mouth. "Is it all gone?" she asked after drinking her fill.

"Almost." A golden bead of juice rested on the luscious curve of her full lower lip. Governed by impulse, Mike bent forward and, with the tip of his tongue, flicked the droplet into his mouth.

Her fingertips gently explored the site. His touch, as soft as velvet, sent blood coursing through her veins with more vigor than it had in days, warming her inside and out.

"I'm sorry. I shouldn't have done that." Mike was

appalled at his action. He had taken unfair advantage
of her vulnerable condition. "I better go." He set the
glass on the bedside table, got up, and started for the
door.

"No, wait! Stay awhile longer."

"If you're sure I won't tire you."

"I'm positive." Becky relaxed back on the pillows.
"What do I usually call you? Mike or Michael?"

"Both." He came toward the bed. "Most of the
time, you call me Mike, but sometimes when we're
alone," he closed his eyes briefly, "you call me
Michael."

Becky was quiet. Was he referring to the more
intimate aspect of their lives together? Judging from
her unbridled reaction of a moment ago, she guessed
those times to be frequent and mutually enjoyable. "I
see," she whispered.

"I'm afraid I've upset you." Once again he prepared to leave. This time his hand was on the door-
knob when her voice stopped him.

"I know this will sound silly, but . . ."

"Never be afraid to ask me anything, love. Anything at all."

"Hold me, Michael. Please, hold me."

He needed no urging. Crossing the room in long
strides, he wrapped her in the tender circle of his arms
and held her to his chest. She pressed her slender
form tightly against him, drawing comfort from his
strength. She could hear the steady even beat of his
heart beneath her ear. His lips brushed the top of her
head, and he inhaled the intoxicating sweet essence
that was uniquely her own.

"Mmm," he breathed contentedly. "Springtime."

"Spring? How can that be?" she questioned, her

voice muffled by his chest. "Maggie said it was November."

"I wasn't talking about the time of year, my love." He gently stroked her tumbled curls. "You have a certain fragrance that's yours alone. Until this moment I could never put a name to it. You smell of springtime. Sweet and delicate. Calling to mind flowers and sunshine."

At last Becky pulled away. "You must think me a terrible baby." She was embarrassed by her display of weakness. "Not being able to see, or to remember, makes me feel as though I'm disconnected from the rest of the world. I needed something solid to hold on to."

"My pleasure," Mike replied softly, gently pushing her down against the pillows and tucking the blanket around her shoulders. "Get a good night's rest. I'll see you tomorrow." He placed a light kiss on her forehead before he left the room.

Immersed in thought, he descended the stairs slowly. God! How he loved her. It had felt so good, so right, just holding Becky again. The curve of her body fit his perfectly, like the two halves of the same coin. To think he had nearly lost her was incomprehensible. Anger began to boil inside of him. Anger directed at a nameless man who had tried to steal what he valued most in all the world.

Adam glanced up as Mike entered the library. His welcoming smile faded at Mike's thunderous expression. Mike stalked across the room and leaned both arms against the mantel, and Adam prudently remained silent.

"I'm going to find the bastard who did this!" Mike gritted. "I'll see him suffer."

Adam strolled to the sideboard and poured each of them a drink. "It's time to get rid of Denby," he said, handing one to Mike. "I have just the plan."

His calm statement drew Mike's attention. There was a trace of ruthlessness in Adam's voice that contradicted his suave, affable appearance. Mike eyed his brother-in-law with speculation. "We can't be certain Denby is guilty."

"As long as Denby is in Oak Ridge, Becky will never be safe."

"What do you propose to do?"

"Get him the hell out of town." Adam allowed a small smile. "By any means available—short of cold-blooded murder."

Mike wore a grim smile when Adam finished outlining his scheme. "To justice." He raised his glass and clinked it against Adam's.

"By the way, I forgot to mention how glad I was to get Becky's telegram saying you two were married. Congratulations!" He reached out and pumped Mike's arm. "That brings up the second matter I wanted to discuss with you."

With part of his mind still mulling over plans to dispose of Denby, Mike only half-listened until something caught his attention. "What did you say?"

"I was saying that as long as you don't object, I'll have the deed for the farm made over in your name." Adam drew a pencil-slim cheroot from a silver case and offered one to Mike. "You can have Becky's name added later, of course. She's been after me to expand, but I told her the only way I'd consent was if she remarried and wanted to make this her permanent home." He lit his cheroot and blew out a stream of smoke.

"What was that you said about a will?"

"I found a loophole in father's will. The clause stipulates the farm can only be sold or willed to a male member of the family. It said nothing about being related by blood. As far as I'm concerned, since you married Becky, you're family. Naturally," Adam gestured expansively with the thin cigar, "I don't expect you to pay market value. A token amount will do. Think of it as my wedding gift."

"That's very generous, Adam, but unnecessary." Mike's voice was clipped. "I have money set aside from serving as army scout. I can well afford to buy my wife her precious piece of land."

Mike felt as though he had been hit in the gut, the wind knocked out of him. He had known for a long time Becky coveted the farm. What he hadn't reckoned with was the extremes she would go to, given the chance. Apparently she needed a husband. Very conveniently fate had dropped one right into her lap—him! Small wonder she hadn't objected to the arrangement. Any guilt was expunged by unlimited access to her very delightful body. Mike felt used, disillusioned. He had trusted Becky. Surely she would never do anything so devious, so reprehensible? Or would she? Old insecurities resurfaced to haunt him.

Becky stood in the center of the room hoping it would stop spinning. Maybe she should have waited for Maggie. But that would have spoiled her surprise. She was tired of being an invalid. Now that the bandages were off, she could start being independent. She advanced another step. Her head felt strange, like a giant balloon that had been inflated and was ready to float away. She swayed unsteadily.

"What in heaven's name do you think you're doing?" Mike's voice boomed out, startling her so that she turned quickly, jeopardizing her precarious balance. He dashed across the room and scooped her into his arms just before her knees gave way.

"I was going to dress and join all of you for dinner," Becky explained. To her chagrin, her voice was thin and faint-sounding.

"I didn't mean to frighten you." The gruff edge left his normally pleasant baritone. "You looked as though you were about to faint."

Her eyes widened. "Mike." It was both statement and question.

Mike stood rooted to the spot with Becky still in his arms. It finally dawned on him. She was seeing him clearly for the first time since the accident!

Openly curious, Becky took his face in both her hands and studied each feature, hoping something would trigger her memory. She trailed her index finger along the scar on his cheek. "Don't pull away," she said softly, sensing he was about to jerk free of her grasp. "Let me look at you."

"Are you disappointed?"

"Not at all," she said with a small smile. "You have an interesting face. It tells me a lot about your character."

"Such as?"

Her fingertip left the scar to lightly trace the lines fanning outward from the corners of his eyes. "These laughlines show you have a sense of humor." Her finger feathered across his lips. "Your firm mouth is that of a man used to making decisions." She outlined his chin and jawline. "Your squared jaw shows strength and a tendency to be obstinate." She tilted her head to one side. "Underneath that tough shell of yours lurks the heart of a romantic and the soul of a poet."

A dark brow shot upward. "You can tell I'm romantic by looking at my face?"

"No." Her ripple of laughter was as welcome as a gentle breeze. "It was what you said last night that gave you away. You said I smelled like springtime. I liked that. And," she added softly, "I like your face."

Mike groaned silently. It was starting all over again. She was ensnaring him in her spell, bewitching him with an exquisite sweetness until he couldn't think straight. He shook his head to clear his confusion. "I'd better get you to bed. If you take your dinner upstairs, I'll bring you down to the library later tonight."

"I don't suppose I have a choice?"

"None."

"All right," she agreed with a sigh. "But tomorrow, I'm coming downstairs for dinner."

"Not even a blow on the head can knock that stubborn streak out of you," he complained as he placed her between the sheets and pulled the covers over her.

Becky hid a yawn behind her hand. "How do you feel about stubborn women?"

He was almost out of the room when he turned back to answer. "If I were smart, I'd avoid them like the plague. There's one, however, I've grown quite fond of."

She was still smiling when he closed the door.

True to his word, Mike returned an hour later to carry Becky downstairs.

"Can't I walk?" she protested. "There's nothing wrong with my legs. Besides, I'm too heavy to be carried around. You might hurt your back."

Ignoring her objections, Mike picked her up. "You weigh no more than a thistle."

Maggie and Adam were waiting for them in the library. Pillows and an afghan had been arranged on the sofa and Mike gently placed her there. Becky looked around with interest, her gaze taking in the walls lined with bookshelves, the cheerful fire crackling in the hearth. A chessboard sat on a table at one end of the room, its figures showing a game in progress. A spinet piano occupied a corner. Everyone waited to see if she recognized these familiar surroundings.

Fighting disappointment, Becky forced a bright smile for their benefit. "Who plays the piano?"

"You do," Adam replied.

"Do I?" Her expression registered surprise.

"Mother insisted, so you learned under protest. Actually you play quite well, when the mood strikes you."

Mike absented himself and returned a short time later holding a large basket covered by a scrap of blanket. He placed it in front of her with a wide smile. "Go ahead," he urged. "See what's inside."

Bewildered, Becky looked from the smiling face of her husband to the basket. Its cover shifted as she watched, and she feared her vision problem was recurring. The puzzle was solved by the appearance of a tan paw followed by a moist black muzzle. With a squeal of delight, Becky snatched away the scrap of fabric.

A fluffy puppy eagerly wagging a white-tipped tail

perched its front paws on the rim of the basket. Becky lifted out the wriggling pup and laughed when it licked her cheek with a rough pink tongue. "He's adorable, Mike. Thank you."

"Hearing you laugh again is all the thanks I need."

"We're going to have to find a suitable name for the little fellow," Maggie said, putting aside her needlework.

"A dog is a good idea, Mike," Adam agreed. "Don't know why I didn't think of it myself."

"Tom Weston mentioned his dog just had pups. He's always bragging what a good watchdog she is. He gave me pick of the litter."

Becky was too engrossed with her new pet to notice the significant looks being exchanged.

"I'm in the mood for a big bowl of buttered popcorn," Adam declared. "I'll scout the pantry for the long-handled popper we used to use in the fireplace."

The puppy's ears picked up. "Follow me, dog," Adam said, laughing. "Let's see if Uncle Adam can find you a treat."

Adam came back brandishing a popper in one hand, a tin of popping corn in the other. The little dog trotted obediently at his heels, its muzzle dusted with fine white crumbs.

They all burst out laughing at the pure satisfaction on the puppy's face.

"For goodness sake, Adam." Maggie clucked her tongue. "Whatever did it get into?"

"While I was looking for the popcorn, he found the biscuits." Adam gave her an apologetic look.

"Not the ones I was saving for breakfast!" the widow said in dismay.

"That's perfect!" Becky cried. "We'll name him Biscuit."

For the remainder of the evening, Becky leaned back on the pillows, content to watch the activity going on around her. After a short while she found her meager store of energy depleted. Mike was the first to notice her drooping eyelids.

"It's time you turned in. You've had enough excitement for one day."

She bid goodnight to Maggie and her brother. This time she didn't protest when Mike picked her up. It felt good to snuggle safe and secure against his rock-hard chest.

"Have you carried me upstairs before?" she asked sleepily.

"Mm-hmm."

"Was it because I was hurt?"

"Uh-uh."

"Why then?"

"Stubborn," he sighed. "And persistent."

"You haven't answered my question."

Mike glanced into her upturned face. The large green eyes mirrored a childlike innocence. Her angelic surface bore little resemblance to the vixen lurking beneath. Should he tell her of the time they made love on the floor of the library? That the embers in the hearth had grown cold long before the flames of their passion? Should he remind her it was nearly dawn before he had carried her naked up the stairs to bed?

"Once, after making love," he said quietly.

"Oh." The unexpected bit of information stained her cheeks a becoming shade of rose.

"Michael?" She unconsciously used the name reserved for intimate interludes. "About making love," she almost faltered. "Is that something we did often?"

"Yes." His voice was harsh. "Very often."

If that were true, she thought to herself long after he had left the room, why was the kiss he gave her so chaste, almost fatherly? Didn't he care anymore?

Chapter Eighteen

BECKY KNEW THE VERY MOMENT THE NIGHTMARES
began. It was exactly one week ago. Adam had come
upon her unexpectedly while she stood at the kitchen
table. The fright culminated in hysteria which neither
Adam nor Maggie could calm. Her screams had
brought Mike running. He had held her, rocking her
back and forth, crooning unintelligible words for
more than an hour before she quieted. The first
nightmare occurred that night.

It was always the same. A man was attacking her,
and she was fighting for her life. When she tried to
rake his face with her nails, there was nothing where

his face should have been. As a result, there were two facts she knew with certainty: Whatever happened had taken place in the kitchen. And it had *not* been an accident. Yet no one was willing to answer her questions, not even Mike.

The same nightmare had occurred twice since. It was getting so she was afraid to fall asleep. Even now, long after the others had gone to bed, she lay awake, her body tense and rigid. Only tonight there was a difference.

Voices. At first she thought she only imagined them, but she heard them again. The sounds of a muffled conversation, the click of a latch, and then the house grew silent. Becky sprang out of bed and padded to the window. A pale glimmer of moonlight illuminated two figures crossing the yard toward the barn. Simple deduction identified them as Mike and Adam. Standing to one side of the window, Becky waited, expecting to see them ride off on horseback. When they still hadn't reappeared after fifteen minutes, Becky impulsively took matters into her own hands.

Minutes later, wrapped in a dark woolen cloak, her head bowed against wintry blasts of cold wind, Becky picked her way across frozen, uneven turf. She paused when she reached the barn, unsure of how to proceed. She couldn't just barge in and demand to know what was going on. She edged cautiously down one side.

Toward the back of the barn she found what she was looking for, a door flush with the exterior, scarcely noticeable until she was upon it. Inching it open, she peered into a storage room. She slipped inside. A feeble shaft of light spilled into the room along with the murmur of male voices. Noiselessly, she tiptoed across its expanse and peeked through a crack in the door.

A lantern's circle of light showed four men. Mike, Adam, and two strangers were seated on bales of hay. The unidentified pair was diverse as the color of their skins. The one Adam referred to as Jim had straggly blond hair with an unkempt beard. His clothes hung loosely on his lanky frame. The other man's dark skin glowed like polished ebony. He was built like a prized bull with a short thick neck and bulging muscles.

"Here's my plan," Adam said, hunching forward. "Friday is a busy day with most folks going to town to do their marketing. There ought to be plenty of witnesses. Jim will pose as a slavecatcher, while you, Luther," he motioned to the black man, "will be the slave. When you show up tomorrow, Jim is to make it known how much trouble he had finding you, that you're a valuable piece of property with a thousand-dollar bounty on your head."

"Sounds easy." Jim bit off a plug of tobacco. "What next?"

"You're to place Luther in the marshal's custody overnight for safekeeping," Mike explained. "Then go down to the Satin Slipper and have yourself a good time. Be sure you stay in plain sight."

"When do I get my good time?" Luther asked with a good-natured grin that showed gaping spaces where teeth once had been.

"Your good time will take place at the jail."

"Whooee!" Luther replied with a deep rolling laugh. "I can hardly wait. Just be sure I don't get to enjoys it for too long."

"No need to worry," Adam assured him. "Mike

284

and I will get you out not long past midnight. We've got a foolproof plan worked out. All you have to do is sit back and wait."

Jim aimed a stream of tobacco juice at an imaginary target. "What do I do next?"

"Show up the next morning to claim your prisoner. When you find out he escaped, make the biggest commotion this town has ever seen. Threaten to charge Denby with dereliction of duty. Allowing a runaway to elude custody is a violation of the new Fugitive Slave Law. That makes the marshal accountable for a slave's full value." Pulling out a thin cigar, Adam lit it and exhaled pleasurably. "A few discreet inquiries told me Denby doesn't have near that kind of money. If he doesn't find Luther, he won't dare show his face again. He can't afford to."

Jim's thin mouth stretched into a parody of a smile. An infectious rumble of laughter broke loose from Luther. Even Becky, who eavesdropped avidly, couldn't resist the compulsion to silently join in the merriment.

This was a good time to leave, she thought, furtively retracing her steps. She had nearly reached the door when her cloak snagged an object lying on a bench and sent it clattering to the floor. She fled outside pressing herself against the side of the barn. Seconds later, the doorway was filled with Mike's shadowy bulk. Not daring to breathe, she flattened herself against the weathered boards hoping to melt into the darkness. Mike started to turn back when a capricious gust of wind whipped open the edges of her cloak. A sliver of her white nightgown was clearly visible.

The next instant Mike's hand was manacled to her wrist. "What the blazes are you doing out here?"

Rational thought deserted her. Becky's mouth felt parched, her tongue clove to the roof of her mouth. A pulse hammered at the base of her throat. Her thoughtful gentle husband had been transformed into this fierce angry giant who frightened her.

Mike wanted to shake her. Couldn't she stay put? Wasn't she aware of the hazards of wandering about alone? What if Denby had been lurking around to finish what he started? Fear tightened his grip to a near threshold of pain.

Adam poked his head out the door and took in the situation at a glance. Annoyance replaced apprehension. "Experience should have prepared me for this. It's not the first time, little sister, you've made a pest of yourself." Sighing, Adam shook his head. "Did you find out what you came for?"

"I heard everything," she croaked.

"Mike, will you escort my inquisitive sibling to the house and see she stays put while I conclude business?"

Mike responded with a curt nod. Not loosening his grip, he propelled Becky away from the barn. She had to run to keep pace with his long strides. Several times she would have tripped if not for his firm hold on her arm. No sooner had Mike thrust her inside the house than she wrenched free.

"I'm not a criminal," she fumed. "All I did was overhear a conversation."

"Don't try to whitewash what you did," Mike growled. "You were spying on us."

Becky's chin jutted defiantly. He was right, but she

wasn't ready to admit it. His highhanded attitude made her resentful. "Why are you trying to force the marshal out of town?"

"Why don't you go to bed?"

"I will." Becky folded her arms across her chest. "After you answer my question."

"Didn't you ever hear the expression curiosity killed the cat?" he grated.

They glared at each other in the darkened kitchen, neither willing to back down.

"You're a meddlesome headstrong woman, Rebecca Ryan."

"And you're an arrogant stubborn man," she retorted. "Are you going to answer my question, or not?"

There was no getting around her determination, so Mike settled on a half-truth. "Adam and I are active in the underground railroad. Denby's a threat to our work. He's already responsible for the death of one runaway. We want him out of town before he causes more trouble."

"Now I understand." Becky pushed back the hood of her cloak, sending a cascade of dark gold curls tumbling around her shoulders. "You're counting on Denby leaving town for good rather than face ridicule and financial ruin?"

"The man's a coward."

She nervously fingered the fastener on her garment. Even in the dim light, her eyes were enormous. "Is your plan dangerous?"

A wave of longing to take her in his arms, to erase her worry, almost swamped his better judgment. But he had promised himself he wouldn't take advantage of her condition by pressing his attention. "It should go off without a hitch. Adam and I took every detail into account."

"Good." There didn't seem to be any more to discuss. Becky left the kitchen with Mike following. She started up the stairs, but hesitated on the first step, turning to face him. "Promise you'll be careful."

"I will." He cleared his throat. "Now go to bed like a good girl."

"Stop treating me like a child!" she snapped, irritated at his patronizing tone.

Humor flickered in dark blue depths. "Once your memory returns," Mike drawled, "you'll know I never treated you like a child."

Standing as she was, Becky's eyes were nearly level with his mouth. Such a beautiful mouth, she thought, with firm, sensually molded lips. What would it feel like, she wondered, to be kissed by that mouth? Not the dispassionate fatherly sort he gave her each night, but that of a man who desires a woman. A slow provocative smile curved her lips. "Show me," she challenged. "Refresh my memory."

"Witch!" he uttered as his lips crushed hers.

His kiss conveyed a wealth of pent-up hunger and yearning. Becky responded with an unquenchable need that sprang from deep within her, devastating in its intensity. Her arms pulled him closer, her body fluid against his, she felt as though she had dissolved in a haze of sensual bliss.

"Oh, Michael," she sighed when he released her. "Is it always like this between us?"

"Always." Mike was angry at his lack of self-control. He ached with need for her. He should have known better than to start something he couldn't finish. "Goodnight, Becky," he said, keeping a tight rein on his emotions.

Becky felt a tremendous sense of loss at the curt dismissal. Her throat clogged with unshed tears as she slowly climbed the stairs.

Shortly before the clock struck twelve the following night, Becky heard Mike and Adam leave the house. Repeating her actions of the previous night, she got out of bed and watched them walk toward the barn. Minutes later they rode past her window on horseback. Shrugging into a dark green velvet robe, she went downstairs to wait.

As the clock chimed two, Becky heaved a heartfelt sigh of relief hearing them return. She ran to the door and opened it just as they reached the porch. Adam's initial amazement ended in a hoot of laughter. He bounded up the steps and caught her in an exuberant embrace, twirling her around. Mike looked on with a tolerant smile.

"All right, you two," Becky laughed breathlessly. "Tell me everything."

"What's all this racket?" Maggie Nelson stood in the doorway, a long gray plait hanging over the shoulder of her flannel wrapper. "Do you have any idea what hour this is?"

Reduced to the status of rowdy children about to be reprimanded, Adam, Mike, and Becky traded guilty looks.

"I don't mind losing beauty sleep," Maggie continued, "but I would be very put out if I missed a good party."

Adam was the first of the trio to recover. "Maggie, my girl, you're just in time for a celebration."

The stern lines of her face softened. "I'll put on the coffee."

Over cake and coffee, the adventure unfolded around the oak table. Even Biscuit joined the group, his bright eyes alert for dropped crumbs.

"I have to hand it to Luther." Adam's admiration was evident in his voice. "I only wish you ladies could have seen it. There was Luther, pleased as punch, his feet propped on Denby's desk like he owned the place."

"Where was the marshal?" Becky asked.

Mike picked up the tale. "Luther got tired of waiting for Adam and me to come to his rescue. So he took matters in his own hands. He tricked Denby into coming into his cell, and when his back was turned, he hit him over the head."

Adam laughed softly. "It'll be morning before anyone finds him a guest in his own jail. By then, Luther will be halfway home."

"Won't Denby swear in a posse and go after him?" Maggie queried.

"Of course, but who would think to look for a runaway slave heading south?" Mike grinned. "Besides, Luther's no slave. He's a free man of color with papers to prove it."

The house seemed unnaturally quiet without Adam or Maggie. Adam had departed the previous day for St. Louis to attend to urgent business, promising to return in time for the Christmas holidays. Maggie had left that morning.

Other than the crackling fire, the only sounds were the click of Becky's knitting needles. From time to time, Mike sent her covert glances as he spread his cards for a game of solitaire. He was deeply worried about her and knew Adam shared his concern. Within the last weeks, she had become a ghost of her former self, wan, listless, jittery. Often at night he would hear her pacing at odd hours.

Mike peppered Doc Nolan with questions about her condition until the poor man had taken to ducking into doorways. Adam had corresponded with physicians from New York to New Orleans in the hope of gaining more knowledge of the little known affliction. One common thread in all the theories was the possibility that Becky didn't want to remember, that part of the past was too painful to acknowledge. With this in mind, Mike and Adam had confronted her with the truth, telling her it was an assault, not an accident, that erased her memory. They stressed Denby was the responsible party, and since their plan had succeeded, he was far away, and no longer a threat to her safety. Nothing made the slightest difference.

The markings on the cards blurred. How could he concentrate on a silly game when Becky's well-being was at stake? Mike was beginning to think that perhaps the assault wasn't the problem. Perhaps there was something even more difficult for her to accept— such as a forced marriage.

What if Becky had only wanted marriage to gain ownership of the farm? Now that it was hers, the idea of being wed to a man not of her choosing was intolerable. If that were so, his leaving would be the best thing for her. Once he was out of her life, recovery could begin. As excruciating as leaving her would be, watching her become more and more depressed would be worse. He couldn't let that happen. He loved her too much.

"Drat!" Becky tossed her knitting down in disgust. The hopeless tangle of yarn and dropped stitches brought tears of frustration to her eyes. What was happening to her lately? She couldn't seem to do anything right.

"Maybe we should call it a night," Mike suggested. The ability to distinguish red from black was proving too much of a challenge for him.

Becky was weary to the point of exhaustion, but the thought of going to sleep terrified her. Though the dream occurred nightly, not once had she seen the face of her attacker. The nightmare generated a growing sense of danger and urgency that permeated every waking moment until her nerves were taut and ready to snap. "It's still early," Becky demurred, delaying the inevitable.

He left his cards to get up and add another log to the fire. Absently he stared into the blaze and rubbed his scarred cheek to relieve its dull ache. A change in the weather never failed to start it throbbing. Snow would probably fall before dawn, he guessed.

The action drew Becky's attention. "Does it hurt?"

"It's nothing." He jammed his hands into his pockets. His face tightened in rigid lines, as if daring her to pursue the subject.

"I don't believe you." Shoving her knitting into a basket, she walked over to stand next to him. "You act like you're ashamed of it."

"What should I be?" he ground out. "Proud?"

"What happened, Michael?" she persisted. "Was it an accident?"

A muscle in his jaw bunched ominously. "No."

"I don't mean to pry." Becky reached out and

placed her hand on his arm. "Please, forget that I asked."

He gazed up at the ceiling, then down into her upturned face. "The last thing I want is to strike out at you. I didn't mean to bite your head off."

"Hasn't whatever happened festered long enough?"

Easy for her to say, he thought bitterly. How would she know what it was like to feel like a circus freak? To watch people stare or turn their heads.

"You know, I could never understand why my scar didn't bother you. What made you different? It bothered Claire."

Becky withdrew her hand from his arm. Her chest constricted at the mention of another woman's name. "Were you in love with her?" It came out scarcely more than a whisper.

"I thought the sun rose and set on Claire McGowen. One glance at my battered face sent her running into another's arms—Patrick's. Granted, I wasn't a pretty sight, but it hurt to see that look in her eyes."

Becky sank to the edge of the sofa and stared down at her laced fingers so he wouldn't notice her tears. "Who did this to you?" Her voice choked.

"My brother." Mike started to walk about the room. "Actually Patrick is my half-brother, three years my senior. People were always comparing the two of us, always saying how I was taller, or stronger, or smarter. Even my eyes were bluer." He gave a short humorless laugh. "Patrick was eaten up by jealousy even before Claire came along. When she chose me over him, it was the final straw.

"One night he came home drunk, ranting how I took Claire away from him. We'd been through this before, so I wasn't paying much attention to his ravings. He picked up a hot poker and smashed it across my face."

Becky's hand flew to her mouth. She wanted to go to Mike, put her arms around him, and make all the hurt go away.

"Naturally," Mike continued, "the next day, after he sobered up, he was filled with remorse. And Claire was filled with doubt. She finally broke down and confessed she could no longer bear to look at me. I left Boston before the wound completely healed."

Becky's heart went out to the man she had married. Intuitively, she knew he didn't want her pity. Along with flesh, the savage act had scarred his pride, his manhood. Guided by instinct, she went to him and placed her hand on his cheek. "It never made you less a man, Michael, but more of one."

Mike sat alone in the silent room, pondering her words long after she went upstairs. He had allowed the incident to poison his attitude. In the ensuing years, he had become overly sensitive, often misinterpreting harmless remarks and simple curiosity. Self-pity had become his sickness just as jealousy had become Patrick's. Becky had been brave enough, wise enough, to point out what he was too blind to see. She had been the cure for his illness; he would be the same for hers. Even if it meant leaving.

Suddenly, a shrill scream broke into his thoughts!

Chapter Nineteen

BECKY SAT BOLT UPRIGHT IN BED, BATHED IN A FILM OF perspiration, her nightgown clinging to her. After the single terrified scream, further sound was locked in her throat. Shock spun a thick cocoon around her, cushioning her from the outside world.

"Becky!" Mike flung the door open. "What is it? Are you all right?" He rushed to the bedside and caught her shoulders. She didn't flinch when his fingers dug roughly into soft flesh. Her pupils were so widely dilated only a small portion of iris was visible.

"Say something! Talk to me!" He gave her a small shake. For the first time in his life, Mike knew panic.

Why wasn't she responding? Wrapping his arms around her, and crushing her to his chest, he rocked her back and forth. "Becky, love, it's all right. You're safe," he repeated over and over until it became an incantation.

After what seemed an eternity, his soothing words penetrated the numbing layers of insulation. The warmth of his body seeped through her pores in slow degrees. Becky emerged from the trancelike stupor as a sob tore from her throat. One followed another until they convulsed her slender frame. Mike continued to hold her until their storm abated.

Becky took in great gulps of air. Gently, Mike wiped away traces of tears with the corner of the bedsheet. "Feel better, love?"

He felt the affirmative nod of her head against his chest. She grew quiescent in the safe shelter of his arms.

"What happened to frighten you so?"

"The nightmare," she hiccoughed.

Mike stroked her hair. "Nightmare?"

"It was worse this time." Mike had to strain to hear her muffled words.

"This time?" His hand stilled. "You've had them before?"

Becky sniffled. "Ever since the time Adam startled me in the kitchen. Only now I get them every night."

"How was this one worse?"

"I could almost see his face. It was as if I knew him."

"The man responsible, Becky, is far away. He can't hurt you." Mike smoothed damp tendrils away from her face. He held her until he could feel tension dissolve, leaving her body liquid and pliant against his. Thinking she was asleep, he peered down at her face.

Her eyes met his, a lambent gleam in their deep evergreen. "Stay with me tonight, Michael."

"I'll sit by your bed all night to make sure you're safe," he agreed readily.

"No, here." She patted the spot next to her. "I want to be able to touch you, to know that you care."

"Oh, sweet witch," he groaned. "I care. Never doubt how much. My love for you knows no boundaries. It's unfathomable as the sea. Only don't ask the impossible. Don't ask me to lay beside you, touch you, hold you, yet not make love to you." *One final time,* he added silently.

"Make me come alive in your arms, truly alive," she pleaded. "Make me forget to fear the past, or to worry about the future. Only the present matters. Make me yours, Michael."

"I do, I will," he vowed, the words spoken as his mouth closed over hers.

It was a bittersweet night of love. It honed the pain of parting to saber sharpness. Mike eased himself out of bed careful not to waken Becky. He looked at her in repose and couldn't resist the temptation to stroke her ivory satin cheek. Responding to the light touch, she smiled in her sleep. His resolve began to weaken. But he had made his decision last night, before emotion clouded his thinking. Lingering would only prolong the agony. Mike silently left the bedroom. The first snowflakes of the season swirled through the air as he rode away.

Becky woke with a delicious sense of well-being. For the first time in a month, she felt rested and able to cope. Her eyes still closed, she reached out to touch the man responsible. Instead of warm flesh, her fingers encountered crisp cotton sheets. Her eyes flew open to find an expanse of rumpled bed linen and a shallow indentation on the pillow next to hers. How like Mike to let her sleep late, she thought.

Her stomach growled with unladylike intensity. Hunger gnawed at her, a sensation almost foreign in recent weeks. Tossing the covers aside, Becky swung her legs out of bed. Eggs, bacon, flapjacks, the works. She'd fix them both a gigantic breakfast. It was time to start living again.

Selecting a lightweight wool dress of dusty pink, she was still fastening its tiny buttons when she walked to the window and pushed back the draperies. She smiled in delight at the sight of cold wet flakes drifting lazily to the ground. It made her remember the time she and Adam had built a six-foot-high snowman and stuck one of father's best cigars in its mouth. Her actions were arrested. *Memories!* Her father had been furious, but her mother had smoothed things over with hot chocolate and sugar cookies. Broken, jagged bits of memory. But it was a beginning. Excitement bubbled up inside of her. She had to find Mike and tell him her news.

"Mike!" Becky called his name going from room to room. He had probably gone to check on the livestock, she thought, as she pushed open the guestroom door where he had slept until last night. It was as neat as a pin. Too neat. No personal items were in evidence, not even a hairbrush was on the polished bureau, only an envelope placed square in the center. She approached it with trepidation. Her name was scrawled across it in bold black letters. Pulse racing, she wiped clammy hands down the sides of her dress. Her fingers trembled as she picked up the envelope and took out a sheet of paper. The handwriting danced crazily; the words refused to make sense. Becky's brows drew together in fierce concentration, reading, then rereading, his message. The sheet of paper floated to the floor.

Icewater circulated where blood used to flow. Chilled to the bone, she hugged her arms around herself to stop the shivering. "Mike's gone." Her lips repeated what her numbed brain couldn't comprehend. "Mike's gone."

With legs that felt like jelly, she walked to the bed and sank down on the edge. When her vision cleared, she realized she was staring at the envelope clutched tightly in her left hand. There was still something inside. Pulling it out, she discovered that it was the deed for the farm made out to Mike, then deeded over to her. At the bottom, he had scribbled he knew how much the farm meant to her. He hoped it would bring a measure of happiness. Becky swallowed back the lump in her throat. How could a piece of paper be a substitute for the man she loved? Even though she didn't know whether she loved him before the accident, or if she had fallen in love with him since, it simply didn't matter.

Two hot tears rolled down her cheeks. Brushing them away with the back of her hand, she tried to think. In Mike's note, he told her he was releasing her from vows made unwillingly. What was that supposed to mean? If he didn't want to stay married to her, he could have at least had the decency to tell her face to face. Were her loss of memory and Mike's leaving connected? Somehow she thought they were. She sniffed back her tears. Blubbering like a baby wouldn't help the situation. She got up and went downstairs.

Vows made unwillingly. The phrase played in her mind like a piece of unfinished music. Becky drifted aimlessly through the house, finally settling on the sofa in the library. She halfheartedly started a fire to ward off the dampness, but it sputtered and smoked. She let it die. When the cold became uncomfortable, she wrapped an afghan around her shoulders and drew herself into a tight ball. She huddled there oblivious to her surroundings, trying to unravel tangled knots of memory. Hours slipped by.

Biscuit pranced into the room, pawing at the afghan and whimpering. Rousing herself, Becky was surprised to discover the room filled with purple shadows heralding an early dusk. She was ashamed at having neglected the little animal. The pup wasn't the only one suffering from lack of nourishment, she realized. She felt lightheaded, and her temples throbbed. Starving wouldn't bring Mike back, neither would sitting around moping. What she needed was a plan of action.

"Come on, Biscuit. We could both use something to eat." She unwound herself from her cramped position and went into the kitchen, the puppy trotting close behind. Biscuit yipped and scratched at the back door making his priorities known, so she let him out.

Tomorrow, she decided over a cup of strong tea and

a thick slice of toasted bread, she would set out to find
Mike if it meant scouring the countryside. Someone
must know of his whereabouts. She'd talk to Maggie,
maybe hire a private detective. Whatever it took,
however much it cost, she would find him. Vows made
unwillingly? She rubbed the persistent ache in her
temples. Last night Mike had told her he loved her.
She had believed him then, and nothing could shake
that belief. She wasn't about to let some half-baked
quixotic notion stand between them.

After awhile, it occurred to her the puppy was still
outside. She looked out the window, but there was no
sign of him in the gathering dusk. Tugging on a pair of
boots and throwing a cape over her shoulders, she
went out onto the porch. A pristine blanket of snow
spread as far as the eye could see. Gunmetal gray
clouds foretold of more to come. Biscuit, his muzzle a
snow-encrusted beard, was frolicking near the woods.
The crimson flash of a cardinal flickered in the drooping boughs of a pine tree. She looked back in time to
see the puppy disappear behind a giant sycamore.

"Biscuit!" After a day spent napping, the little pup
had too much stored energy to heed the command.
Exasperated, Becky went after him. The snowfall left
a scant two inches on the ground making the tracks
easy to follow. Skirting around the massive trunk, she
called again. The puppy looked back but seemed to
think this was a game and ran ahead.

A light dusting of snow had penetrated the thick
canopy of branches overhead. In the dim light, Becky
could make out a faint trail that wound through the
trees. It was familiar. The flush of excitement she felt
earlier that day stirred to life. She could no more turn

back than she could stop breathing. She followed the path.

Driven by a compulsion to discover what lay ahead, she forgot the puppy scampering ahead of her, forgot everything. Becky felt as though she were being pulled by a powerful magnet. The path opened into a clearing. A rough-hewn cabin and small shed wearing years of neglect stood in its center. It, too, was familiar. The magnetic tug became stronger. She went closer and pushed open the unlatched door. Not questioning her knowledge, she knew there would be matches on a shelf near the door and a lantern close by.

At the scrape of a match, the sparsely furnished cabin glowed with life. Oddly enough, the light illuminated dark recesses of her mind as well. Disembodied faces, bits of conversation swirled inside her head. Isaac, Celia, Ben. Mike! Dear Lord, she remembered. *Vows made unwillingly.* Now she understood Mike's note and why he left. She wanted to laugh and cry at the same time.

Biscuit's frenzied bark jerked her back to the present. Turning toward the sound, she froze. A large burly figure stood in the doorway. Her nightmare had a face. Pete Mitchell's!

"You!" she gasped.

Taking an instant dislike to the man, Biscuit sank his sharp teeth into Pete's ankle. "You mangy mutt!" A kick in the ribs sent the little dog flying out the door. Pete quickly closed it. "Too bad you remember me, Becky."

She retreated further into the cabin. The horrible realization that she was totally helpless engulfed her.

A deserted cabin. Deep in the woods. Nothing to defend herself with. She was at his mercy. And he knew it.

"Mike knows where I am," she bluffed. "He'll come looking for me."

Pete laughed and shook his head. "Nice try, but it won't work. Your husband paid me a visit on his way out of town. Told me he'd be gone for a spell. Asked me to keep an eye peeled in case Denby decided to return."

"What are you going to do?" she asked. Her imagination was already painting graphic pictures.

"With your husband gone, I thought I'd make sure you didn't remember anything. Seein' how you do, I'll have to finish what I started."

"Just let me go. There's no harm done. I won't tell anyone." Becky tried to reason with him.

He stood in front of the door, thumbs hooked casually through his belt loops, blocking the only exit. "I make it a point never to take a woman's word. The minute my back's turned you'll go blabbing. Things are nice and cozy as town marshal. I'm not about to let you spoil them."

"You won't get away with this."

"Easy as taking candy from a baby," he bragged. "In the course of doing my duty, I find your body. By sheer coincidence, your husband took off to parts unknown that very morning. What will folks think? They're bound to draw certain conclusions. Naturally, bein' marshal, I'll head up the search party to find him. Can't be helped if I'm called out of town same night there's a lynch mob."

Becky's heart stopped, then began to pound with

thick heavy beats. Not only was her life at stake, but Mike's as well. She mustn't allow fear to scatter her wits. Maybe she could draw Pete away from the door and make a break for it. It was dark and once outside, she could hide. Keeping her eyes on him, she began edging around the room.

"You sure are a pretty little thing," he said, starting after her as though he had all the time in the world. "Gave me quite a start when I sobered up and found out you weren't dead. Hadn't been for Jed Rawlins comin' by with that damn telegram, I would have stuck around to make sure. As it was, I didn't want to take any chances."

Inch by slow inch, she circled the table. There was a gun in a holster slung low on his hips. Maybe he would shoot when she made a run for it. A bullet would at least be quick. There was no time left; she had to act. Shoving the table at him with all her might, she sprinted toward the door.

But Pete's reaction was quick as he caught the table in one hand and sidestepped, once again effectively barring her exit. "Only cats have nine lives, Becky," he snarled. "Your luck has just run out." He drew his pistol and pointed it at her heaving chest. "On the bed. Flat on your back."

"No." Becky shook her head, her refusal a choked whisper.

He brought his hand down and slapped her, sending her reeling backward to sprawl across the mattress. "Right where I've always wanted you," he smiled evilly. "Flat on your back."

The gun was aimed at her heart. Becky watched in wide-eyed horror as he unbuckled his holster and let it drop. His pants followed. Shifting the gun to his left hand, he placed one knee on the bed. The mattress dipped beneath his weight. He reached out and stroked her throat with his right hand. "Pretty neck. Just the right size for a string of pearls, or a man's hands." The heel of his hand pressed against her windpipe. "You're going to be real cooperative now, ain'tcha?"

Becky couldn't answer. She tried to pry his hand from her throat.

"No use fightin' me." The pressure on her throat increased and his smile became a leer. Satisfied when she ceased her struggle, he laid the gun on the floor beside the bed. He shoved her skirts around her waist and clawed at her underthings. "Spread your legs," he commanded.

Becky felt him nudge her thighs apart, and prayed the end would come soon. It was so hard to breathe. It took all her concentration, all her energy, to suck air into her oxygen-starved lungs. Tiny stars sparkled in the dark mist before her eyes.

Then she was dimly aware of a crash, followed by loud voices, and then shots were fired. The acrid smell of gunpowder was heavy in the small cabin; a curtain of smoke hung in the air. She barely noticed, because Mike's beloved face loomed in front of her, filling her vision.

"Michael?" Her mouth moved, but no sound came out. Not sure if he was real, or if she was dreaming, she reached up and gently traced his scarred cheek.

"You're safe, my love. No one will ever hurt you again," he said, taking her in his arms.

Becky wasn't certain if the vibrating shudder came from her, or the man who held her so protectively. Closing her eyes, she buried her face in his broad shoulder and held on.

"God I love you. It terrifies me to think I nearly lost you, not once, but twice. Can you forgive me for doubting your love?" Need roughened his voice.

"I could forgive you anything," she whispered softly. "Take me home, Michael."

He lifted her in his arms. Becky glimpsed Pete's crumpled form lying on the floor, an ever-widening circle of red stained the back of his jacket, his hand reaching for his gun.

"Don't look." Mike pressed her face into his shoulder. "He left me no choice."

Leaving the cabin behind, he retraced the path to the house. "Biscuit deserves a bone." Mike motioned to the little dog trotting close at his heels. "When I didn't find you in the house, I tracked your footprints to the edge of the woods. But it was Biscuit's barking that brought me running."

"What made you come back?" Becky murmured contentedly.

He gave her the lopsided grin she found so endearing. "It took awhile to get it through my thick skull, but I finally figured out that the special magic between us went far beyond the physical." He paused, looking into her upturned face. "What could it be, but love?"

"What indeed!" Becky smiled. The glow in her eyes was eloquent.

At last they emerged from the woods, their home in

view. Becky wove her fingers through his ebony locks, and gently coaxed his mouth to meet hers. Snow started to fall once again, resting on their heads and shoulders like a silent benediction, each crystalline flake as perfect as the kiss they shared, as flawless as their love.

Tapestry

HISTORICAL ROMANCES

POCKET BOOKS

879

TAPESTRY ROMANCES